TROWCHESTER BLUES

ALEX BEECROFT

RIPTIDE
PUBLISHING

Riptide Publishing
PO Box 6652
Hillsborough, NJ 08844
www.riptidepublishing.com

Trowchester Blues
Copyright © 2015 by Alex Beecroft

Cover art: Lou Harper, louharper.com
Editor: Sarah Frantz
Layout: L.C. Chase, lcchase.com/design.htm

ISBN: 978-1-62649-199-1

First edition
February, 2015

Also available in ebook:
ISBN: 978-1-62649-198-4

TROWCHESTER
BLUES

ALEX BEECROFT

RIPTIDE
PUBLISHING

To everyone who likes this kind of thing,
I salute you.
To those who believed in it enough to publish and buy it,
all my thanks.
To those who believed in me, in this and many other things,
all my love.

TABLE OF
CONTENTS

CHAPTER
ONE

Thirty seconds after Smith knocked at the front door, the suspect threw open the back and charged out. Michael May, standing to one side waiting, kicked the guy's knees out from under him, and moved in to try to seize an arm, get the bastard in a half nelson, under control.

But this guy—Watkins—was tougher than these white-collar city boys usually came. He took the fall like a pro, used the momentum to roll, and came up running. He was a wiry git, taller than May—most men were—with long legs. That damn kung fu fall set off all kinds of alarms in May's head, but at this stage it was fight or lose him, and he was not going to let the bastard get away.

A wheelie bin in the narrow passage between the back of the house and the street slowed the perp up enough so May could throw himself at those long legs and rugby tackle him to the ground. Watkins went down, but he squirmed like an eel. May took a heel to the balls, and blessed his own foresight in wearing rugby protection down there. He held on tight, not wanting to walk his hold up the guy's body and potentially give him a better angle to use his fists. Pinned by May's considerable weight, facedown on the pavement, there wasn't a lot the guy could do to him. May could lie here just fine until Reed or Smith got round to coming to help.

The perp tried rolling. No luck. He pushed himself up on his arms, trying with better leverage. Failed again. In terms of sheer physical force, May outclassed him easily.

"Nigel Howard Watkins"—this was an unusual position from which to make an arrest, but May wasn't going to turn down anything that worked—"you are under arrest for—"

Watkins flopped flat. One of his long, flailing arms went to the back of his designer suit trousers. His jacket shifted, and there was the bulge of a gun stuffed down the back of his waistband.

May's heart kicked up beneath his ribs. Fuck, every villain had a gun these days, and they hadn't brought any armed officers with them. His mind went white and clear even as his lips tingled with cold adrenaline. *Don't let him draw it.*

He punched Watkins in the kidney with his left hand, reached up with the right to try to grab for the gun. The moment his hold loosened, Watkins squirmed again, got one leg out from under him and kneed May in the ribs with it. May body-slammed the guy back to the pavement, swarmed up him, got his hand on Watkins's hand just as it grasped the gun, and kept it pressed down hard against the guy's back, so if he did pull the trigger, he'd shoot his own arse.

"May?" Acting Detective Constable Reed called from the exit to the road.

"Here! I could use a little help."

The yard gate swung open. Reed—a tall, skinny kid who lived up to his name—ran through, pushed past the wheelie bin, and got his knees on Watkins's shoulders.

"You're not going anywhere, sir." May managed to get his thumb on the pressure point of Watkins's wrist. Watkins jerked like he knew exactly what May was doing, knew that as soon as May dug in there, his hand would go numb, he would let go of the gun, and it would be all over.

If the man was going to shoot at all, it would be now. And yes, the bullet would go through his own buttock on the way to tearing into May's belly, lodging itself in his pelvis or his spine, but May would still be dead, and he'd be alive. Could he be tough enough for that? Tough enough to get another shot off afterwards, take Reed down too, and escape?

"You're not going anywhere," May said again, digging in to the pressure point with his fingers, pushing with his own resolve against Watkins's determination. "Nigel Howard Watkins, you are under arrest for kidnapping and unlawful imprisonment of a minor."

Watkins struggled against May's hold, but his fingers opened involuntarily, and May wrenched the gun out of his hand, threw it out of reach. The high, shrill edge to May's mood quietened down into a more familiar wariness. *Okay, okay. Thank God, we're all fine.*

He breathed out hard, pushing the panic aside, and drew on the comforting blanket of routine. "You do not have to say anything, but it may harm your defence if you do not mention, when questioned, something you later rely on in court. Anything you do say may be given in evidence."

Reed passed him handcuffs. He snapped them on, breathed again two, three times before giving the ADC a smile. "Good work. Let's get him up."

The fight had gone out of their prisoner. He rose easily enough, stood between them meekly with his smart white shirt black all over with the exhaust residue and smut of London's streets. Jermyn Street tailoring, gold watch, this season's spiky City cut on his muddy-blond hair, manicured hands. Maybe with blood under the nails, they'd have to check.

"You can't touch me," he said, obviously trying for suave and not quite making it.

"You got him?" Smith appeared at the yard door, wiping her hands over and over against her jeans. Jenny Smith, May's longtime partner, was hard and clear as diamond. His already queasy stomach—roiling with the comedown of that sudden flood of fight or flight—sank at the sight of her. Mouth pale, skin greenish, creases of strain between her eyebrows. It was bad.

"Bag the gun," he replied, nodding to it.

She knelt down to do it, not looking at him, not looking at Watkins. "Is he going to be secure in the car? You should see inside."

May could almost feel the confidence coming back to his prisoner, as if he were a vase being filled under a tap of it. Being physically overwhelmed and disarmed tended to knock even the most egotistical down a peg, but this guy was bouncing back from it with all the arrogance of his suit. He wasn't going to sit still and be a good boy while he waited for the police to gather evidence.

"We'll bring him."

Inside the man's house, it was glossy. A whole Victorian terrace house, not even split into flats. The ground floor was open plan, finished in pale wood, with a floating staircase up to the second and third floors. The bannisters were wrought iron. Nice and sturdy, so May used his own cuffs in addition to Reed's and secured Walker there, each wrist cuffed to a different spoke.

Smith passed the bagged gun to Reed. "Stay here. Make sure he stays too."

May caught Smith's gaze and raised his eyebrows. *Reed's staying here?*

She shoved a tendril of barley-sugar-coloured hair back into her plait and gave him a twist of the lips that said, *ADC Reed is twenty-one. Too young for this.* "I've already called for forensics, but you should see, so you can corroborate my evidence."

The smell began halfway down the stairs to the cellar. Very clean stairs. They ended in a small stone room full of racks of wine. Not a speck of dust on the floor, probably because if there had been, the place where the far wall swung out to reveal a hidden room would have been obvious at a glance. May drew on gloves, though he didn't intend to touch anything.

His educated nose picked up the bouquet of blood and burned flesh, layered with the fainter and yet more disturbing scents of semen and corpse. The energy of the fight had well and truly worn off now. His hands in his pockets shook no matter how hard he clenched them. He stopped where the false wall, cheerful with green bottles, still blocked his view, and closed his eyes for good measure.

"Jenny, I . . ."

But she was a woman and a mother. She'd seen everything he'd seen over their shared career. If she could take it, what kind of a pathetic excuse for a man did it make him that he could not?

Smith looked at him with a kind of cold fury that meant, *You are not leaving this all to me. Pull yourself together*, but what she said was, "No, you know, on second thoughts, why don't you and Reed just take him in? I'll wait for forensics." And see, he was letting down his partner with his weakness. She'd have to go home at night and know she was the only one with this stuff in her head. She'd have no one to talk to about it, no one to understand the pain that came out as morbid jokes and obsessive hand washing and one too many beers on a Friday night, if you were lucky.

No one needed to tell him he'd been flaky lately. He knew he'd been unravelling for the better part of the last year. That didn't mean he had to give in to it. He could try acting like a man and suck it up.

"Let me see," he said. Didn't miss her look of relief and guilt. No matter how concerned she might be about him, she didn't want to be alone with this.

The victim was a fourteen-year-old girl. Quite dead. By the look of her, she'd been dead for a couple of days. Her wrists, where she'd been chained to the radiator, had melted into the metal. Stacey Merriweather: ran away from home after a family argument over her grades at school, failed to return.

Cameras on Platform 3 of Piccadilly Station had seen her sitting with her back to the wall, crying. A disconsolate little package of short skirt and Hello Kitty hairband. Had seen the camel-coated back of the kind gentleman who'd comforted her, and a flash of his pocket watch as he'd reached down to help her to her feet.

They'd traced that watch to waterfront properties, a high-powered job in the City, every luxury money could buy and then some. A slew of false names, this house belonging to one of them. And then they'd followed the trail down and down again to this room with its operating table and its instruments and its chains. To this corpse with its internal organs removed and placed in labelled jars. With its lips sewn shut and its eyes sewn open and a Hello Kitty hairband in its hair.

May thought he said something. Pretty sure the strangled noise was his voice. But he'd mostly lost himself, not quite following who was striding back up the stairs with Smith's shouts chasing him and a head full of such rage that the skull had shattered under the pressure and the fury was smoking behind him in a tail like a dark comet.

Footsteps came running behind him, but he was in the living room now, looking at white furniture, deep white carpets like clouds. Looking at polish and varnish and golden autumn light slanting through high windows onto a monster in an Armani suit.

"Sir!" Reed squeaked as May reached out a lazy hand and shoved him aside.

Fingers tried to grab hold of his jacket from the back. "May! May! Michael! Listen to me."

He twitched them aside, drew back, and punched Watkins straight in the gut, the satisfying impact reverberating through his knuckles into every bone of his body. How about he show the bastard what it was like when *his* internal organs were pulped?

Watkins tried to double over, still cuffed to the stair rods like a crucifixion. It brought his smug mouth down perfectly to the level of May's fists, and May hit him twice more, splitting his lip, bloodying his nose, making spittle and blood fly. He grinned, fierce, righteous, because this was just what the guy deserved. No. He deserved more, so much more. May drew back his hand to strike again.

But something was stopping him from swinging. He tried his hardest, succeeded in unbalancing Smith and dragging her forwards, but she kept right on clinging to his arm as Reed's long grasp locked around his waist and the ADC fought to pull him away.

May could have shaken them both off without much effort, but the contact, their grip, their concerned voices, started to wake up something human in him again. He was coming to after having been unconscious, all the madness that had been spiralling around his head contracting into a little black hole that he swallowed back down.

Just because the guy deserved this didn't mean May could go around beating up defenceless citizens. He was not fucking Batman. He was better than this.

"Shit," he said, appalled, and stepped away from the prisoner. "Shit. Jenny, Mark. I'm sorry."

They let him go. Stood, looking at him with shocked and unsettled eyes, Jenny with that guilt back, all over her face like she somehow thought any of this was her fault.

Silence while it all sank in, and then Watkins raised his head and smiled. "I have friends in places so high you don't even know they exist. I'm going to be fine. But you? I'm going to see you broken for police brutality at the least. At the very least."

It was later, and he was standing in DS Egmont's office, breathing in the smell of cardboard files, hot ink from the laser printer, and the sergeant's cheap cologne that he wore in bucketfuls and refreshed every time he went to the toilet.

May wished it was stronger. Strong enough to scour the remembered scents out of him, take the inside off his nose and make it impossible for him to smell anything again. He couldn't stand in front of the sergeant with his hands in his pockets, so he locked them together behind his back and felt the tremor travel up his arms, across his shoulders, and jangle the headache that sat like a fat crow on the crown of his head.

"Sit down, May."

DS Egmont looked like he'd been left out too long in the sun. White shirt, grey tie, grey skin, white hair, white rims around his pale, pale-blue eyes. Rumours had it he wasn't as old as he looked, nor as washed-up, but maybe he didn't have the ruthlessness he needed to get promoted. Maybe he'd had so much of the stuffing knocked out of him as a lowly copper that there wasn't anything left to rise up the chain. May figured he knew how that felt.

He sat down carefully, tucking his hands under his thighs to keep them still.

Egmont nodded at them. "You hiding the split knuckles, or are you hiding the shakes?"

Stuffing or not, he was a wily old bastard. "Shakes, sir."

Shame was perhaps ninety percent of the weight lodged under May's breastbone where a heart should be, but he had enough experience of the stuff to know the shame was only a sugar coating on something more insidious, so deep, so hollow he often wondered why he didn't implode. Take himself out of existence, like a soap bubble with all the air sucked out. Right at this moment, he'd welcome it. Just to be able to stop. Stop thinking. Stop hurting. Stop being him. That would be fantastic.

Of course it carried on not happening. He bowed his head and addressed the blotter and pen set on Egmont's desk. "I'm sorry, sir."

Egmont got up and took his crumpled suit and dandelion hair over to the window. "First of all, good job on getting that sick bastard. He thinks he's walking free from this, but he's not. If there ever was an open-and-shut case, this would be it."

"Yes, sir." May wished he could believe it. Half of him still did. Under all the despair, part of him still believed in justice. Even in the criminal justice system. It was creaky and slow and weighted towards the criminal, but it wasn't systemically corrupt.

It didn't have to be, though. "I don't know. He seemed pretty sure. Lots of money, best lawyer, one bad judge. What're the chances?"

"That's not our concern." Egmont looked out over the scrubby miniature roses in their faded window box to the rooftops of his metropolis. "But it's hard to coerce a whole jury, and if he tries, we'll charge him with that too." He took in a long breath. "That's not what I want to talk to you about."

In the light from the window he had all but disappeared: only a pair of dark trousers and a belt visible against the light; everything else a haze of white against a white sky. May's imagination tasered him with the memory of a man literally severed at the waist. He'd seen one once, as a new constable: a man who had committed suicide by jumping in front of an underground train; his lower half intact, his upper half smeared along the train tracks for three miles.

He closed his eyes in an attempt to force the picture back into the dark, but all the graves were opening now, and his head was full of horrors he couldn't even say he'd imagined.

"No, sir. I assaulted a prisoner. In . . . in my defence, sir, he deserved it."

Egmont turned around, but it didn't do much to make him more visible. He was just a condemning voice from the corner, disembodied, like a judgement handed down by God. "He deserves hanging, and not the long-drop kind either. But maybe you can comfort yourself with the thought of what he's going to get when he's banged up with the decent cons."

He sighed, drifting back to his desk, suddenly visible again, a man made out of paper and regrets. "But you, May. I can't have you going round assaulting my suspects. I don't give a shit what he deserves. *I* deserve not to have my station under investigation for police brutality. Do you hear me? I need you to get yourself together and be absolutely squeaky clean from now on, or I will not go to the wall for you. As it is, I'm tempted to let you face this one on your own. The man was tied hand and foot, for God's sake. You didn't even have the excuse of an affray."

May took his hands out from under his legs and tipped his face into them. How the hell had it come to this? He'd known he wanted to be a policeman from the age of five. He'd spent his school life getting between the bullies and their prey. He could no more walk away from someone else's danger than he could leave his own arm behind, but . . .

But he was starting to think he couldn't do it anymore. If he had to walk into another room with another dead girl in it, he couldn't guarantee that anyone would be able to hold him back again. He wanted it all to stop so badly, he'd started fantasising about choking the next rapist with his bare hands, and if he ever met Watkins again . . . He could almost feel the man's neck under his fingers, the cartilage cracking under his thumbs.

"Are you losing it, May? Is that what's going on?"

It wasn't such a hard question to answer after all. "Yes, sir. I think so. I think maybe I should resign before you have to throw me out."

"You can't promise me it will never happen again?"

"No, sir. I'm fairly sure it will."

Egmont sighed. May could feel the pale gaze on the top of his bent head. Then the sergeant sat down and hunted in his desk before drawing out the appropriate form. "I understand your father just died?"

That was an unexpected stab. Smith must have mentioned it. May hadn't taken time off for the funeral, just arranged it over the phone, and hoped the old bastard had at least one mourner, but it damn sure wasn't going to be him. "Yes, sir."

Another sigh and some warmth in the wintery old voice. "Well, I think I can sell this to the powers that be as an incident brought on by grief. With that and your resignation, we should be able to put it to bed in such a way that your pension is secure and your record is clean."

"Yes, sir." The prospect of being dishonourably dismissed hadn't felt real until he narrowly avoided it. Grief and horror overwhelmed him again at the reprieve. "Could I . . . Could I come back? If I get this under control—some kind of anger-management thing—could I be reinstated?"

It was like asking, *If I sort myself out, could I be Michael May again?* The job was so integral to who he was.

But Egmont shook his head. "Maybe you could reapply, start again on the beat in some little peaceful station out in the sticks, but no one's going to want you like this, Michael. Just be glad that you got out before you fucked it up any worse."

CHAPTER
TWO

"I can't believe it." Jenny tucked the ends of her scarf back into her green greatcoat and glanced away. Her mouth set hard and her chin crumpled a little in an effort not to cry. Out of solidarity, May looked in the opposite direction, over the lawns and trees of St. James's Park to where the fountains were playing in the Serpentine.

October's wet cold had taken a brief break in favour of the kind of autumnal weather you saw on postcards. The sky was clear deep blue, the ashes and oaks of the park had turned a dozen shades of burnt umber and orange and gold. Blown leaves whispered down the paths and the water in the fountains glittered like diamonds.

He watched London's bundled-up passersby hurry along and saw murderers and their victims as though the day had been rolling in spilled blood.

"I shouldn't have insisted you went in," Jenny was saying, her voice under control now. He looked back, and her face was smooth again, her eyes only a little brilliant, and that could pass for the effect of the wind. "I could tell something was wrong. I shouldn't have—"

"It was going to come out sooner or later," he said, nudging a fallen conker with the toe of his shoe. It reminded him of childhood's small pleasures, such as they were. At least his school days were all behind him. He'd have to go a long way before his life got that bad again.

"But you were holding it together until then, and I—"

The wind plucked the ends of her scarf out of her coat. A silvery thing that looked soft. She'd tied it in some kind of elaborate knot, and he hadn't even teased her for it—that was how bad things had got.

"You know—" he started them walking again, over towards Paddington and Khan's Indian restaurant, where they traditionally ate when everything was shit and they needed to be reminded that something was worth carrying on for "—I'm not sure I've been normal for months."

Jenny laughed. "You've never been normal, May. It's what I like about you. I ask myself every morning, 'What kind of freak show are we going to get today?' It keeps things interesting."

The wind tussled with her hair, unravelling it from its braid. It never stayed as sharp as she wished. Two hours into the day she always ended up looking like she'd rammed it into a hedge full of teasels. Then she would bitch about it and spend twenty minutes in the toilets redoing it. He once suggested shaving it all off. She actually had the kind of strong-boned face that would look good under a buzz cut. But she'd just called him a wanker and laughed.

And now she isn't your partner anymore. Like taking hold of an electric fence, the thought tensed all his muscles to the point of pain, but he couldn't let it go. He stopped and put his head in his hands. After a while, she took his elbow and tugged, and they walked on with her leading him, like a plough boy with his horse.

"But yes," she conceded, "you haven't been quite the life and soul of the party you normally are. I've missed the deadpan snarking. What happened?"

"I don't know."

"Come on!"

He managed the glimmer of a smile at her scepticism as they skirted the fountains and the little Victorian glasshouse that looked in the long rays of the setting sun as though it were made out of light.

"I don't."

A final screen of trees and they stepped out onto Bayswater Road, glowered over by monumental hotels. Had to run full pelt over one carriageway, then stand on the white line for ten minutes waiting for the chance to get across the second. Then they disappeared into the warren of narrow streets lined with white-terraced houses just like the one belonging to Watkins.

Queensway Tube station fell behind them in silence, then Bayswater.

"I just stopped being able to switch it off," he volunteered finally as they proceeded past gardens full of chained-up bikes. Chained like her. A squat little discoloured church broke up the neoclassical façades with unexpected Gothic, and he thought about pederastic priests and the people behind them in the shadows whom he could never take on and win. It was like being a child forever in a house of fear, forever powerless to make the misery stop.

"You know? We get one guy and there's always another. There's always someone who'll protect the criminals and the rich, and there's an unending supply of victims, and nothing we can do to dismantle the whole . . . the whole fucking structure that props it up."

She flinched, and he wished he hadn't said anything. This whole talking-about-your-feelings lark was fine when your feelings were fit to be seen, but it just spread the shit around when they weren't.

"We," Jenny said. "*We* are the structure that stands against all of that, Michael. You, me, the unit, the CID, all the button mob on the beat. We're here to stop it. And we did, today. We stopped him."

"Too late for Stacey, though." May's turn to hide his face so she wouldn't see him fight off tears. He fixed his gaze on black-painted railings rather than see wheelie bins just like the ones under which he'd lain wondering if he was going to be shot. He wouldn't have to imagine the light flooding in from the sash windows they passed, that were the same ubiquitous pattern as the ones in the house where he'd found that little corpse. "I can't look at these streets and not think of going down into every basement, finding it flooded with blood. The whole fucking city's just floating on blood."

Jenny took his elbow again, but she was quiet until they turned onto Westbourne Grove. The shopping centre's cupola was lit up magenta pink against London's orange night sky. Golden palm trees outside Khan's gleamed with familiar welcome.

"Maybe this is a good thing, then," she said gently. "I don't want you to go, but it sounds like you really need to get away."

Inside, Tahir showed them to their usual table, but maybe he recognised when a man was so bowed with shame he could barely stand up, because he forwent his usual banter in favour of turning up with two whiskeys and a basket of bread, then leaving them so May could pull himself together in peace.

What kind of a man was he, that he could believe in this so much and still find himself unable to do it? Maybe his father had been right all along; he was useless and just too stupid to realise it until now. He was a mummy's boy, a cringing little crybaby who would never amount to anything. Well, that had turned out to be true, hadn't it?

And perhaps he could live with that part, if only the anger would go away, the terrible werewolf anger that was his father's true legacy. Could he be turning into the bastard? This explosion of fury, could it be some kind of late-onset psychosis that would eat him out from within, leave him bitter and cruel, delighted by his loved ones' fear? He'd rather slit his wrists right now than let that happen.

He sipped the drink, the burn and buzz setting a thin film of gold between him and the darkness. The bread seemed to solidify him, and he remembered he had not eaten today, too rushed for breakfast, too broken for lunch.

Sighing, he looked up into Smith's smile as she nodded Tahir back over and ordered for him. There was a finality in her gaze he didn't want to think about. "So what are you going to do now?"

May got the pieces of himself together enough to smile up at Tahir. Another person he was going to miss, another regret. They could have got closer if he'd taken the time.

"Is it a funeral?" Tahir asked and put his hand down tentatively on May's shoulder. He was a beautiful guy, with his black curling hair and his strong brows and eyes dark as polished obsidian. He'd made a couple of passes at May since his divorce, which May had rebuffed because the force was old-fashioned about queers and he was married to his work.

Wrong choices everywhere. He reached up and covered Tahir's long hand with his own squarer paw. Too beautiful a boy for a forty-year-old failure like him anyway. The guy deserved better. "Kind of," he said, distracted and regretful at the way Tahir's fingers tightened on the sore muscles. "Funeral for my career. I'm leaving the force, leaving London." He indicated a spare seat. "You want to sit down?"

"You wait until now to ask me?" Tahir took his hand back. There was a brief moment of indecision, and then May could practically see him make the decision to disengage. He was very gentle about it, though. "But I mustn't." He nodded at the rest of the room, where the tables had begun to fill up. "My father will have my guts if I sit and chat during the dinner rush."

He patted May's shoulder again, maybe consolingly, certainly in farewell. "We should have seized the day sooner. But I hope it goes well, your new life."

May watched him leave with the sense that everything was being cut away. A new life, eh? But he didn't want to have to let go of the old.

"So." Jenny applied herself to tearing her naan into orderly rectangles, eating first the curved pieces around the edges that disrupted its neat lines. For the first time that day, there was something resembling her normal liveliness in her eyes. "You didn't shut him down this time. That's interesting."

May relaxed minutely. If she was teasing him, then one thing at least was still all right. "Just leave it."

"I'm having new thoughts about why your wife left you." She shuffled to one side to let Tahir put down rice, balti, and a bottle of Tiger beer.

"Yeah, bringing that up is guaranteed to raise my mood." May smiled back, because oddly enough it was true. The shit in his life was hard enough without having to go home to arguments and recriminations and guilt. At least he was alone now, where he could drink himself into a stupor and pass out on the couch with no one there to tell him how pathetic he was.

"That's what I thought," she said, and partitioned her food into two careful camps, curry on one side of the plate, rice the other, a perfect straight line where they touched. "You know, I always thought she was a terrible bitch. But it can't have been much fun being some dour copper's full-time beard."

He wasn't sure how they'd got to this of all subjects. He'd been so careful on the job, never a one-night stand, never a lingering glance, just "unhappily married straight guy" leading to "divorced and bitter." It wasn't even that he expected her to be biphobic, just that the days when it wasn't safe for people to know he was bi were not exactly long ago. "You knew?"

She waved a naan soldier at him in triumph. "Not until right then. You walked straight into that one." She had relaxed enough to slump against the back of her seat, cross her legs, and rest her cowboy-booted foot against the pillar of the table. He recognised the pose. Tea-break time. Watercooler moment. Shooting the shit.

"Seriously. I can see why you haven't told anyone before, but—like Tahir says—you have a new life now. You could find someone, settle down. You know? Actually have a chance to be happy. It could be great. Anyone in mind?"

"Are you joking? In my state? What if they got on my wick and I punched them? I'm not . . . really not fit to be with myself at the moment, let alone someone else."

"You wouldn't do that." She nudged the balti pan over to his side of the table so that he could eat the quarter of it that she didn't have space for. "I know you. You're a lamb in wolf's clothing—"

"But I don't trust myself."

"No." Her smile turned bitter again. "No, and I guess you don't want to have to deal with someone else until you at least know where you stand with yourself. Fine, then. No boyfriend just yet. But what *are* you going to do?"

He'd been trying to avoid this realisation from the moment he'd cleared out his desk, but hey, that was cowardly too. He should face the facts as they were. Not facing them would not make them go away.

"My dad left me the house." A little clench of anxiety, a pain in his chest like a stomach ulcer. "From all accounts it's a tip." Brown patterned wallpaper. Brown curtains with great cream-coloured roses on them like moonlight seen through the slats of a trap. "But it's a waterfront property. There's a boatyard next door and a narrowboat docked at the end of the garden. I'm going to go there . . ."

Ramming his head back between the bars.

He's not actually there anymore. And even if he was, it's been a long time since he could hurt you.

"And I'm going to do it up, see if I can sell it for a profit, buy something else with the money, do the same again. You know? I like making stuff with my hands."

"You're good at it too," she agreed. "Those bookshelves you put in for me? They. Are. Awesome. All my friends think they're some kind of bespoke designer ware, with that curve. And yes. It'll do you good to repair things, make ugly stuff beautiful. Come to terms with the past. All that jazz."

He had the sneaking suspicion that at some point she had stopped talking about shelves and segued seamlessly into suggesting that he could make some peace with his memories, with the old bastard and the place where he grew up. That seemed needlessly optimistic, but he was not going to tell her so now that they'd both crawled their way out of the morass of despair and grief. It was a fake hope, but a fake hope was better than none.

"Yeah," he agreed. "Maybe it's time to clear out some old stuff and make way for the new. After all, I'm about due for a midlife crisis. I should buy a sports car. Get a tattoo. Drive off and see the world."

"Have a few one-night stands." Jenny's smile made a good attempt at impish. Didn't quite get there, but he wasn't going to point out the deficit. "I'm sure you've got a lot of good sex to catch up with."

"Is that you objectifying me now? Is that like one final indignity?"

She made up the shortfall with interest, her smile flicking straight through to delighted laughter. "If only I'd known earlier. You could have been my sassy gay friend."

That pinged him wrong. He thought of saying, *Listen, I'm not gay, yeah? I'm bi. Different thing.* But that seemed a little harsh and this was a bad time to start an argument. Best to let it pass for now.

"Hey, I still can be your sassy bi friend, I hope." He reached over the table and took her hand. It turned in his grasp, clasped back, and squeezed.

"Absolutely." Her smile had an element of apology in it. "You'd better expect me at weekends and Christmases. Holidays too maybe. Where is it you're from anyway? Is it nice?"

Her enthusiasm was catching. He remembered that he'd liked the town, everywhere that wasn't his parents' house at least. "Yes, it's good. Trowchester. Fourth smallest city in the country. Takes three-quarters of an hour to walk across it by foot from one side to the other, and half of that's river and floodplain, but it's got a cathedral and a charter, so it's a city, officially."

Tahir rematerialised to clear the empty plates, returned with a platter of halva, cham cham, and rosewater rasgulla, which he put down with an air of apology. "The meal is on the house, of course. Father said if we had known you were going, we would have done something better."

May bent his head over the sweets while he worked on smoothing out his anguished look, thrown straight back into grief by the kindness. "I didn't know either," he managed at last. "It was— It was kind of sudden."

"But you will come back?"

And that was the killer, wasn't it? He didn't know who he was anymore. He couldn't stand London. He couldn't stand himself. But he had a hard time believing anything would be better in the place he'd left as soon as it was legal to go. "I don't know. I don't know what's going to be left of me to come back."

He should have kept his mouth shut because Jenny's smile fell off like rotten plaster. "Phone me," she said. "Whenever. I'm always going to be here. You're not alone."

CHAPTER
THREE

He could have waited, could have clung on until the bitter end, watching daytime TV, or walking aimlessly down the streets where he expected every loose paving slab to tip up and reveal a corpse.

But having made up his mind to leave, he was impatient to get it over with.

He found a leasing company to take responsibility for his flat, put his belongings in storage to be reclaimed or thrown out later when he had the energy to deal with them, and set out ill-advisedly late on Wednesday evening, feeling like Major Tom in the song—high above everything, the world spinning by without him. It was nice of Jenny to say he wasn't alone, but she was wrong. He was alone, and he was unimportant, and if he died on the motorway on the way to the Midlands, there was no one in his life for the authorities to contact about it.

This realisation gave everything a surreal, disconnected feel. The traffic on the M25, bumper-to-bumper jams, insane drivers, interminable crawling chaos? It was like he wasn't involved with it at all. Someone else was piloting his body through the turns.

Night fell with a rolling of clouds as if the world had drawn on a blanket, and as he finally freed himself from London's traffic, the rain began to fall. He reached for a CD, refused to sink to the level of listening to Pink Floyd while depressed, and put on Vangelis instead. It did nothing to counter the sense of being alone in a tiny vehicle while the world did its thing without him, but at least it made him feel like Rick Deckard from *Blade Runner*. Washed up, yes, but unaware that he was about to embark on an adventure that would change his life. If he was going to be a retired and pathetic wreck, he might as well model himself on a retired and pathetic hero.

He'd managed to achieve some kind of Zen acceptance of fate for most of the drive, but when the landscape became familiar, when he started to recognise the hills, know the names on the signposts, everything closed back in.

His mouth dried. He rotated his jaw to try to work the stiffness out of it, but as soon as he stopped, his aching teeth would go right back to grinding. And it was stupid to feel like this, but knowing as much hardly made it stop.

He drove past the water tower on the outskirts of town. A retail park had sprung up under its bulbous shadow, and he stopped at the McDonald's there to eat a cheerless dinner and brace himself for the last gasp.

New nightclub on the high street with a neon dragon twisting around its door and a queue of implausibly dressed young people under umbrellas waiting to go in. Looked like the cinema had shut. If he let himself, he would feel regret at that—he'd spent so much of his teenage years there. Even on a good day, the potential of his father's anger filled the house with land mines. Home was where a wrong word or a wrong gesture, or being alive in the wrong room at the wrong moment, could trigger an explosion. The rules changed from moment to moment, so he and his mother never learned how to be safe—because that was the point, of course. They never were.

So the cinema had been a fantastic escape on rainy weekends. But regretting its absence would mean thinking about the past, and he was not going there. That was not what he was doing here. This was all about the present moment, nothing more.

Most of the shops were shut. The DIY shop had moved to a less salubrious venue at the bottom of the street, and the space had been taken over by an alternative-therapy beauty parlour. Otherwise the city was pretty much the same as it had been when he'd left. Even in the rain it managed to project a ghost of charm with its eclectic architecture and its drenched flower boxes. Its wet streets winding up to the cathedral, whose twisted spire was floodlit blue.

The golden angel at the very top of it looked down on May as he turned left from the high street, wiggled through narrow lanes congested with parked cars, and came at last to his old home.

He drew the car into the gravel drive and stopped with the house picked out by his headlights. The rain felt colder here, pouring off the porch, flooding the pots of the bay trees that stood by the front door. The front garden hadn't been tended for years and was now a wilderness of brambles behind a towering leylandii hedge.

Curtains were drawn over all the upstairs windows, and shutters locked behind the lower. He got the impression the house didn't want him inside any more than he wanted to go in. But he couldn't sit out here in the car all night.

He pulled his coat over his head and ran for the front door. Goose bumps stood up over his arms as he fumbled with the key. The wind blew water under the porch roof and spattered him with it as he finally got the key in the lock and tried to turn it.

It wouldn't open. He tried again, but the lock wasn't stiff—the key simply didn't fit. Now that he looked, there was a second lock farther down that took a deadlock key, something he'd never had.

He shrugged his coat on properly and buttoned it tight against the cold. It was very like his father to leave him the house while changing all the locks so he couldn't get in. It wasn't worth feeling more than a moment's irritation about it.

Jamming the useless keys back in his pocket, he left the relative shelter of the porch and stepped out into the drenching rain. The pea shingle of the garden path scuffed his London shoes and water soaked into the leather as he rounded the side of the house to get to the back garden.

New fence. Locked gate. But there was a drainpipe up the side of the house that his father had not reckoned with. He took a run up to the wall, jumped, and used the pipe to scramble farther, got a hand and foot on the top of the fence and let himself drop into the long, sloping back garden.

No lights on the opposite bank. With the willows whispering down to the water's edge, it was profoundly dark except for a wavering yellow glimmer to the right, where next door's land joined his.

He was already as wet as it was possible to get, so he followed the glint, curious to see what it was. The fences down here were much less intimidating. Great swathes of slats had been knocked over or were missing. He could step through onto the concrete frontage of a boatbuilder's workshop, in which a channel had been dug out to the river and a single-boat dock built. A rusty gantry crane straddled the dock, its taut chains still tight around the decaying hull of a coal barge that had been hauled out of the water for repair when May was five and left there to rot ever since.

Beyond it lay a larger boatyard, closed up tight for the night. More-fortunate boats stood in dry dock to be repaired, and in a larger basin beyond the offices, a dozen narrowboats drowsed with lights behind their windows and thin smoke trickling from their generators.

But the fire or candlelight he'd seen earlier spilled out of the belly of the rotting barge, showing off her great ribs. He wished for a torch or his badge or both as he crept closer, suspecting the local ne'er-do-wells were making an incompetent attempt at arson. "Hello?"

There was no reply, but his policeman's instincts told him that something had stirred, something had pricked up its ears and was now listening to him approach.

"Is there someone in there?" He came two quiet steps closer. Still no movement. A less experienced hunter might have doubted their prey's existence, but he just eased his weight onto his toes to go more quietly and listened harder for the crackle of a fire. He snuffed the air but only smelled diesel from the distant pumps and the dank, depressing scent of waterlogged wood.

He thought of saying, *It's the police*, but it wasn't, and at that bitter reflection he almost walked away. It was no longer his job to investigate suspicious things. Let someone else phone for the fire brigade or disturb the drug addicts in their den. Not his business.

He considered, *I mean you no harm*, as an opener. But if it *was* drug addicts or petty vandals, then *I mean to scare the shit out of you and get you off my neighbour's property* would be closer to the mark.

It had been so long since he'd been a private individual, nothing to back him up at all—no station, no sergeant, no authority. His step faltered at the knowledge, and he felt a pang of bereavement a hundred times stronger than he had felt when they told him his father had died. It made him gasp, rub a hand over his face to wash away the distress.

His fingers were still over his eyes when the rotting boat erupted with scrabbling noise. He dropped them, looked up in time to see a flash of white on top of a dark figure scrambling over the far gunwale and dropping onto the concrete forecourt of the boatyard. The instinctive reaction to a hooded figure running away was to give chase, but God, it was fast. Chains and detritus on the ground kept breaking his step, breaking his concentration. He got around the concrete lip of the pool in time to see the two luminous stripes on the back of the fugitive's trainers sprint around a distant shed.

He pushed himself hard to catch up, rejoicing in the familiar thrill, but when he got to the shed, there was no one in sight and no further glint of light. Panting, he put his hands on his knees and caught his breath. "Damn it." Then he returned to the dead barge and its crane.

He used a stepladder attached to the rear right leg of the crane to scramble onto the deck of the barge. The wood felt spongy under his feet, and as he got to the edge of the cabin his heel went through, sending a rain of punk through into the hold.

The light filtering out of the boat was not strong, but in the almost absolute darkness it was enough to show a rope descending through a hacked hole in the deck, disappearing into the gold-lit dim of the hold. No guarantee there wasn't someone else down there, someone braver, waiting in ambush for him to lower himself through the hole, eyes dazzled and hands occupied.

He went anyway, half because he refused to be afraid, half because he wasn't entirely sure he cared if there was a bullet with his name on it tonight.

Rain dripped from his hair into his eyes, pittered into the puddles awash across the keel. The stink of stagnant water mingled with the sweet rankness he was familiar with among London's homeless, the ones who had pissed themselves and then slept in it, had it dry into their clothes over days of damp body heat while they sheltered in cold doorways.

Gleaned wood from supermarket pallets had been laid over the ribs of the boat at the stern, where two layers of deck still kept a watertight roof over the hollow. On this dry platform flickered a pumpkin-spiced candle in a glass holder traced with decorative golden glitter, and a single dirty blanket with its end trailing over the platform into the bilge.

Around the platform, on every accessible space, flowers had been drawn—silvery ones scraped into the mould with a fingernail, huge black ones burnt on, maybe with the flame of this very candle.

May hunkered down and fished the corner of the blanket out of the puddle before it could sop up all the water. He looked at the little nest and blew out a long sad breath. When he was young, he'd thought everyone in Trowchester lived in snug stone houses. And yes, he'd gone so far as to hoard food under the bed in preparation for running away, but he'd never really had the courage. He didn't want to think that this place, this corner of old England where there *was* honey still for tea, could have anything in common with the uncaring metropolis.

There couldn't be blood on the pavements here too. There couldn't be, or where would he go to escape?

Pulling himself together, he took his notebook out and wrote *Sorry.* Tore out the page and pinned it to the blanket with a two-pound coin. Chances were whoever lived here was a petty shoplifter—he'd stake his life that candle had not been paid for—but it was a small measure of freedom that it was no longer his duty to care about that part. Anyone who lived like this deserved a little treat, now and again.

Climbing back out, he stumbled blindly through the fence and into his own garden. Knowing his father, cracking the house was going to be a serious business, and he would need light for it. He followed the slope of the ground down to the river's edge and waded among sedge and grebe nests before his outstretched hands found the hard edge of the narrowboat's stern. It too was locked, but it was a great deal easier to lift the small doors off their hinges and crawl through to the cabin than it would have been to do the same to the house doors.

He stumbled and cursed, knocking his knees against piles of hard-edged stuff his father had clearly put in here to hoard. Broken dishwasher. Valve-powered TV. Microwave with the glass shattered. Even a bookcase. He reached the bed eventually, blindly groped for the covers, stripped off his soaked clothes, and crawled in to shiver.

The bedding clearly hadn't been aired since his father's cancer was diagnosed six months ago. It smelled of damp and dust and mildew. Worse, it smelled of wariness and cruel laughter. It tightened around him like a fist. With the roof so low and the walls so close, he might have been lying in a coffin, but that was obscurely comforting. If he were dead, then he could stop. He could lie down and rest. He could let go.

He hoped he had not frightened his vagrant neighbour out of their night's sleep. The rain kept coming down, and no one deserved to be out in it alone. Maybe that could be his project. Not the house, but plugging up the leaks in the hulk of the barge. Give the poor bastard somewhere dry to sleep and a proper address, so they could start looking for a job . . .

"You're a lamb in wolf's clothing," Jenny had said, and yes, he didn't see why he should stop trying to protect people just because he could no longer be official about it. He only hoped his homeless neighbour wouldn't die of exposure before they had the chance to find out that Michael was a soft touch for a hard luck story right now.

The morning came early and bright. Condensation trickled down the narrowboat's tiny windows, pooling even under the cut-glass roundel in the toilet. The gas did not want to play but yielded to his persistence, and he boiled hot water before discovering there was neither tea nor coffee aboard.

"Urgh," he said, clambering back into damp, clingy clothes. "Fuck that. Fuck all of this. All of it. Every last bit." Then he drank his hot water and scrambled out to face the day.

Morning light revealed that the back of the house was easier than the front. A yellow plum tree grew close to the conservatory, so he could climb up the tree, across a branch that was dropping plums outside the conservatory door, and gingerly edge along the main supporting beam of the roof until he came to the spare bedroom windows. They were locked too, of course, but with a simple latch he could jimmy with a credit card.

He swung them open, crawled inside.

The place still smelled of misery, though if he was reporting it at the station he would have described it as the scent of decaying carpet and toilet cleaner, old age and dust. Since it was bright outside, he left the window wide. Sidling into the other bedrooms, feeling like a burglar, he opened all the windows in the hope of flushing out the smell with fresh air.

First things first. Downstairs, he chipped a chunk of semidissolved granules out of the cracked container in which his father kept the coffee, went to turn the kettle on, and discovered that the electricity had been turned off. He stood far too long facing the countertop, stymied by the silent appliance while his mind took a brief absence of leave. Reassembling himself to do anything else seemed to take more resilience than he had left. But he did it eventually, sighing and raising his head.

There were coffee shops in town. He only had to locate the house keys, then he could drive to the nearest and get his first coffee of the morning there, with something good to eat thrown in.

Long experience both of searching houses and of his father's sense of humour let him turn up the house keys in only half an hour: bundled in a plastic ziplock bag and taped inside the cistern of the upstairs toilet.

"He's such a card, your father. It must be a laugh a minute living with him," the old lads at the bowling club used to say to Michael as he stood dumbly in the corner of the room, waiting for his father to stop showing off and take him home, before the dinner his mother was cooking was spoiled to the point she could be blamed and harangued for it. And yeah, yeah, it was hilarious being the butt of the joke all day, every day, all your life.

"It's not funny, Dad," he'd dared to mutter once or twice, when the unfairness of it had got to him, and he'd been in a public setting and therefore relatively safe.

His father would beam from ear to ear, implore his friends to sympathise with his plight. *"You see what I have to deal with? The boy's got no sense of humour, and his mother is worse. I try to keep things cheerful, but these two? Sour as Scotsmen and twice as mean. For God's sake, don't be so uptight!"* Then—when they were home—there would be three-quarters of an hour of shouting about how Michael had let the side down, how Michael had shamed him in front of his friends, how he should throw Michael out on the street, though it would break his mother's heart . . .

His father's little jokes—they were just the petty nastiness on top of a whole berg of malice. Further proof, maybe, that his father enjoyed making life hard for him, but not worth getting too riled up about. He threw his useless keys into a plant pot, went down, and opened the front door.

Only to narrowly avoid being punched in the nose by the woman who had raised her fist to knock. They both ducked and recoiled. She laughed. She was a motherly-looking Chinese lady, with her plaited hair tied back in a headscarf. She wore an apron whose pockets were stuffed with bottles of spray cleaner and bright-yellow cleaning cloths.

May gave her what he hoped was a politely inquisitive look.

"Are you young Mr. May?" Unbelievably, she handed him a red thermos.

"I am." He unscrewed the top of the flask and inhaled deeply the smell of instant coffee, more watery than Michael's caffeine dependency might have preferred but oh so welcome. "I'm sorry, I don't . . ."

"Mrs. Li." She watched him struggle with the desire to pour and drink, and her smile settled into a beam of smugness. "My husband and I own the boatyard next door. I came outside to clean the unused boats and saw your car. You arrived during the night?"

"Yes." He ushered her inside, ashamed of the cold shabbiness of the place, although to be honest the ghost of unhappiness that clung around every piece of furniture might not be visible to her. "I couldn't get in. I had to sleep in the narrowboat."

"But you had keys?"

He decided not to embark on a full retelling of his father's last prank. The bastard loved to be talked about, and May had long ago decided he never would. "It turned out I brought the wrong ones. But it's okay. I knew where he kept the spares, so I'm all good now. Just got to get the gas and electric back on, and then we'll be set. So I'm afraid I can't offer you—"

Mrs. Li's smile broadened. "I thought that might be the case, and that you would need something hot to pick you up. You can bring the flask back when you've finished in town, and meet the rest of my family."

"There was an old codger who owned the boatyard when I was little," May offered, not quite sure what to do with a conversation that wasn't a questioning. "Looked a proper old salt. Aran sweater, beard, and pipe and all."

Her smile didn't falter, but her eyes took on a considering look, as if wondering if he was working up to something annoying. *I thought you people only ran restaurants*, for example.

"Yes. He retired in 1990 and we took over. You've never been back in all that time?"

Oh no, her faint disapproval must be more a reflection on his filial piety. "We didn't get on well, my father and I."

She wrapped her right hand around the handgrip of a spray-cleaner bottle as if it were a gun, and sighed. "But still I am sorry for you that he's dead. It's hard to lose a parent, no matter what."

This time May did pour the coffee and wrap his hands around the cup to chase away the cold. He sipped, and his entire body sighed with relief. "Oh. You are a lifesaver, Mrs. Li. I needed this. Here . . ."

He dived into the kitchen for a cup, filled it, and gestured her to one of the sofas. "Well, I can't offer you my own coffee, but I can offer you yours."

She waved it away with a resurgence of the smile. "I shouldn't. I have five boats to clean and pump out before the next batch of tourists arrives at nine to hire them. You enjoy that and come over, meet us properly later."

"That sounds like a lot of hard work." He escorted her to the door feeling marginally better about the day. Good neighbours were a blessing.

"Oh, it is. My . . . uh . . . my child helps, but only on the holidays. I don't want anything getting in the way of their schoolwork during the terms."

"I can see that." He held the door open for her. Coffee had given him the mental alertness to begin to grapple with his problems, so he added, "Is the crane and the barge in it part of your yard?"

Her step faltered a little, and her expression became unambiguously complicated. "I presume you noticed the state of the fences?"

Folding her arms and looking at where the tip-top of the rusting crane could just be seen over the hedge, she admitted, "The ownership of that strip of land is disputed. Your father has deeds to the dock, but so do we. Sometimes your father would put a fence up to claim the land as his, and my husband would knock it down. Sometimes my husband would fence around the land where our deed claims the boundaries, and your father would knock it down. This—" she made a gesture he thought indicated their introduction, the chat "—was partly in hope that we could talk to you more reasonably than we could to him."

"He liked to jerk people around as a hobby," May offered, feeling guilty and tired again. It was always this way. He ended up talking about the old man no matter how many times he vowed he would not. "He was never going to settle with you. He'd have been having far too much fun knowing he was pissing you off. I'm not like that."

Truth was he'd set out from the age of five to be the exact opposite. To be reliable and straightforward and honest. To have people know that they could trust him, and not to betray that trust. He heaved a great sigh of weariness, and followed her gaze to the beam of the crane from which the dead boat hung. He was still determined to do something for its mysterious occupant, if only they could be lured to come back.

May drained his first cup and refilled it. "I'd really like to be able to do some work on that old barge. Maybe see if it can be repaired. But I'd rather have the goodwill of my neighbours. We can talk about the deeds, figure something out that'll suit us all, I'm sure."

Mrs. Li's smile took on a shade more softness. "Well. You need time to move in before we pester you. How about you come over for dinner on Friday, and we'll talk about it then?"

Dinner on Friday gave him a point to steer by, like the North Star seen through clouds. With that as a goal, he could probably make it through the week. Maybe the boat restoration project wasn't so mad after all. And presumably he'd find out what was up with her . . . child as well, because the trained investigator in him just didn't want to leave that one alone.

"Thank you," he said again, ushering her out into the cold yellow morning. "For the coffee and the welcome and everything. I needed it."

She waved a cloth over her shoulder as she walked away. "Anytime."

May went inside so that he could phone for the amenities to be turned back on. But the house phone was dead too, and his mobile dangerously low on battery. The empty house surrounded him with silent recriminations, inviting him to sit and contemplate how very badly he had messed up his one chance to do what he'd always wanted to do with his life. Misery flowed out from under the tables, from under the carpet, down from the spiders' webs in the corners, and whispered at him with its soft, inexorable voice.

So he finished all the coffee in the thermos and went out.

CHAPTER
FOUR

Trowchester looked better in daylight than it had when he'd driven through it in the rain and under the influence of disappointment. With its great cathedral, its castle, the ruins of the Roman walls, the holiday traffic up and down the river, and its apparent location on some sort of Stone Age Zen pathway he wasn't entirely clear about, it owed a significant proportion of its wealth to tourism. And while the natives complained about this incessantly, it did mean the place made an effort to keep itself pretty.

The tourist hordes were thinning now as autumn added a bite to the wind and clogged the gutters with bronze leaves, but hanging baskets still filled the streets with colour and softened the predominantly grey stone buildings. Tourism meant there was not only a Starbucks and a Costa, but there were three other independent coffee shops and one tea shop far too splendid for an impromptu breakfast.

May got a fry-up in Sandra's Café, where he didn't have to worry about spilling sauce on the plastic tablecloths, and then headed for the town hall and the government buildings that surrounded it.

He spent several hours in the offices of British Telecom, British Gas, and Northern Electric, receiving promises that the power and phone service would be restored to his home in due course. They would of course try to do it today, but he should be prepared to spend another night without.

With that in mind, he bought supplies for the narrowboat: another gas canister to power the fridge and cooker, the kind of groceries that could be cooked on a two-ring hot plate, a duvet and sheets, smokeless fuel for the stove. As he packed them into his car, loneliness hit him like a physical blow, taking him by surprise. He felt the universe all around him, huge and busy, and himself, utterly irrelevant to its purposes, untethered from everything that made human life worth living.

So he wasn't going back to the house in that state of mind. He dumped the groceries in the boot, locked the car, and headed for the library, where he could read in the warmth, surrounded by people, and pretend not to be so acutely on his own.

As he passed the stone cross on Castle Street, a little bookshop caught his eye. Wedged between a glittery emporium selling implausibly coloured dream catchers woven out of nylon thread, and a sweet shop that claimed it was Ye Olde Candy Shoppe, which made him wince and had certainly not been there when he was young, the bookshop with its awning and small table of rummage books looked too classy for its company.

Its green-painted door had a knocker shaped like a giant squid, and was forbiddingly closed. The frontage of the shop was so narrow its display window was scarcely wider than a second door. There was only one thing in it: a single volume on a book stand, open at two carpet pages of illumination. Tangled swathes of colour drew his eye. Patches of gold burned under noon's strong light. May approached until he could see the delicate, intensely detailed pictures more closely.

On the right, a castle was being built out of a field of flames. Little stone masons in medieval clothes proved on a second glance to be animals on their hind legs. A giant hare with a cunning expression was operating a treadwheel on the top turret to hoist up a pallet full of hedgehogs. On the left was a sea full of monsters with the keel of Noah's ark just visible at the top.

Above this astonishing volume, old-fashioned golden letters had been applied to the shop window in a similar style to the fake Victorianism of Ye Olde Candy Shoppe. May looked up and burst out laughing. They read, "Bibliophile Bookshop: If this book doesn't bring you inside, I don't want you. Piss off."

The door opened silently onto coconut matting and a long pale corridor with cream walls, on the right hand of which was painted in careful copperplate, "Don't say I didn't warn you."

The steps up, with a handrail of ship's cable, had been roped off. Two steps down, through an arch to the right, and he stepped into a wizard's study. Heavy wooden bookcases lined the room and stood three deep freestanding in the centre of it. The smell of leather and paper and knowledge permeated the air. A great bench littered with tapestry cushions reclined beneath the window. Two enormous volumes were chained to reading desks just before the shelves began, their covers embossed with ravens.

Brass astrolabes glinted in spare corners and a distant alcove held a great Pegasus of glittering glass. He looked up and laughed again because yes, there was an embalmed dragon hanging from the ceiling, and it was giving him a peculiarly reptilian sneer.

The sound of his laugh brought movement from the distance. He walked forwards, saw more steps down into a further series of cave-like rooms where a young man with blue hair was just edging himself out from behind a large desk half taken up with a steampunk monstrosity of a till.

The young man straightened, looked at May, and froze for a long, telling moment. Not a bad-looking lad, but with a round scar on one cheek that spoke of having been bottled in a bar fight. Toned physique, square hands with tattoos over the knuckles, something indefinable about him that said gay, and something much, much stronger that said ex-con, but May was keeping an open mind on the *ex*. Maybe it was the flinch, or the way he had obviously IDed May as a copper and was now wondering what to do about it, but they recognised one another as predator and prey at a glance.

Except that May wasn't a copper anymore, and he had better not forget it. He swallowed down the stab of grief just as the shop clerk swallowed down his own reaction and said, "Can I help you?"

He should have expected that question and had an answer prepared. Instead he was thrown. "I . . . uh. I don't know."

"No, you can't help this gentleman, Kevin," a voice came from behind him. An older voice, amused, urbane. Just a little touch of Irish accent. "This is a man who needs something he himself doesn't recognise. Something he can't express. Am I right?"

Now May was amused too, because yeah, he'd just said that, but when this guy rephrased it in his intellectual doublespeak, with that smooth voice, it sounded deep. It sounded like he was here on some kind of quest. He turned with a smile to meet the person who was obviously the wizard in charge of this establishment.

The guy was shorter than him. That was always a pleasant surprise. But whereas May was wide enough across the shoulders to feel square, this guy was perfectly shaped for his height. He should have looked small, delicate even, but something about his personality turned it around, made him seem lean, capable, beautifully built and proportioned. Made everything else in the world seem out of scale.

He wore pale flannel trousers and a tweed jacket with a crescent moon tiepin worn in one lapel like a brooch. His white shirt was unbuttoned to the top of his waistcoat, his oak-blond hair cut in a floppy 1920s' style. Right down to the clever, ironic expression in his green eyes, he could have stepped out of an episode of *Poirot*, and though May had seen young intellectuals in London attempt the same look often enough, this was the first time he'd seen it really pulled off.

This vision of elegance waved a hand dismissively at his clerk. "Be off with you."

From the corner of his eye, May watched as Kevin took the hint. Stopping to haul a box of books out from under the desk, the young man disappeared through a distant door with a nervous backwards glance in May's direction, trying to look like he was busy doing his job and not running away.

Rocking his weight back on his heels, the wizard considered May with a small smile, as though May were one of his pieces of art, or a volume he was appraising to buy.

"You liked what you saw?"

May could have dealt with camp easily enough. This wasn't quite camp, or if it was, it was camp done sideways, undermining itself. He had no idea what to make of the man's attitude or demeanour. He thought he was being checked out, but he honestly couldn't tell for sure.

The guy's impish smile spread at his confusion. "The book in the window?"

"I like it," said May. "But it can't be real, right? You'd never put a real medieval manuscript out in the sunlight like that."

"Well, well." Everything about the guy seemed calculated to be soft. The oatmeal-coloured trousers, the whimsical fringe of his hair, and the lowered, lilting voice. But May got the impression that he was marshmallow wrapped round barbed wire. He liked it.

"They do say 'Don't judge a book by its cover,'" said the wizard approvingly. "It's obviously true in your case." He held out an ink-stained hand for May to shake. The grip would have crushed his bones together if he hadn't expected it and braced beforehand. "I'm Fintan. Fintan Hulme, the proprietor of this marvellous emporium. Call me Finn, why don't you? Everyone does."

"Michael. Michael May."

"What can I do for you, Michael May? More to the point, why haven't I seen you in here before? A man who knows enough not to expose a valuable manuscript to the light, but can appreciate a more robust copy . . . I would have thought a man like that would have had the good taste to come in sooner."

Okay, so now he was pretty sure he was being flirted with. A long way away from home with no career to lose and no one to disappoint, he was being hit on by an extraordinary guy. It occurred to him with a thrill of wonder that he didn't have to shut this down, and then with an accompanying thrill of terror that he didn't know how not to. He glanced aside, discovering that someone had drawn a mousehole on the skirting board with a little cartoon mouse beside it.

He admired the whimsy of it, wished he had something equally offbeat and interesting to say, but could think of nothing but the truth. "I . . . um. I just moved in. Into town. My dad died, left me the house. Though I'm actually in the narrowboat at the bottom of the garden." Catching himself rambling, he ducked his head, tried to pull himself back together. "And you don't need to know that, do you? Sorry. But I arrived yesterday evening. You were closed then."

When he looked up again, ashamed of his inarticulacy, his bald, unimaginative earnestness, Finn was so close he could see the faded freckles over the bridge of the guy's nose, laughter lines like spidery writing in the corners of his eyes. They were blue, close to. Blue with scatters of yellow spots around the pupil that made them seem green at a distance. And they were full to the brim with amusement.

Finn leaned in even closer, making May freeze, afraid to do anything in case he got it wrong.

"I'd open anytime for you."

Finn laughed at the expression on May's face. Nipping his upper lip between his teeth as if to stifle a triumphant smirk, he retreated and let May catch his aborted breath, struggle to slow his runaway heart. Wow.

Teasing. That had been teasing, nothing more. But shit. The visceral need to grab hold with both hands and taste that mocking mouth was brutal. Like nothing he'd ever felt before. He almost . . . It was almost scary. So unexpected, so unprecedented. He didn't know where to go from here, what he should say or do to put things back to normal. He covered his face with his hands to try to hide the fact that it was burning.

Silence from Finn, and then footsteps approaching him. He startled as a narrow hand wrapped around his wrist and tugged, making him uncover his face.

Finn looked older, with the impish expression dropped to make way for concern. Lines on his forehead and bracketing his mouth said he was about the same age as May, just doing a better job of not crumpling under the years. "I'm sorry," he said gently. "That was too much, wasn't it? You're bereaved. I shouldn't make fun."

Embarrassingly enough, May had to pull his hand back and cover his face again as his eyes stung. He didn't care about the old bastard dying. He didn't. But bereaved just about covered everything else.

"Let's find you a book." Finn touched his wrist gently again, leaving a fleeting impression of warmth. "Books cure all ills. What will it be?"

May rubbed his knuckles under his eyes to be sure they were dry, raised his head in time to see Finn trailing his fingertips lovingly along the polished wood of the bookshelves. Maybe age and experience was why he wore the clothes well—because for him they were a self-expression rather than a costume.

"I would recommend a happy ending, but there are too few antiquarian books where things work out well for men like us. So . . .?"

He turned to give May a quizzical look. In the muted light of the globe lantern that hung overhead, the posture bared the long line of his throat. May wanted to touch it so much he could hardly think of a reply, but inspiration came at length. "I— I have a boat I want to renovate. Have you got anything on boatbuilding?"

He braced himself for Finn to reduce him to the level of a tongue-tied teenager again with some kind of quip about being good with his hands. But Finn just beckoned.

It looked like the bookshop pierced the terrace of shops only to expand out in either direction behind them. There was a warren of rooms back here, all as idiosyncratic as the first. Mostly books, but with two or three beautiful things on pedestals in each room, vases that seemed to shine from within, automata that turned to watch them as they passed and that May found intensely creepy.

They stopped in a room that put him in mind of the Natural History Museum, where single-page illustrations, magazines, plans, and maps were stacked in sliding teak chests of drawers. Finn went directly to one and brought out a leather document folder which he pressed into May's hands.

May opened it with the care it deserved, conscious of the stiffened, cracking leather, the brittleness of the paper. It wasn't a book on boat repair; it was a plan for building a new one from the keel up.

"It's a traditional colliery barge," said Finn with an air of academic approval, "which is a little more spacious than a narrowboat but still fits in the locks. What better way to learn how to repair something broken than to build something better from scratch?"

"I . . . uh." May felt as if he was hanging halfway down a cliff. Finn, on the top of it, was holding on to the rope that was the only thing preventing him from falling. It was intensely unsettling to feel something so strong, so essential, for a man he hadn't known existed ten minutes ago. He also had no idea what to say about it, defaulted to the safest option, which was trying not to let it show at all. "How much?"

Finn tilted his head so that his asymmetric fringe fell entirely over one eye. A quizzical, birdlike look, as if he were a raven wondering if May was yet dead enough to be safe to eat. "Well, that's quite a question. If you follow this plan to the letter from beginning to end, not only will you end up with a new boat—a habitation, a form of transport, of freedom—but you will also have taught your hands and your body and your mind a dozen skills you never had before. In this plan you have the seeds of a new life, a new business, a new you. So you tell me. How much is that worth?"

The voice was peaty as whiskey and just as warm. May would have said it wheedled or cajoled, but those words were too weak to give the proper taste. It enchanted, and it filled the world with wonder. He found himself laughing at it as he had laughed at the warning on the window. Charmed and willing to go with it.

"How about you try again including the facts on what you paid for it yourself?"

"Oh!" Finn touched two fingertips to his mouth as if to hold in his own laugh. "You philistine. You wound me. And really, such a dreary way of estimating a thing's value. No wonder there isn't much joy in your life." He brushed his lopsided hair out of his eye with a theatrical gesture. "But if you insist. It cost me five pounds. Such is the folly of mankind, that inestimable knowledge is valued a little less than a burger and fries."

"I'll give you a tenner for it then. Hundred percent profit, you can't say fairer than that."

Finn opened another drawer. This one full of glossy leaflets, some of which May recognised from the local tourist information board. He brought out one that had been edged in silver, like a posh party invitation, and held it to his waistcoat as he gave May a sly look. "Are we bargaining?"

"I guess."

"Very well, then. How about you give me fifteen, and then you will value it all the more."

May laughed again. This guy was outrageous, and he knew it himself, and he still managed to pull it off somehow. "I don't think you know how this bargaining thing really works."

"I'm using the auction-house method." Oh. Finn didn't like having his competence questioned, even in jest. May found the brief coldness in the guy's voice a little reassuring. There was something real under the play, and he wasn't ashamed to show it. Good. That was good, because the only people May had ever met who were unfailingly pleasant all the time had been the most careful of psychopaths.

He stepped back, lowered his head in acknowledgement and heard the guy's tone warm right back up, though his words still gave no quarter. "I think you should quit while you're ahead."

"Fair enough." May leafed through the plans again. They were pretty extensive. Scale them up and he could see how all the pieces would fit together. He'd need a big, flat bare space to lay it all out in, but the disputed land was exactly that. None of it looked beyond his technical capabilities. With the first stirring of excitement since leaving London, he handed over fifteen pounds.

Finn gave him the flier in return. "I run a book club," he said, watching as May read the details. "Here on Friday evenings. We concentrate mostly on queer literature, and so in practice we are also Trowchester's equivalent of a gay club. You should come. Unless I read you wrong?"

May considered for a moment saying, *Yeah, you did. I'm straight as an arrow.* But he couldn't find the impetus to lie. So he'd never been out in his life? Then maybe it was due. "Apparently I'm an open book."

"I value that." Finn gave him a smile that was a little less like a weapon than his previous smirk, and leaned in to press the folder against May's chest. "So I'll see you there? We generally buy in fish and chips, so don't eat dinner first."

That jogged May's memory, which had been clouded by the experience of being leaned against confidingly by a perfectly shaped armful of mature, bohemian gentleman. He shook off the urge to reach out and grab the back of Finn's blazer, drag him close, and crush the plans between them. "Ah. No, I'm having dinner with my neighbours, Friday. Ah, I can't."

Finn stepped away but didn't stop smiling. "Well, stop by here early on. You can say hello to everyone, and I can give you the book for next week. Then you can come Friday week. There's no rush, after all. We'll be here when you're ready."

With his plan and flier in hand, May staggered back out into the early-afternoon light with a sense of having left a parallel world. A better one. The bookshop door closed behind him with a sense of finality, and although he was perfectly aware it was because there was a stiff spring bolted to it at the top, it still felt like a portent—as though the magic had decreed that was all he was allowed for today.

Probably just as well. He was going to have to think about this with some deliberation, give himself time to turn it over in his head and pry it all apart. Something was definitely nagging at him, beneath the worrying flutter of butterflies and heat. Abandoning the idea of a day spent idling in the library, and unable to progress on the boat until he had cleared the use of the land with the Lis, he went home and spent the rest of the day stripping his father's wallpaper from every room.

CHAPTER
FIVE

"**Y**ou know he's fucking filth, man. Right?"

Kevin had been fidgeting in the corner of Finn's eye all afternoon, clearly working up to this. Finn appreciated that he had kept it to himself until he'd ushered all the customers out, closed the shutters on the window, and locked the door.

"Your grammar, boy," he lamented, trying to turn the conversation away from himself. "Could you put that in a form your teachers would recognise?"

Kevin smoothed down his T-shirt and fiddled with his rainbow dog tags. He was a pretty little thing and hardly needed to wear the flag to advertise what he was. His face had been cut open once already because he was so gamine, so slender and effete it wasn't possible for him to hide. Finn admired that about him, but it fortunately did little to stir his loins.

What he liked was something a little more rugged. Something with wider shoulders, with lots of bruising physical power.

"That bloke you were all over today. He is a policeman." Kevin managed to produce one-and-a-half unobjectionable sentences. It deserved a response for sheer effort.

"And I am an honest businessman with nothing to hide. As, I hope, are you."

The trouble with the fucking bruisers was that they liked to think they were in control. Generally they took one look at Finn and assumed he wanted someone to tell him what to do. They were so preoccupied with being macho that they couldn't recognise his strength when they saw it, couldn't reconcile themselves to being bossed around by anyone as small, as breakable, and as offside as him.

But Michael May had stood in his shop like a lost child waiting for a parent to pick him up. With his stupid curly hair and his bull neck and the open shirt he'd been wearing over his T-shirt that utterly failed to hide pecs like steel. Twice as wide as Finn, and he was willing to bet that all of it was muscle . . .

"I'm just saying," Kevin said, sullenly as though he knew it was useless, "he's probably come from London, recognised your mug shot, and is checking you out for the plod down there."

"He's welcome to check me out anytime." Finn suppressed a stir of discomfort at the boy's words. It seemed unusually subtle of the police to send in bait so perfectly calculated to appeal to his tastes, but he supposed it could be true.

It made no difference if it was, because Finn had put it all behind him with his partner's death, buried it six feet deep, and run away to mourn and become an honest man. If the police were here to investigate him, they would find nothing worthy of their scrutiny.

And maybe that was part of what called to him about Michael May—the fact that he knew how it was to have left everything behind and started again utterly new. He recognised the fragility of the man as something he had lived through himself. And when it came wrapped up in such a sturdy little package, all vulnerable and lost, well, how could he stay away? He loved a paradox.

It occurred to him perhaps belatedly that Kevin might be concerned on his own behalf rather than on Finn's. "You *are* currently unobjectionably employed and not entangled with the criminal fraternity?"

Kevin took a moment to parse this into something closer to the form of English he preferred, his restless hands constantly tweaking at the careful disorder of his hair. "Yeah," he said at length, giving the inside of the locked door a worried glance. "But you know how they are. They don't let you go, not ever. Did you see how he looked at me? Like he was just waiting for a chance to have a go. Like I was fucking scum. You get a record, and they never let you forget it."

Finn had seen. He'd been lurking behind a bookshelf when Michael ambled in, all compact muscularity and aimless curiosity, like an inquisitive bear. He'd been checking out the man's very fine arse in those blue jeans when Kevin had made his move, and he'd seen it perfectly. The way all that unassuming, shambling gentleness had hardened and grown taut with the threat of imminent violence, terrifying and arousing all at once.

"Oh, I saw. It was delicious. Tell me you didn't want to just lie down in the middle of the floor and let him have his way with you right there?"

Kevin dropped his head into his hands and shook it. "You're fucking weird, man. Me, I like a nice college boy. Someone you can talk to, you know? Not that they look twice at losers like me."

"You should enrol." Finn picked up the old argument with a sense of relief. Thankfully Kevin had had enough of talking about his employer and had returned to the safer subject of himself. "It's not as though we're overflowing with business every moment of the hour. You could study for A levels when there are no customers in the shop and apply to the university next year."

Kevin gave him a complex look he interpreted to mean, *You're so old you don't have the faintest idea how things work anymore, but thank you anyway*, and said, "Yeah. Maybe. I gotta go."

"Cheerio. See you tomorrow." Finn followed the boy through to the back door and gave him an ironic wave as he decoupled his bicycle from the drainpipe and pushed it out between the planters of geraniums, under the arch of brick wall, and onto Cattlegate Street, where the rush-hour traffic was simmering bumper to bumper from one medieval wall to the next. Their windscreens reflected the sunset like so many panes of glorious stained glass.

He locked the door behind the lad, and put the books to bed, closing those that had been left open, reshelving those that had been half-read by his regulars, Old Mrs. Granger and Reverend Thomas, who came in most days to occupy his cushioned bench and while away an empty day in the warmth.

When the shop was tidied and dusted, he took the rope off the stairs and went up to his flat. Unlocking the single door on the upstairs landing, he stepped through into the pokey little hall from which all his rooms opened. He'd occasionally thought of knocking some walls down, making everything more open-plan, but when no one saw the flat but him, it hardly seemed worthwhile to beautify it. He spent so much more of his life downstairs. The kitchen had a pleasant air, though, with its window that opened towards the sunset, its view on the back garden, and the vintage French country table he'd found at a car boot sale.

His cookbooks rested snugly in a glass-fronted cabinet which boring people might have used for plates. He gave them an affectionate look but left them alone, having no patience for recipes tonight. There was spinach in the fridge, and thyme and parsley growing in the window box. He put a pan of pasta on to boil, finely chopped some garlic and herbs, then sautéed them in olive oil with salt and pepper. Added the chopped spinach and then the cooked pasta, served it onto two plates and shaved a little Parmesan on top.

Then he put his own plate into the oven to keep warm, took the other downstairs into the back garden, and set it on the iron table where sometimes in midsummer he took his midday meal.

Once back upstairs, he switched off the electric light, lit a candle, poured himself the last glass of the nice rosé he'd been drinking since Monday, and looked out of the window just in time for his dark-adapted eyes to pick out a slender, hooded form eeling down the garden path. It took the plate, dropped into a cross-legged sitting position, its back against a table leg, and wolfed down his cooking in indiscriminate gulps.

Smiling, he took his own dinner out of the oven and tucked in. It wasn't at all like the companionship he'd once had, but there was still something comforting in knowing he wasn't eating alone.

Candlelight always brought memories of Tom. In the early days of his loss it used to conjure him out of the darkness in strokes of gold. He'd be looking away and would catch the curve of Tom's cheek, the glint of his wheat-blond hair in the corner of his eye. He'd turn to it with a stab of anguished hope, desperate for a ghost, a vision, *something* real. But there would be nothing.

Thank God, there was nothing about Michael May that reminded him of Tom. The man was as dark as Tom had been fair, with something Greek—or Italian perhaps—about his looks. Tom had been six feet tall, which made kissing an exercise in a cricked neck, had Finn not moved it horizontal more often than not. Michael was scarcely taller than Finn himself.

Tom had spent so much time in the gym, he'd been sculpted to perfection, a living work of art almost too perfect to be real. He'd been vain of it too, Finn admitted with fondness. Always wearing the tightest garments, and as few of them as he could get away with, so everyone could see and marvel at what he'd made of himself.

Michael on the other hand dressed like a straight man. A man unaware that anyone might be looking at his figure with interest. Loose trousers. The shape of his shoulders and waist concealed under the unbuttoned shirt he'd shrugged over his T-shirt. It hadn't quite managed to disguise the fact that he was built like a brick shit house, but it had played coy with the exact details.

And that just made Finn's fingers itch to unwrap and explore and discover, out of pure academic curiosity. Pure academic curiosity being in Finn's case a drive almost as strong as lust.

"Don't be jealous, darling," he murmured to the empty chair opposite his, careful not to stir up a grief that had finally burnt down into embers. "I'm going to assume that if you can hear me at all, it's because you're in a place where everything makes you happy. So . . ." Ah, perhaps this train of thought had been unwise after all. His throat was closing and his eyes welling up despite his care. He pushed on through it because it was important. Because he would not be defeated by anything as mundane as death. "Be happy for me that I'm still alive."

He pushed the wine away, knowing better than to drink while morose. Five years was enough. It was enough by anyone's standards. He had perhaps, barring accidents, another forty, fifty years to live. He was not going to spend them alone, not even for Tom.

"You'd have hated this growing-old lark anyway." He forced a smile, picked up the one-sided conversation again. Man could not logically prove the world existed. Even Descartes's proof that he himself existed was flawed at base. Since the universe had to be taken on faith, he felt he could hardly rule out other things more up front about their lack of proof. It was possible Heaven existed, and that Tom still listened when he spoke, even though he never replied. "Wrinkles. Sagging. You'd have despised it."

But that sentence led to *Perhaps it was for the best you died while you were still flawless*, and he was appalled he'd almost thought it.

Candlelight appeared to be detrimental to his mood. He blew the flame out, went to curl up in the corner of the sofa in his tiny living room, and picked a book at random from the piles that balanced around its feet.

Typically, he'd just got comfortable, just found his place, when someone hammered at the squid knocker of the front door like a judge's gavel. He pulled a piece of junk mail out from behind the cushion for a bookmark, closing the book on it with a scowl.

His pocket watch said ten thirty, which was—in his now unobjectionable small-town life—a little late for visitors. Something about the urgency of the knocking lit up warning signs in his head, making him consider grabbing the fire poker before he investigated. But violence, however sexy, was not really his forte, so he made do with slipping his mobile into his pocket, so he could call the police if necessary.

The door admitted more rain, the dark bulk outside it not distinguishable until it stepped into the corridor and dripped on his matting. He let go of the sides of his phone and stepped back. Not a physical threat, then. That would have been too easy.

Howey Briggs rubbed a hand over his bald head to wipe off the water, and looked down on him with an expression of mingled smugness and disdain. "Well, this is nice. They said you'd skipped town. I had such a time figuring out where you'd gone. You should've given out cards, you know? Change of address."

"Change of life." Finn tried to root his weight in the corridor, to prevent Briggs from coming further in, but Briggs simply walked forwards, shouldered past him, knocking him into the wall in the process, and turned into the shop.

It was symptomatic of their entire relationship. Even the man's face was raw as a slab of beef, unaltered by evidence of thought, his eyes flat, suspicious, hostile, his body as ungenerous as a clenched fist.

He stood in the largest room of the shop, running his eyes along the bookshelves, lingering over the glass Pegasus and the other curiosities, all too obviously wondering how much money they were worth. "You done well for yourself, clearly. I've got something that will interest you."

"No." Finn second-guessed himself, put his hand back in his pocket, and punched in 999 on his phone, keeping his finger lightly hovering over the Call button. "You don't. Whatever it is, I'm not interested. I'm out of the business."

"They did tell me you'd been scared off. I didn't believe it. A little court case? I'd have thought a man of your calibre would have viewed all that as part of the game."

He had, at first. And then—perhaps because of the stress, perhaps because it was simply his time—Tom had had a funny turn the day before the trial. He'd been rushed off to hospital, stabilised, and tested. The doctors had said it was probably nothing to worry about, but they wanted him kept in overnight just to be sure. So Tom had kissed Finn and wished him luck, said he would see him tomorrow, victorious, and while Finn was being cross-examined, Tom had had a massive heart attack in the CT scanner and died. Alone. Tom had died alone, abandoned, because Finn had thought it would be fun to dabble a little in the resale of antiquities acquired by methods into which it did not do to enquire. That was the moment when it had all stopped being even moderately entertaining.

Finn bit the inside of his cheek to derail memories and nerves alike. "I am three seconds away from calling the police. I don't know how you found me, but please go back to whomever it was you spoke to and tell them I am done. Go. Now."

"You see." Briggs reached in to his messenger bag and brought out a palm-sized book. Even the glimpse of the binding through his callused knuckles made Finn's breath catch. That shade of oxblood red . . . that dusty-but-waxy look. The embossing, with some kind of ivy-like plant drawn in a style that went out in the tenth century.

His mouth dried. He let go of the phone and pulled cotton gloves from his inside pocket. After putting them on, he held out both hands. "God, don't hold it like that. Give it here, carefully."

Parchment leaves, folded in quires, hand sewn onto wooden boards, covered in Hiberno-Saxon decoration. Traces of pigments on the interlace. One or two flecks of gold leaf that hadn't yet rubbed off. He eased it gently open and fell even more deeply in lust.

Irish cursive script with the initial capitals surrounded by flocks of red dots.

Briggs, grinning, made a sudden lunge for it. "You gotta turn to this page, look—"

Finn snatched it away before it could be bruised by the impious touch. He separated the pages carefully and turned them until he could see the illumination Briggs had been trying to show him. An oddly elongated angel holding a flower out to Mary, Mother of God.

He had to sit down in a hurry on the step between one room and the other. "This is from L—" He didn't have anywhere safe to put it down, and his hands were shaking too much to hold it properly. "This is from Lindisfarne. A private psalter for the abbot, done in the same style. This is . . . It's as old as Cuthbert's prayer book. Where did you get it?"

"Come on, prof, you know better than to ask. So how much'll you give me for it?"

It rested in his hands so helplessly. A legacy a thousand years old. "This shouldn't be sold. It should be in a museum. Do you know—"

He had been about to say, *Do you know how rare these things are? This is a national treasure, beyond price,* but shopkeeper's instincts kicked back in. "Do you know how impossible something like this would be to sell on? With no provenance? Any reputable collector would arrest me the moment I tried."

"Mmm." Briggs held out a hand for it. "Yeah, that's what the other bloke said. I just thought of you because you used to be something special. And you allus had a fondness for books. Never mind. I made my profit in other things. I'll just take this back and put it on the fire when I get home."

The man was enough of a savage to actually mean it. Finn hugged the book closer to himself. He'd as soon have abandoned a baby to the flames. Law be damned, morality was all on his side. He did a quick mental inventory of what was left in both tills. "I could give you two hundred pounds, but that's my uppermost offer."

"I'll take it."

Briggs watched with an air of friendly interest as he scraped the notes together. "It don't pay so well, honesty?"

Finn counted the money out into the man's palm and then pushed him to the door. "Perhaps not. But I never want to see you again. Do you understand? This is the last time. Never again."

"Sure," said Briggs with a lack of conviction that made Finn queasy. But he did at least go away.

Finn's whole house settled around the book on the counter. Every particle of air, every empty space, seemed to focus on it while he fell apart in a burst of nervous shuddering. Oh God. Oh God. It couldn't stay here. Michael May the policeman was due to visit again on Friday. What if he somehow stumbled on it? What if he could tell it was here, the way these people sometimes knew?

He had to find it a good home. And now.

CHAPTER
SIX

"I thought you said you were out of the business." Dr. Martina Whinnery perched herself on the edge of a chair designed more for pretentiousness than for comfort. She had completely revamped her style in the six years since he'd last seen her—swapped faux orientalism for a charmless industrial aesthetic replete with polished concrete and galvanised steel.

She had done herself over in the same style, now aggressively tubular in a silvery-grey dress that hardly moved when she did. Her plum-coloured hair looked positively dishevelled by comparison despite being lacquered as heavily as her nails.

Finn had had second thoughts the moment he'd located her new address. No longer in the bohemian environs of Bayswater, but now in a waterfront property in London's dockyards. Clearly doing well for herself and determined to flaunt it whether or not the In Thing spoke to her on any honest level.

Her bookcases were built into the walls, covered with sliding doors of polished aluminium. He hugged his briefcase to his chest as he stood in the middle of the area in her warehouse designated as a living room by the possession of three Eames chairs all facing a blank white wall. Presumably some kind of projection system would, when desired, throw moving pictures up there, and perhaps give the place the illusion of colour for an hour or so a week.

He didn't like the thought of the abbot's book being left in those morgue-like shelves.

"I *am* out of the business," he said, and tried to rest on the edge of one of the chairs. It flexed in a disconcerting way under his weight. "This is a one-off, I assure you. But the book . . . the book! I couldn't leave it in the hands of philistines. You'll know why, when you see it."

Dr. Whinnery smiled at him with a professionally warm and encouraging smile. Shrink to the stars as she was, it wouldn't do to exhibit her own monomania in any clearer way, but he saw it. He recognised it as one enthusiast to another. Behind the polite face, something ravenous had just perked up. "Then by all means let me see it."

He had tried to make the book feel at home by wrapping it in a burgundy silk handkerchief and nestling it in its own little casket—in this case an old letter-writing box with its innards removed. He placed the whole thing on a coffee table badly made out of spoons and noted how the presentation intrigued her. "You're in love with this one?" she asked.

"Of course," he agreed. "Of course I am. Anyone would be."

She unbent a little, taking the box onto her knee. Opening, unwrapping. And then her purple-painted mouth fell open. "It's genuine?" She pulled on her own gloves and reached inside.

"So far as I can tell."

His conscience was a little assuaged by the tenderness with which she lifted the book from its setting, the care in her fingertips, the way she kept her face slightly tilted away so as not to breathe moisture on it. "Where did you get it?"

"You know that," he brushed the question off with a theatrical hand gesture. "Its owner sold it to me, of course. I have all the necessary documents and affidavits here."

In fact he had smudges on the side of his right hand where he had written them out, concocting a believable provenance for the thing and forging the paperwork to match. That part he still quite enjoyed—giving the book a backstory, telling the tale of its heroic survival down the years.

She barely glanced at them, having seen enough of his work in the past to know it was good. Instead she stood with the book in one hand and drifted to her coffin-like shelves. Hauling a chatelaine of keys up from inside her skirt, she unlocked and opened one. Inside not a bookshelf at all, but a second door, this one with fingerprint sensors and a twelve-digit pass code.

"Do you want to see?" The glance over her shoulder might have been taken as flirtation, but he was fairly sure it was just pride. She wanted him to look and want and know he couldn't have. Given that he wanted to brain most people who took a precious volume out of his shop, he was familiar with the feeling.

"Love to."

It was another room that looked as if it had been reassembled wholesale from the belly of a submarine, the dim lighting and the scent of desiccation in the air perfect for the long-term storage of books. Around the walls, the larger volumes lay on wide shelves, somehow dispirited and drained by the blue light. Smaller volumes stood isolated between marble bookends like prisoners in chains. He hadn't the heart to read their titles or to touch them, so tired they looked.

Maybe it was regret that made him realise suddenly—and clearly far too late—that he could have taken the book to the authorities, who would have restored it to its original owner. But no, when he tried to imagine himself voluntarily entering a police station, giving a statement in the face of their thinly veiled officious hostility, well. It didn't compute. He couldn't see that happening, ever. This, therefore, was the only choice.

"Here." She placed the abbot's psalter into an empty niche just above a red-painted Mexica codex and below an extraordinary fan of knotted cords that he thought must be a quipu. "Here will be perfect."

"With the South American books?"

She looked at him as if he were stupid. "With the other books I can't read. I don't know about you, but I'm not fluent in Anglo-Saxon and have no desire to become so."

Perhaps he *was* stupid, because it hadn't occurred to him at all. "You're just going to look at the pictures?"

"What a romantic you are." She smiled as she ushered him back out and closed the two doors firmly on the secret room. "I don't even need to do that. Every so often I let a fellow collector in here, and I look at their faces when they see all the books they will never possess. *That's* my prize. I spend my entire career healing psychological hurts. Which, when you think about it, is not very balanced. It's such a refreshing change to be able to pour salt into the wound and rub it in hard."

CHAPTER
SEVEN

Friday morning, he took the five thousand pounds he had charged her into the bank. "Come into a windfall, Mr. Hulme?" said the cashier, far too cheerily for a day on which dank leaves were sticking to the gutters and everyone around him smelled like wet sheep.

"Blood money," he replied, shocking himself. Five years out of the business, and he had evidently got into a bad habit of being honest. Fortunately his eccentricity saved him. The cashier giggled and looked at him with the half-worried, half-expectant look of a girl who didn't know what he would do next and wasn't sure if she liked it.

"Don't tell me it was one of those books where you have to sell your soul to be able to open it?"

Finn covered a wince by raising his eyebrows at her, and redirected her interest as well as he could. "Well, you sound like someone who would enjoy the fine selection of fantasy novels I have in the Jules Verne room. Why don't I see you in my shop more?"

"I don't like all that old stuff," she said, bundling the notes together with an elastic band and printing him a receipt. "Now if you started stocking real books—stuff published this century, I mean—then you might be talking."

"Alas, I have no room for your modern trash." He tucked the receipt into his waistcoat pocket with his heart beating faster than it should and a tremble in his fingers he found most irritating. "If it's not bound in leather, I'm not interested."

The cashier tipped him a wink. "Said the actress to the bishop, eh?" And they both laughed as he made his way back out into the rain.

It was a good recovery from letting slip an accidental truth, but the regret came back almost as soon as he was alone. Was it really any better for the abbot's psalter to be locked in a sterile cage where it would never be read than it was for it to be burned? And if it wasn't any better, then for what reason had he just sold the integrity he'd been working so hard to establish since Tom died?

He bought Danish pastries at Bernadette's on the way back for himself and for Kevin, but couldn't muster much appetite for them, tainted as they were by the pieces of silver with which he'd bought them. He felt as hunted and as defenceless as he'd been in the police station the day they'd arrested him. They'd put him in the cells to wait for Tom to arrive with the bail money, and he'd seen how easily he could end up spending *years* in this place where an ability to talk fast was always going to lose out to the clenched fist. If he was honest, that experience had scared the shit out of him, and he couldn't face it again. Even the thought that tonight Michael might be looking in at the book club made him queasy with guilt.

Stopping outside the shop to adjust the awning over his table of charity books (*Take and donate as it pleases you. If you have no money, take anyway.*) to make sure they were out of the rain, his gaze was caught by the wet cobbles, by the long street of receding shop fronts, now populated only by one other human being bundled into a dark coat and disguised under a yellow umbrella. It was a moment where everything stopped. Everything stopped and waited for him to reach his decision.

"Never again," he said, inviting the rain as a witness. "That was it. That was the last time. You hear me, rain? This time I really mean it."

He thought perhaps something had heard. The weight eased a little off his chest. The clouds chose that moment to part, and the street glittered as though diamonds had been spilled underfoot. At the touch of sunlight on his face, he breathed in, and something released in him. Who would have thought he'd been carrying that reservation all these years without even knowing it? That little hidden place that said, "I know we've gone straight, but perhaps . . . If the reason is good enough. If it seems like fun . . . we might go back. We don't want to be boring, after all."

And now it was gone. Five years later, and he'd finally accepted this was the right move.

He found himself smiling as he walked in the door. All of his leather chairs, armchairs, and window seats were occupied. Kevin took his feet off the desk abruptly at his presence but failed to look convincingly guilty. And it was Friday, a busy time, but he'd just had a revelation, and he deserved to celebrate that. He put the pastries down on the desk and gave Kevin a smile that made the boy side-eye him in return.

"Sweets for the sweet. My boy, how do you fancy holding down the fort here while I give myself a well-earned holiday?"

"Do I get paid for doing your job as well as mine?"

"I suppose you do."

"Then have a great time."

Boatbuilding plans and a house with a narrowboat at the bottom of the garden. Finn walked along the towpath, looking up at the expensive grey stone houses that lined the river. A less self-aware man might have tried to pretend he was not hoping to accidentally bump into the object of his interest, but Finn was not that man. It was ridiculous to have to wait the many hours until this evening when a little application of reason and effort could engineer a meeting earlier.

He clambered over Petty Curie lock, its great black wooden levers jutting out into the path in the shut position, as a blue-painted canal boat with a willow-pattern theme began to float up to the higher level. A charmless concrete arch of a bridge spanned the river here, and when he stood on it, he could see a neat little marina on the left-hand side, a rotting barge in a rusty crane, and beyond that a faded red narrowboat veiled under willows at the end of a garden. Glimpses of a house were all solemn stone walls and wrought iron, but he spared it scarcely a glance, because there was a figure by the river's edge, clearing junk out of the narrowboat, and there was his quarry, as large as life and twice as handsome.

Finn strolled down from the centre of the bridge and stood on the same side of the canal as Michael, thinking. If he was a cop on active duty, merely lying to pique Finn's interest, then he would surely be at work right now, plodding round the district with his partner. He would not be at home alone like this in the middle of the day, trying to deal with his dead parents' detritus.

Yet here he was. Clearly, the poor man needed company. It would be an act of goodwill to go and say hello. And of course it didn't hurt that today Michael had left off his overshirt and had obviously been working in the rain. The way his T-shirt clung across his chest left very little to the imagination and confirmed Finn's initial impression that the man was ridiculously hot.

"Hello," he said, walking up just as Michael was bending to lift a TV the size of Scandinavia. He paused to unashamedly admire the line of the man's back and his arse and the way the strain made his shoulders and biceps bulge. "What a surprise running into you here. Here in your own back garden."

Michael put the TV down on the footpath and straightened up, turning to Finn with an expression of wary surprise. Finn had been remembering him a little wrong. He recalibrated. It was a heavy face, to be sure, with sturdy bones, but there was a classical handsomeness to it that he had underestimated in memory. The eyes that he had taken for brown, in his shop, proved under autumn sunshine to be a light hazel that verged on gold. And he had almost forgotten the soul inside, the impression of something powerful reduced to helplessness, trapped and lost and waiting to be rescued.

What he hadn't seen before was the misery behind that uncertain gaze. He was just having second thoughts—did he really want to play the part of rescuer, which seemed like hard work—when Michael smiled. Only a little smile but very sweet. And Finn stayed.

"You showed up at my house." Michael bowed his head to smile at the ground before Finn's feet. "Are you stalking me?"

He hadn't forgotten the tragic directness, though. Bless the man, he made himself so vulnerable, being utterly transparent like that. "If I was, would you object?"

Michael raised his head as though something else was holding it down. But when he looked Finn in the eye, finally, the challenge in his gaze went straight to Finn's groin. "I think I can handle you."

"Oh, you'd be surprised."

They smiled at one another, as if aware how ridiculous the exchange was, and Michael lost some of his wariness. He picked the TV back up again and nodded in the direction of the house. "My father filled the boat and the house with crap. Let me just take this to the skip."

"I know some people who could use a TV." Finn thought of Kevin's pregnant sister and her ne'er-do-well boyfriend in their squat. "If you're just throwing it out."

"It doesn't work." Michael stood with the great bulky thing in both arms. One of the old-fashioned ones made of thick glass and thick wood that Finn probably couldn't raise off the ground at all, and Michael apparently hadn't yet begun to notice the weight. "Nothing around here works. If it had worked, he would have sold it before he died."

A yellow skip stood in the drive, on top of a flattened fence that had evidently once separated the front and back gardens. Michael tossed the TV on top of sheets of old wallpaper, broken chairs, and tables. One or two whole mugs and unbroken white plates with gold rims said that not everything had been rubbish *before* it was trashed. Even the blanket box with its lid torn off was broken from the inside out with marks that seemed to match the sledgehammer that stood by the back door.

"You want a coffee?" Michael gestured him inside. Finn was pretty sure he recognised rage in the heaps of broken things piled in the skip, but he'd been curious as a cat all his life, so he went in.

The kitchen had been completely stripped. Tiles and paper gone from the stained plaster of the walls. Carpet torn up and standing in a roll by the fridge. Dismantled cupboard doors that matched some of the carcasses outside had been stacked by the boiler, which together with the sink were the only two things left standing. A kettle stood on the bare concrete floor in an island of jars, looking like a refugee in the middle of a minefield.

Even more curious now, Finn put his head into the living room. The rage tornado had not yet reached this room, but Michael was probably right that the stereo didn't work. It must have been made in the seventies. A second TV was a little more modern, on a carpet that was bland and blue. The cream upholstered sofa had probably been bought in the fifties and was stained with brown streaks on one side. The kitchen was a war zone, but this was something worse.

Finn had a vivid imagination and this room was like something undead. He expected the walls to start leaking blood at any moment and all the doors to open onto emptiness with eyes outside.

The kitchen was comforting by comparison when he backed carefully into it and found Michael watching him with interest. "You can do the tour if you like."

"Is it haunted?" Finn asked, trying to put his finger on the feeling that was making his hair stir and prickle all over his body.

"To me, yeah." Michael's shoulders hunched as he followed Finn's gaze to the rest of the house. "But I'm surprised you feel anything." He gave a self-deprecating snort. "Haunted by memories, I mean. I hate the place, but I assumed that was just me."

"I'm very sensitive that way," Finn admitted, and added together the house's aura of malevolence and the misery Michael had been carrying like a weight for the whole conversation. "I'm gathering it wasn't a place where you were happy."

"You could say that."

Hmm. Big, strong guy with anger-management issues? Possible cop. Finn told himself to walk away and close a mental door on this attraction as firmly as he could. Padlock it too.

"So how about I take you out for coffee?" he found himself saying instead. "Or tea. The best tea shop in the county is only about a mile farther down the towpath. They do curried parsnip soup and cheese scones to die for. Or if that doesn't appeal, there are two pubs and an ice cream van around the same park. Come, let us disport ourselves among the dairy products."

The desolation in Michael's eyes was covered over by a wash of amusement. "Is it expensive? I'm between jobs right now."

Finn could have kissed him twice. Amusement suited him, gentling some of his more brutal edges. And he wasn't a policeman at all, so Finn had been fretting for nothing.

"Well, I'm feeling flush at the moment," he admitted. "Call it my treat."

"This is . . . um. A bit genteel for me." Michael looked up at the Mermaid Tea Rooms as Cinderella in her rags must have looked at the ball. Finn suppressed a smile and wondered what exactly it was that the man found intimidating.

The river had been widened here into a basin in which the boats could moor up and turn around. In harmony, the towpath had also spread out into a little paved plaza lined with pubs, an independent cinema, a neatly kept stand of public toilets and an avant-garde statue of what Finn believed was a crayfish made out of fibre optics, which was subtly coloured in the daytime but unpleasantly garish at night.

The tea shop on the south of the plaza, by contrast, was a study in how to do English countryside right. Its white-and-yellow façade was half-obscured by climbing roses. Its window boxes trailed verbena almost to the ground, and its door had the perfect balance of aged, peeling paint and bright door knocker. The door stood open on two large rooms where half a dozen tables were visible, draped in white tablecloths and centred with flowers.

When they sat, they were brought two menus, the first with a choice of light lunches, the second with 108 varieties of tea. Finn was trying to calculate the odds on whether Michael would go for Number 1: Ordinary Tea, or whether he would be more adventurous than that.

"The owner is one of my book club members—Idris," Finn said, enjoying the return of Michael's slight smile. "They told him the town wasn't big enough for another coffee shop, so he came up with this."

"And blew the competition out of the water?"

"Exactly."

Molly, the waitress, returned to take their orders. Finn lost a fiver to himself when Michael ordered the tiger tea—black tea laced with ginger. His raised eyebrows must not have been as subtle as he thought, because Michael gave him that look of challenge again. It dried his mouth right out and made his body sing like a taut string.

"What? You figured I'd play it safe?"

"I admit the thought had occurred to me. You seem a man who's comfortable with convention."

Michael snorted. "I've always tried to be."

Finn watched the waitress put down a china teapot on a tray with a milk jug and a pot of hot water, a strainer, and a lace-covered sugar bowl with silver tongs for each of them. A teacup and a plate for cakes came next, followed by a cake fork and a five-tiered cake rack with a selection of sandwiches and sweets. The table shrank to crowded patches beneath the onslaught of delicately flower-patterned tableware.

Michael poured himself tea and looked at the kitsch with a disbelieving eye.

"I can't believe we're having a talk about how macho I am about my tea." Michael's smile spread into the crow's-feet around his eyes. "I don't know what the hell has happened to my life."

"Ah, well." Finn relaxed, pouring his own Lady Grey and smirking. "I'm like the Spanish Inquisition."

"Nobody expects you?" Michael's speaking voice was a pleasant low growl, his laugh a few tones higher, more boyish.

"And I take care to keep it that way. So tell me all about yourself, Michael May. Why do you live in a house of horrors? What is the tragedy that shadows you? And more importantly, why has some discerning boy not snapped you up already?"

Away from the house, the vague sense of danger Finn had been getting from Michael was ebbing slowly away, leaving him oddly comforting to be around, like a big dog flopped on a hearth rug, dozing.

Michael filled his plate with a selection of sandwiches and lived down to Finn's expectations by putting milk in his tea, still with a faint, almost ironic smile.

"I don't know where to start on all that," he admitted, with a quick glance up to check if Finn was still looking. Shy didn't seem the right word for his mannerisms, but it was close. He shrugged one shoulder. "But you should probably know I've been bisexual passing as straight most of my life. So, no discerning boys because I've been married ten years, and divorced and bitter for another three."

"And then one day you decided, 'Sod that for a lark. Time to come out'?" Finn wasn't quite sure how a man could go half his life fighting against who he really was and then turn it about in three days, but perhaps it had been boiling under the surface for a while, like a long-expected volcano.

"I wish I could say it was that deliberate." Michael frowned at the tabletop. The expression made him look five years older, scored deep gashes in his forehead and his brows. His face had grown so used to stress it had remodelled itself around the expression. "But no. I lost my job. I was with the Met? And antiharassment laws aside, it wasn't a good move to be openly queer in the force. I'd been gradually resenting that more and more over the years, so when I left I thought, 'Fuck that. Fuck that. Why am I even bothering anymore?' And I stopped."

The Met? Finn dropped a slice of cucumber sandwich on the floor, dipped his face out of sight until he could control his expression. The Met was the force that knew him in his old life. God, they were the enemy. What the fuck was he doing, consorting even with an ex-member of the Metropolitan police?

Some of Michael's rage made sudden sense to him. If it had scared Finn shitless to be in their hands for a day, what must it have been like trying to be one of them, hiding your differences all your life in an environment full of judgemental people, every one of whom was trained to meddle?

But why would you try? Why wouldn't you run as far away as fast as you could?

"You okay?" Michael asked as he came back up. And of course the man had noticed his flinch. Of course he had. That was what he was trained for. Part of the bulldog breed. Get their jaws in, and you'll never pry their teeth out of you again . . .

But this freak-out was not helping. Finn forced himself to laugh, scrambling for a way to turn Michael's attention away until he could get himself under control. "Just. Well, just recalibrating my expectations. I never met a forty-year-old virgin before. I should have handled you more carefully."

Michael laughed. "I'm not—"

"Ah, ah. Women don't count." He waved aside Molly's narrow glance with a quick, "In this context. How many men? Go on, you can tell me."

Michael bowed his head, looking hugely amused, a little embarrassed, and very definitely distracted from Finn's business. His hair was growing out of what must have been a very short cut. Rebellious wisps of black curls had begun to stray over the nape of his neck and his ears, but they could not quite hide the blush.

"I. Uh. I don't have to answer that."

And Finn couldn't help it, he was charmed.

He didn't make an excuse to leave, though he probably should have done. Michael was a long way from London, apparently hacking himself out of his old life with a machete. Finn was here to celebrate leaving his own. So maybe it wasn't time to run quite yet. He did, however, change the subject. "So tell me about the house? Was someone murdered there?"

Michael lifted his head and skewered Finn with a gaze like he was driving an icicle through Finn's eyes.

God, they were?

"You can feel . . .?" When smiling, Michael had sensuous lips, but they thinned to white lines under the pressure with which he cut off this thought. "'Murder' is not the right word."

Outside, the light dimmed to grey and a faint spatter of rain hit the panes of the windows. Molly came out of the kitchen with an arm full of logs and knelt to light the fire in the grate, while Idris leaned in the doorframe and waited until Michael was watching the flames. Then he gave Finn a subtle thumbs-up.

Finn waggled his hand in return. Undecided. "So if 'murder' is the wrong word, what would be the right one?"

Michael was all gentleness again by the time he looked back. A big, gentle puppy of a guy. "'Neglect,' I guess," he said slowly. "Or, I don't know. What would you call a cat that played with its prey but never actually harmed it? That was what he was like, my dad. You could hardly call it abuse. He was just having fun, lying, jerking you around, you know? I mean, yes, he had a temper, but he never *hit us* or anything. I always think I'm remembering it worse than it was, but then I go back there and I can't breathe."

Or maybe not gentle at all, but soft—like a garment that's had all the stiffness beaten out of it. Finn swallowed against an upwelling of pity so strong he hadn't known he had such sympathy in him. He remembered calling Michael *bereaved*—the sudden collapse the word had caused—and adjusted all of his assumptions again to take into account the fact that this was Michael alone, raw with loss and having a succession of bad days. He was meeting a Michael who was at his lowest ebb, and he was still all but hooked. How much better would it get when the man began to recover? "Your father's the one who recently died?"

"Yeah." Michael watched the flames catch in the grate. One eye gold in the light, the other dark. "I should be happy he's finally gone. I don't know why I'm not."

Finn gave up on trying to figure out the pluses and minuses of pursuing this relationship, let his instinct take him. He reached out and closed his hand around Michael's square fingers. "The human heart isn't well-known for doing what it should."

Michael's head turned. His deep and thoughtful gaze locked with Finn's. And yes there were edges and hardness in it that scared him, but there was such a sweetness underneath that came welling up slow and warm and strong to spill like honey over Finn's skin. His breath caught and the hollow of his chest filled with exultation. Before he knew what he was doing he had pressed Michael's hand into the table, immobilising it, leaned across the stacks of chinaware, the porcelain cups, and brushed a first, exploratory kiss over Michael's closed lips. The flare and dazzle of arousal was like a firework going up.

Michael gasped and pulled away. Reflexively, Finn thought. Reflexes built up from years of playing straight. But he didn't take his hand from under Finn's. He caught Finn's eye and licked his lips as though he was deliberately trying to sample the taste.

To their left, a tableful of teenagers burst out in giggles. From the kitchen doorway, Idris gave Finn an *I told you so* look. Even Michael was smiling. What could Finn do but give in? "And if the heart is going to err," he finished his thought, "it's surely always best to err on the side of love."

Which was surely far too strong a sentiment for a first date, if this meeting could even be called such a thing. Finn prepared to backpedal for comfort, but Michael's smile just sweetened a fraction as, with a strange diffident tact, he let the matter drop.

A half an hour later, they had finished their tea. Michael glanced up as the sun struggled out once more and gave the flowers hanging over the window an air of being preserved in amber. "I'd better get back to clearing out the boat. If I can get that sorted this week, I'll at least have a bed to call my own."

He eyed Finn warily, obviously wondering if Finn would turn the observation into some kind of double entendre, but Finn despised the double entendre as juvenile, and besides, this one was far too obvious. He just rose and accompanied Michael to the door. An awkward moment, when neither of them could decide what was appropriate. He held out his hand to be shaken, and Michael took it.

Brief disappointment turned into a delighted mixture of embarrassment and shock when instead of shaking it, Michael raised Finn's hand to his lips and kissed his knuckles.

"Oh," Finn said, taken aback and touched all at once. How old-fashioned, how unexpected, and how offbeat. "Oh, you're delightful."

"Will I see you again?"

It wasn't a question he could answer right now, for all he wanted to say yes. Deciding he'd been a widower long enough was one thing; deciding to take up with a guy with so many problems of his own was another. "Whenever you're least expecting it."

One of the advantages of them both being grown-up: Michael took the ambiguous response without melodrama, simply nodding and walking away. Finn watched him amble along the riverbank, his black jeans, black T-shirt, and black hair stark against the silvery sheen of the water, until he was swallowed up in the shadow of a bridge. Then he went back inside to pay the bill and field Idris's enthusiastic curiosity.

"Come into the kitchen and tell us all about your mystery friend," Idris said, catching him by the wrist and pulling him into the steamy warmth. Idris's cousin Lalima waved a spatula at him in acknowledgement as she smoothed lemon icing over a newly baked drizzle cake.

"There's nothing to tell," he said, feeling unusually tight-lipped. "He's just moved into town and knows no one. I felt sorry for him, so I thought I would invite him to the book club."

"And kiss him, in public, in my highly reputable tea rooms."

"Oh, I'm sorry, am I bringing down the tone?"

Idris stepped back, raised his hands. "Defensive *and* evasive. What do you think, Lalima? I think it's serious."

"I think you should mind your own business and get those scones out of the oven before they burn."

"My friends' happiness *is* my business," Idris protested. But he gave Finn a sympathetic glance nevertheless. "Is he coming to the book club? Because if he is, I don't think a lot of literary criticism is going to get done tonight. Eligible bachelor comes to town, and you snap him up before the rest of us even get to lay an eye on him? That's going to cause a stir."

Lalima looked at Finn's face and smacked her cousin on the back of his hand with a wooden spoon. "Leave it. I'm not joking."

It worried him a little that she could see the uncertainty on his face. "I'll tell you what's going on when I have it worked out myself," he offered. "It's . . ." *Too fragile, too frightening. I wish I knew what Tom would think of it. I wish I could ask him. Apologise to him. I haven't been so nervous, so full of butterflies and dread and desire since I was in my teens.* "It's too early to say anything for definite."

Idris took pity on him and let him go after that. He walked back into the centre of town along the towpath, with wet gardens sloping up from him on one side and the slow push of the river on his other. He had a good life, such as it was, alone in his little flat, with no one to tell him what to do. Master of his own fate and king of his own little kingdom. He wasn't sure if he had it in him to sacrifice that after all this time. But increasingly when he thought of Michael, it was with a tug and current as strong as the river, desire rising through him as irresistibly as a flood.

He went back to work annoyed at the poets who had neglected to mention how distracting and irritating and disruptive this falling-in-love lark could be, and annoyed at himself for being unable to manage a simple flirtation and potential roll in the hay without getting all . . . involved.

He shut the door on the last customer and ushered Kevin out with a feeling of liberation. Two hours to calm down before book group. He should make some dinner and—

The bell rang just as he was switching off the lights in the shop. He raised his eyes to heaven and unlocked the front door again, throwing it wide. "What?"

And oh fuck. They barged straight in, jostling past his raised hands. Benny and Lisa. The twins. Both mousy haired and high cheekboned, thin and swift and nervous as the speed-freaks they were.

"We heard you were—"

"Back in business."

"So we brought you—"

"This fucking—"

"Vase."

They separated as soon as they were in, heading in different directions. He could only stop one of them physically, so he stood in the stairwell and blocked Benny out of his flat.

"I don't know who told you I was here, but I'm *not interested.* All right? I am not back in the business, and in fact, if you don't get out of my house immediately, I am calling the police."

They know, he thought, tasting despair in the back of his throat like warm copper. *Briggs must have told them about the book. Who the hell else has he told? Do any of them have* proof?

"You wouldn't do that," Lisa called. He could see only a shadow in the darkness of the bookshop's main room, a suggestion of a white-gloved hand resting on blown glass. It was the sculpture of Pegasus, made out of glass reclaimed from the sea pebble by pebble over twenty years of the artist's life. "You know why not?"

"Because we would be—" Benny shifted the bulky parcel he was carrying into his other arm so he could shove Finn in the chest unhindered.

"Very displeased."

Twenty years of the artist's life and all of her care and genius expended over six months of intensive creation. Finn clenched his shaking hands and mourned preemptively. *I meant it. I meant it. No more.*

He pushed Benny back down the stairs. "Get. Out. Of. My. Fucking. House."

"Ooh, I'm—"

"So scared." Lisa gave a grunt of effort and a moment later came the thud and crack and tinkle of ten pounds of glass hitting the floor.

Finn saw red. Before he knew what he was doing, his fist was in Benny's teeth, and that fucking hurt, damn it, but Benny recoiled with a shout, sounding flabbergasted and betrayed.

Lisa came tearing out of the room at the sound of it, gaped at Benny's split lip, and gave Finn a glare that was like being splashed in the face with vitriol. "You fucking whore. Benny, you okay?"

"Yes. I think we should—" Benny backed towards the door, dabbing at the flow of blood from his mouth.

"Come back later," said Lisa darkly, ushering him tenderly out. She paused on the step to look Finn up and down. It was like being eyed by a starving wolf. "You don't get to say yes to Briggs and no to us," she said. "And you don't get to hurt Benny. We may be going away right now, but this ain't over. Is that clear?"

He shut the door in her face. But yes, it was crystal clear.

CHAPTER EIGHT

"**C**ome in, come in." Mrs. Li opened the door to him with a beaming smile. Michael was instantly glad he'd taken the time to root through the boxes of his possessions that had arrived this morning and find his suit, because she was very smart indeed in a soft-pink mohair twinset and a pair of Harris Tweed slacks.

"Thanks," he said, and offered the requisite bottle of wine and bunch of flowers. He knew very little about wine, but the guy at the shop had said it was a good one, which would have to be enough. He offered a nervous smile back, trying to be on his best behaviour, but not sure what was expected of him.

"Oh, you shouldn't!" She took them from him with pleasure, ducking her head to sniff at the roses as he had a good look around the hall and noticed the shelf of shoes by the door.

Coming up from the flowers, she caught his eye and nodded at him. "You can leave your shoes there and then come through. I'll just put these in some water."

As he was unlacing the second shoe, she returned, offered him a pair of white slippers, and guided him straight through into the dining room, where a man and a youth stood up to greet him.

"This is my husband, Aiguo, and my child Tai. And you should call me Lian."

He shook hands, resisting the impulse to peer at Tai's throat. They were as androgynous a person as it was possible to get. Longish spiky hair that would have suited an anime hero or a rock chick alike, a faint tracing of eye shadow on a face that was beautiful no matter which way you leaned. Flat chest, narrow wrists. He caught himself trying to guess again and firmly drew a line through his curiosity. The kid had obviously put a lot of thought into not letting their body dictate how others saw them. Michael knew enough to leave it at that.

"Michael," he said. "Michael May. I'm very pleased to meet you."

"Sit, please." Mr. Li drew out a chair for him opposite the door, while Mrs. Li bustled in and out, setting a dozen different dishes on the lazy Susan in the centre of the table. She put a bowl of white rice down in front of him, filled his glass with something that smelled like alcohol but about which he was too ignorant to go any further. Then she settled into her own seat and sighed.

Mr. Li raised his glass. "To new neighbours," and when they had all drunk, Michael gathered from the expectant gazes that it was his turn.

"To friends."

A certain air of relaxation entered the room.

Aiguo leaned forwards onto his elbows. "Please, start." And as Michael took a dab from each bowl and laid it on top of his rice, he said, "I was very pleased to hear that the house next door was no longer empty. Your father and I, well. Maybe we didn't have the best of relationships, but I was sorry to hear of his death."

"He, uh, only had good relationships with people who didn't know him," Michael said. "By which I mean he was charming to strangers, but if he was unpleasant to you, that meant he considered you . . ." A real person, a challenge, a worthy adversary—none of those were appropriate dinner-party fare. "Important."

"Well, so he should. I wonder if you brought your deeds so that we can fix this question of whose land is whose, once and for all."

On either side of him Lian and Tai gave identical eye rolls. "Let the poor man eat his dinner first," said Lian, rotating the turntable to put the dry-fried bean curd within easy reach—the one thing he hadn't yet tried. He duly sampled some, and then went back for more. It was amazing.

"So, um." He scrambled for small talk, aware that he had a tendency either to sit in silence or to conduct an interrogation, neither of which would do. "Why the boatyard?"

"Boats are in my family." Aiguo smiled. "We've always been river people. We didn't see why we should change that simply because we had new rivers. My wife tells me that you are interested in the old barge on the disputed land. Why?"

"I . . ." *hadn't really thought about it.* "I guess because it's there." Everyone wanted to know his business, it seemed, and maybe telling them was a good place to start getting over it. "I was a police officer in London, but—"

"Cool!" Tai's voice was a gruff alto, or perhaps a light tenor. "Did you investigate murders, like on TV?"

He had a flash of Stacey. Looking at Tai's narrow hands, he had a flash of Stacey's wrists, melted into the radiator. Pushing away from it, instinctively, he came back to find himself panting hard. Everyone watching him with horror. He took a shaky gulp of the pale green tea that had mysteriously materialised at his elbow. "Sorry. But yeah. Yeah, I did. And that's why the barge."

With concentration, he stabilised his breathing, managed an apologetic smile. "It got to be too much. So I quit and came home, to do something peaceful with my hands." He pulled himself together enough to raise his head and look at Tai, who was so young. "Murder, it's not . . . it's not as much fun as it looks on the TV."

"But it's important," they said, with a hint of sullenness. "Important to stop it, I mean."

"Tai wants to become a detective." Aiguo smiled at his child fondly. "And is doing very well at school, so I see no reason why xe should not."

May pulled himself together as hard as he could tug and smiled at the youth. "You're right. There is no better thing in the world to do. And you are obviously already a damn sight stronger than me. I'm sure you'll do fine."

The awkwardness passed. Lian topped up his glass and made sure he had seconds of everything before she said, "So you mean to become a boatbuilder, to support yourself in future?"

"I guess I do," he said, surprised that an idle thought had become a business plan while he wasn't paying attention. "I met this amazing guy in the antiquarian bookshop in town, and he sold me some plans. They seem straightforward enough. All I need is enough flat land to cut out the pieces and assemble them, and some means of putting the thing in the water after."

"And so we come back to the question of the crane." Aiguo gave him a considering look and pushed away his bowl. "I may have something to show you, when dinner is over."

He refused to be drawn on what.

Later, when Michael genuinely could not eat another bite, they went out together into the boatyard. Around the marina, everything was scrubbed and neat. The tourist boats slumbered like horses in their stalls. The huts where they replenished their water and fuel, pumped out their waste, were freshly painted and well looked after. A little grocery shop, now with its shutters closed, completed the spick-and-span circuit. Farther from the water's edge, the boats whose owners rented space for dry docking rested forlorn on their pilings.

Farther on again, behind the alders that curtained the back of the crane, a warehouse stood empty. Aiguo led him inside the echoing chamber. Dusty concrete, a distant corrugated iron roof, and a set of stairs up to a mezzanine floor where bulks of rusting machinery were overturned amid spiders' webs.

"What do you think?"

"It's a . . ." He'd seen a documentary about the *Titanic* and it came back to him in a flood of sudden understanding once he adjusted the scale. "It's a cutting floor?"

"Yes, and space to build downstairs. When we bought it, the boatyard used to do repairs. We found that side of the business lost too much money, so we shut it down. But you could use the premises, if you thought you could do better."

"And for rent?"

"Let's talk about those land boundaries again and see what we can work out."

They shook hands on a deal, not half an hour later, in which Michael ceded the disputed land to the Lis, but in return was granted use of the warehouse and crane for a peppercorn rent of dinner once a year. Terms to be reviewed in ten years. After the agreement was made, Michael excused himself to go and turf the last abandoned microwave out of the houseboat, so that he could begin to see it as a place to live and not just a tipping ground for his father's old rubbish. Perhaps he belonged with the rest of the trash, but right now he was feeling pretty positive about his chances of correcting that—of gutting everything that carried ghosts and making a new start.

Good people made such a difference.

"I really want to thank you for, um . . . reaching out to me like this," he said as he shook Lian's hand in farewell. Which was probably a little American in its earnestness, but there was too much dishonesty in this world. A little earnest truth was sometimes exactly what was needed. "It's been a hard time for me recently, and you've made me feel that there's hope for better things."

"Thank you." She ducked her head as if to let the praise pass above it. "But we are also glad to see an improvement. And in that vein—" she twisted her blue-black hair tighter and reclosed the diamante grip on it, her round face doubtful "—I don't know whether I should say anything, but, do you know him well? The man who called here earlier today?"

Michael's new little hope tripped and sprawled on its face. He tried not to let it show. "Mr. Hulme? From the bookshop in town?"

"Yes." She directed a troubled look at one of the bay trees that stood outside her front door. "When he arrived in Trowchester five years ago, there were many rumours. He's the kind of person who gets talked about. He turned a rather dull butcher's shop into that eccentric tourist trap of his, so many people had many things to say about him."

"I can imagine." Michael put a foot on his dread and tried to strangle it. Small towns and gossip made a famous pairing. This was probably just something of that sort.

"But you seem to like him, and I feel it's the responsible thing to tell you there were rumours he was fleeing London because he was wanted by the police there. Our local bobbies were in and out of his shop for months."

Michael remembered the dropped sandwich and the quick way Finn had redirected the conversation when he'd mentioned being a detective. Put that together with the fact that Lian seemed a reliable witness, and it added up to something he didn't want to think about.

"To be fair—" She raised her gaze and made fleeting eye contact before he looked away. "After that they left him alone. But then he went and hired Kevin Watts, who's already been in jail twice for burglary. The Watts family is notorious. Always fighting in the street and yelling at three o'clock in the morning. Setting cars on fire, stealing people's plants from their gardens. So. I don't want to speak ill of anyone without cause, but . . ."

"You thought I should be warned." With an effort, Michael kept the dread down long enough to say with civility, "I appreciate that, and everything else. Thank you again."

It was only when he walked over the collapsed fence onto his own land that his nascent good mood popped like a soap bubble, and his mind replayed Finn's flinch again and again like an earworm he couldn't scrape out.

He cleared the last of the rubbish from the boat, closed the doors, and ran up the generator. The space was bare now, chipboard furnishings standing unpainted, the only splash of colour the bright-red duvet cover and the faded blue curtains. He wondered what had possessed him to buy bedding the colour of freshly spilled blood.

That led him to wondering where Finn lived and what kind of high-fantasy concept his rooms were modelled on.

And that led him to wonder again whether Lian was right and there was something dodgy about the guy. Maybe something he used his charm and his eccentricity to cover up, to distract from? A tease of a memory kept almost forming at the back of his mind, telling him he had seen Finn before, and where else was there but in the police database? Well. There was an easy way to find out.

Once the generator had settled down, he plugged his computer in. He checked Google first just in case, but nothing came up except for the bookshop, so he Skyped Jenny next. She was slow to answer, and wearing a fluffy pink-and-mint-green dressing gown when she did. Surprised, he checked the time, and it was half past midnight.

"Sorry." He smiled apologetically at her bleary look. "I didn't realise it was so late."

She rubbed the sleep out of her eyes and gave him a rueful grin. "No problem. I'm glad to hear from you. How's it doing?"

"Fine," Michael said, automatically.

She raised an eyebrow. Rebuked, he rubbed both hands over his face and tried again. "The house is shit. He locked me out. I had to crawl across the roof and break into an upstairs window to open it up. The removal men have just arrived. My stuff is piled in boxes in the middle of each floor, and I'm not unpacking until I've gutted the place."

The other brow went up to join the first. "Fair enough. Where are you living now?"

"Boat at the bottom of the garden."

"And that's okay?"

"Yeah," he said, looking again at the bare boards. A lick of white paint and a couple of Moroccan-style cushions. Maybe a rug. He could see himself warming to this space easily enough. "Yeah, that's one of the good parts."

"There's already more than one good part?" she picked up with a grin. "I'm impressed. Such as?"

"The neighbours seem nice. And I . . . I met a guy."

"Oh." She pulled a hair tie from off her wrist and bound up her messy caramel-coloured hair in a sign that she meant business. "That was quick! Tell me all."

Michael bowed his head and tried to sort through his thoughts. They were deeply conflicted. On the one hand a shy, almost sly joy—a joy that knew it wasn't safe in his neighbourhood but was sidling in regardless, turning the lights on and softening what it touched. On the other, a kind of dull suspicious ache, the fruit of too many stones turned over to reveal hidden monsters—a certainty of betrayal and the anger that went with it.

He didn't know how to get all of that out in words, or what Jenny could be expected to do about it if he tried. "Well, I kind of want you to tell me."

"Because my psychic powers have never been stronger?"

"Because you've got access to the database. He's, um . . ." Michael attempted to marshal a description of Finn—the big, clever eyes and the way his hands and his body moved with such grace and such crackling energy. The hawklike delicacy of his face and his slender collarbones peeking from the open collar of his shirt, the way he unsettled and soothed and mocked Michael all at once, mercurial and fascinating.

He couldn't say any of it. "His name is Fintan Hulme. He runs a bookshop here in Trowchester, but he apparently came up from London five years ago following some kind of brush with the law. If local rumour can be believed. Can you hunt him up? Tell me what you find?"

Jenny leaned back in her chair, taking the top of her head out of frame, giving him a good view of the shape her mouth made as she sighed out uncertainty. It was paler than usual, bereft of its daytime shade of rosy lipstick. "Michael, don't do this to me."

"Do what?" he said, although he knew.

"Don't make me remind you that you're not in the force anymore. I can't just go giving out police information to private citizens. You know that, and you shouldn't be asking me."

"I do know," he agreed, the rejection biting like winter. "And I'm sorry, I shouldn't have asked. But— I guess I really like this guy, you know? And I thought I'd better know before I got in too deep. But I can check from here. I guess I could just ask him, right?"

"Communication." She tipped back into view again, relieved. "It's a radical new thing in relationships, so I hear. Louise did mention you had problems in that area, so maybe you could work on that, this time around."

He flashed back on long evenings spent with Louise, side by side on the sofa, each absorbed in a different book. He'd thought it was an idyllic form of companionship, right up until she started yelling at him for being *emotionally cold* and *negligent* and *withholding*.

"Yeah," he said, unconvinced. "I'll just come out and ask him if he's some kind of criminal. I'm sure that will go well."

"Ooh," Jenny laughed. "Burn. I've really been missing that sarcasm of yours."

"I've been missing you."

Another moment where he had said too much with too little disguise. Jenny's chin crumpled as she looked away. "Yeah. Listen. I'll see what I can do about the database. But this is the last time, all right?"

He wasn't sure if he felt more relief or fear. "I promise. Thank you." For a moment, they were both in danger of crying, and then the kettle boiled on its gas ring and he got up to pour water on his coffee. When he sat down again he had it back under wraps. "So tell me any news you can. What's been going on in your part of the world?"

"You won't believe this." She too was a little overbright. Neither of them mentioned it. "DI Cartwright is pregnant. No idea who the father is, but says she's going to keep it anyway, and DC Howard is already eyeing her office . . ."

When she signed off, the place felt emptier, lonelier, a million miles away from anywhere. The boat looked bare and the bed cold. Michael tried sitting on it, but in the small space, the curving walls seemed to be clenching around him, crushing him. He wondered how long it would take before whatever it was that was gnawing away at his insides would finally swallow them and let him die.

Okay, so it was a choice between lying here sleepless and watching the ceiling, or going out to walk aimlessly around town. It had been a while since he'd had any sort of beat, but he yearned for it, the measured peace of it, a strange kind of meditation.

Pointless wandering around town it was, then. He tugged his boots on, picked up the torch he kept by his bedside for late-night reading. And maybe he could stroll past Finn's place, see if there were any lights in the window. Decide what to do about it when he was there.

Naturally, the night was soft with rain, the weightless drifting drizzle that was the closest anyone could get to being inside a cloud. Michael pulled the hood of his duffle coat over his head, stuffed his hands in his pockets and headed upstream.

The hulk on its crane loomed out of the darkness to his right, the chains that supported it groaning as the wind tried to set it swinging. He stopped and examined it for a moment before climbing inside.

His money was gone, as was the blanket. The empty glass which had once contained a candle glimmered from beneath two inches of water in the well. He found a stick and fished it out, wiping the scum from it and putting it back on the platform of scrap wood at the stern with a sigh.

So he had frightened them away, whoever it was. Damn. One more thing to feel guilty about, one more poor soul out there in the world without a roof because he just had to pry.

As he climbed down, the beam of his torch caught muddy footprints to the side of where he landed. Sneakers, by the look of things, both with treads so worn down that the most recognisable thing about them was the crack across the ball of the left foot. He followed them across the yard, behind the boat shed, and to the far boundary, where a child-sized gap had been pushed through the hornbeam hedge.

Getting scratched and prodded for his trouble, he tracked the sneakers across a brook, up into the car park behind the Methodist church, where he lost them on the smooth tarmac. The tall backs of three-storey houses squared off against each other around the empty parking lot. A single streetlamp gave an amber cast to the rain and showed a distant children's playground, fenced with railings, with a wet slide glinting yellow, empty swings, and a spidery climbing dome of ropes.

That hadn't been there when Michael was a child—truth was, nothing had been on either side of the river but fields in those days. But he found himself drawn to it nevertheless, with some idea of sitting on the swings and rocking until he lulled himself to sleep.

He hadn't got to the gate before his idly sweeping torch picked out something that made him stop dead. In the far corner of the playground, a huge pipe had been set into the ground and covered with earth and grass to form a tunnel. From the near end of this trailed the corner of a blanket he recognised.

Instinctively, his gait smoothed, his footsteps growing silent. He lifted the latch of the gate with both hands to prevent it clanging and swung it quietly open. Pressing the bulb of the torch against his coat to conceal the light, he came within six feet of the tunnel end and hunkered down to try to see into the inadequate shelter. It was too dark.

Cautiously, he aimed the beam of the torch into the tunnel. There was a gasp and a stir. An impression of eyes, their pupils gleaming red-gold. Whoever it was, they were about to bolt, and he would lose them again.

"Sorry!" he said and flipped the torch, aiming it at himself. He could almost feel the light as it streamed past his face. "Hi. I'm sorry I disturbed you the other night, but it's okay. Come back and sleep in the barge where you were, if you like. It's no problem, and it's got to be better than this, right?"

His straining ears could just about pick up breathing, rapid and nervous, but no other sound of movement. This was going better than last time at least.

"It's up to me what happens to the barge," he offered, trying to sound soothing. "So if I'm fine with you being there, no one else can kick you out."

A long, long pause. He thought the sound of breathing evened and slowed a little. Then there came the scuff of a worn-down sneaker against pipe. "You're not going to call social services?"

Michael had to put both knees down in the mud to keep from falling. He covered his face. It was a girl's voice. Midteens, he thought. Same age as Stacey. The desire to weep took a slow swing into the desire to hit something. He unclenched his fists carefully and bowed his head into them.

"Shouldn't I? How old are you? You shouldn't be sleeping out here in the—" he swallowed a *fucking* in case it frightened her "—mud all alone. You should have a proper roof over your head and someone to look after you. And social services would—"

He was hunched forwards, blinded by the beam of the torch and his own hands. About as vulnerable and unthreatening as it was possible for him to get. Although he hadn't intended it that way, it seemed to lure her out. He heard the whisper of cloth against cloth and the all-but-silent footsteps as she moved.

"Social services would put me in a fucking home again," she said, bitterly. Nearer to him. He began to wonder whether she was armed. A baseball bat or a length of four-by-four to the back of the neck and he could be waking up—if he was lucky—two days later stripped of his wallet and his keys.

He'd told her which was his house. She'd have time to rifle through it for stuff to take or sell, and with the money she could buy a ticket to London to seek her fortune. God, he must at all costs prevent her from going to London.

He uncurled, reached down to grab the torch and aimed the beam at her. Caught in the light, she froze. Fourteen or fifteen, was his guess. Thin and nervous as a whippet yet bulky in many layers of coats, her dazzled eyes squinting beneath a tracker hat the colour of mud. She reeked like a fox.

"Would that be so bad? You'd have food and warmth and safety—"

"Safety?" She hissed it at him, catlike, backing away. "The last time I was in one of them, three boys tried to do me. Three of them and one of me, so of course everyone believes them, even though I'm the one with the bruises. I'm not going back there. Never!"

Another pace back. He could see her reaching the end of the invisible tether that connected them. If he wasn't careful, she would snap it and bolt, and he wasn't sanguine enough to believe he would ever meet her again. If he was to do her any good, it must be now. He raised his hands in surrender. "It's okay. It's fine. I won't tell them you're here. I promise."

"What's it to you anyway?"

As she edged away, he could see there was no weapon in her hand after all. Only the blanket with its dirty pink stripes.

"My dad died, recently. I guess I know what it's like to be alone. What about *your* family? Can't you go to them?"

"They're the ones who fucking threw me out in the first place, aren't they? Just 'cause I had a girlfriend, and how sick is that? They threw me out in the street! They were supposed to—"

She seemed to realise she was yelling, her words rapid-fire and all but unintelligible with tears. Another step back and she breathed like a weight lifter, calming herself down.

"Come back to the boat," Michael insisted gently, hurting for her, and scared. "We'll pretend I don't know you're there. Or here's a thought . . ." He could do this. If the alternative was letting her run off to London to get scooped off the streets by the next psycho, he damn well would live in the damn house if it killed him. "I have a narrowboat at the bottom of the garden. It's dry and warm. There's a proper bed and a shower. Somewhere to cook. Winter is going to be here soon, and you'll die if you try to tough it out without shelter. Come and sleep in my narrowboat instead."

She gave an ugly chuckle, her little heart-shaped face hard with grown-up cynicism. The big, star-grey eyes swept him up and down sullenly. He knew perfectly well what she saw—a harsh-faced, brutal-looking man three times her size wheedling with her to come back to his house? Yeah. He wouldn't have bought that one either.

Fuck. Fuck being a man anyway; sometimes the guilt-by-association was paralysing. What could he do? If he lunged for her to try and get her by force, that would be the very end of any kind of trust between them, but if he let her run away . . . Well, Watkins wasn't the only psycho out there.

"I only want to help you."

"Yeah," she said, and laughed again. "But the price of that is always too high."

"Don't—" He got up on one knee, arm outstretched, but it was too late. A flash of white from the soles of her sneakers, and she was gone. Driven out of another refuge by him.

So, that was the end of any possibility of sleep for the night. Feeling like he no longer deserved to seek out comfort for himself, Michael went back to the house and started on the deconstruction of the living room. The sofa . . . the sofa with the bloodstains down the arm of his mother's seat. Yeah, that had had retribution a long time in coming. He got the sledgehammer out of the porch and went to town.

The heft of the heavy lump of metal pulled at his shoulders like a butcher's hook as he laid into the wooden frame. Dull impacts thudded through his hands, down his back, made his head throb, and could not keep the memories away.

His mum had cut her arms to the bone and sat there bleeding. She'd sat there weeping, rocking to and fro, while the old bastard called her names. Called her a psycho bitch, a failure of a mother, a useless wife. Called her selfish, lazy, a waste of air and space.

Sweat made the sledgehammer slip in his grasp, but he only felt blood in his palm. He'd been eleven. He'd run to her side, kneeling there, her hand in his, her blood running over his fingers and his tears falling like salt into her wounds.

"I'm sorry," she choked, as he tried to pry the knife from her hands. "I'm sorry, darling, but I can't. I can't do it anymore. I just can't." And he knew exactly what she meant because he couldn't either. But he had to.

The back of the sofa separated with a tearing crack, and he whaled into it like it was a body, the soft resistance satisfying now, so much like the softness of flesh, of ribs.

He never knew what made his father finish once the man had started. He'd just run out of steam eventually, rise and walk away, and with the predator out of the room the two of them could move again. Michael had torn up his sheets for bandages. Together he and his mother had staunched the blood and wept themselves dry and picked themselves up to carry on another day.

But neither had the energy or courage to insist on going to a doctor. His father did not approve of needing the doctor, didn't approve of weakness or sickness. Even if they were too worthless to avoid illness altogether, they had both been trained for *years* not to let such a sin show. When the cuts swelled and reddened and began to seep, Michael had bought antiseptic cream from the chemist with his pocket money, and his mother had smilingly told him he was her angel, that everything was all right, that she was much better now, even as she began to stink.

There were stains from infection on the sofa too, because when she died of it, Michael had put the covers through a hot wash on the washing machine, not knowing that would fix the stain in and make it indelible.

Infection, and the blood poisoning that came with it, was a fucking awful way to go, and he didn't understand—even now, thirty years later, he didn't understand how his father could bear to sit on the fucking couch, in the same fucking house where she had been driven to do that to herself, and look at the bloodstains while he watched the TV.

Bastard. The bastard. The fucking, fucking bastard.

And he kind of resented her a little bit too, because she'd gone away and left him alone with it. But that was shit and unworthy of him, and he wished he could cut that feeling right out. Maybe with the same knife.

He choked in a strangled breath and stopped. The sofa lay dismembered about him, the room covered in fluff and horsehair. His hair and clothes were drenched with sweat and gritty with dust, and his limbs shook. Picking up the biggest of the pieces, he levered it through the doors and dumped it in the skip. When the whole thing was gone, he felt a little better. Calmer. Emptier.

Might as well follow it with everything else: the TV, the ornaments, the paintings, the hi-fi, the chairs, and the carpet.

By four in the morning he was ready to drop, but he stood in a reclaimed space, torn back to the bones. His hands and knees were like water. He fumbled whatever he tried to pick up. Opening the door, stumbling down the garden, finding his bed in the narrowboat felt like an unattainable goal. Kneeling in the bared room, he toppled slowly sideways, just to rest for a few moments while he got up the energy to move.

He awoke two hours later, stiff as hell and freezing, with a headache like a diamond drill boring its way through his skull above his right eye. He wanted a coffee and a shower and painkillers. Lots and lots of painkillers. But he still didn't think he could face the journey down to the bottom of the garden to get them.

Necessity drove him upstairs to the bathroom, where he soaked for half an hour in a scalding bath before the cold was fully driven from his bones and some flexibility returned to his overexerted muscles. The bathroom wasn't so bad. As the only room in the house with a lockable door, it had often been his refuge as a child, and it still carried echoes of safety. But he could hardly stay in here all day, and he wanted coffee.

Locating fresh clothes from a box in the hallway, he dressed and brewed coffee in the kitchen with a small feeling of satisfaction. It wasn't much, but he'd conquered two rooms and spent some part of the night here. He could do this—reclaim this territory for himself, not have it reclaim him.

When the coffee and ibuprofen had eased the headache a little, he went back upstairs, put his hand on the handle of his parents' bedroom and tried to turn it. He made it halfway before love and despair and hopeless bitterness lanced out from the metal and pierced his hand.

"Fuck." He dropped it and backed away. Stood in the centre of the upstairs landing breathing hard and holding his clenched hand against his chest. "Damn it!" They were fucking memories, nothing more. Why was he so bloody pathetic? Such a waste of space and air?

Okay, okay. He unclenched his fist and used it to cover his face. So he wasn't doing that today. There were other useful things he could do.

He tried to enumerate them as he fled downstairs, stuffing his feet in his shoes and his arms in his coat like he was being pursued. He could order wood and begin the process of laying out the new boat. He could buy paint and paint the narrowboat so it was a decent place to live. He could drive back to London and beg to be reinstated in his job.

Instead, he locked the front door behind him and, without thought, snapped there like a pole of a magnet to its opposite, he found himself knocking on the cephalopod knocker of Finn's bookshop. The only thing moving on an early-morning street that hadn't yet begun to wake.

No answer. But he wasn't having that. He carried on knocking. He was going to carry on knocking until Finn came, because there simply wasn't anything else to do.

CHAPTER NINE

Footsteps in the hall. "I fucking swear." Finn's voice made it through the door, sharp and flat with annoyance and something Michael might almost have called fear. "If that's you two . . ."

Rattle of key in the lock and the door swung partially open, stopping at the taut end of a short security chain that Michael could have broken with one good push. He was going to have to say something to Finn about putting a spyhole in the door, particularly if the man was already having trouble of some sort.

They looked at one another through the gap. Finn in a pine-coloured dressing gown atop soft blue cotton pyjama trousers, with his asymmetric hair flattened by the pillow as if tiny aliens had been making crop circles in it. His face morphed out of threat and into greeting in a way that might have been funny had he not also been carrying a raised cricket bat as an obvious weapon.

"Hey," said Michael gently, surprised to find that his voice sounded hoarser than normal, as though his throat was raw. "You having some kind of problem with the neighbours?"

"It's these e-book retailers." Finn closed the door briefly to slip off the chain, then opened it wide and made an elegant gesture suggesting he should come in. "Amazon, you know. They're not joking when they say Amazon is driving small booksellers out of business. You should see some of the toughs they send around."

Michael gave an uneasy smile and came in from the cold. He didn't like being lied to, no matter how transparent and how harmless the lie was. But he also had nowhere else to go that could teach him how to be human again. He needed . . . He didn't know what he needed, but he was pretty sure he would find it here.

"I'd ask what brings you here this early—" Finn tucked the bat under one arm and took Michael's elbow with his other hand, leaning towards him in a strangely formal contact-free hug. "But I can see it's urgent. Come on up, and I'll make you breakfast."

Abruptly, Michael was ashamed of himself for imposing. "I'm sorry," he said, following Finn up the narrow stairs and into a large, bright kitchen lined with bookshelves. A country-style, scrubbed oak table in the centre of it held a tragic pile of glister, within which the morning sunlight was picking out feathers and hooves and the curls of a glassy mane.

"What happened?" Drawn to it as to a corpse, Michael recognised in the wrecked pieces the Pegasus statue he had admired in the bookshop's biggest room.

Finn turned from putting beans in the coffeemaker, gave him an oblique look, his bottom lip nipped between his teeth. "My theory is he tried to fly. It's tragic when one has a nature that doesn't fit one's form."

"So." Michael sat at the table amid the scatter of pieces and glue. "You don't want to tell me anything." He fitted two pieces of lower hind leg together, located the third at the base of a stack of notebooks. "Fair enough. But bear me in mind if you need any help."

"You're sweet." Finn set velvet-black coffee down in front of him, with cream and croissants, butter, and jam. "And you're good at that." He examined the entire leg Michael had already reassembled. "Stick it together while I shower?"

"You got anything other than this yellow glue? Because this is going to show every crack like a road map."

Finn smiled. "That's the idea. It's my take on *kintsukuroi*. There are flecks of gold in the glue. It will dry clear except for those, and all the cracks will become trails of golden stars."

"*Kintsukuroi?*" Michael asked, trying to wrap his head around the idea that you would want the damage to show.

"The art of putting a broken thing back together in a way that makes it more beautiful than it was before. It's a Japanese idea." Finn's face pinched for a moment, the encroachment of middle-age showing in the creases around his mouth. "Something I think that offers a little hope to us all."

Michael caught his hand and pressed it. They stilled for a moment in silence before Finn pulled away to disappear up another flight of stairs. Michael drank his coffee and began to piece Pegasus back together. He had a whole wing done by the time Finn got back, pink from the shower, dressed in nautical style in navy flannels and a navy-piped white woollen jumper. His entrance perturbed the net curtains at the window and let a band of sunlight fall across the wing, showing the golden galaxies aswirl within the feathers.

The beauty of the thing brought out a disbelieving anguish in Michael's chest. "It really is better."

"Oh ye of little faith." Finn sat down opposite him, cradling his own coffee between both hands. There was a bruised darkness to his eyes that Michael didn't like, as though Finn felt just as fragile this morning as Michael did. "So what brings you to my door at this ungodly hour?"

"I . . ." Michael turned away from the man's riddling green gaze as too much emotion choked him. He wanted to tell Finn everything, have the man piece him back together in such a way that he too was better than before. He just didn't know where to start. Didn't dare. "I had a bad night. With my ghosts, you know? In the house."

"And you came to me to soothe your pain?" Finn reached over and snatched the last bite of croissant from Michael's plate, licking his fingers delicately to catch the crumbs after. "Good choice."

He leaned into Michael's space, close enough to bring his mouth within whispering distance of Michael's ear. The stir of his warm breath and the faint butterfly wing graze of his lips made every inch of Michael's skin shiver with sensitivity.

"Do you know what I suggest?"

Right now, Michael could only think of one thing. He swallowed, turned quickly, and managed to catch the edge of Finn's smile between his lips before Finn drew away. The little touch still filled his mouth with the taste of tin, spiking him through with the intensity of his need.

"Let's go to the fair." Finn stood, smiling down on him as though he knew exactly what had just happened and it delighted him to know he was a vicious, ball-breaking tease.

"The fair?" Michael managed at length, steadying his voice by a heroic application of will.

"Farnham Food Festival." Finn picked his overcoat from the back of the door and folded it over his arm. "Twenty minutes away by car. I can ask young Kevin to man the shop—he appreciates the hazard pay of working alone—and they always have three good secondhand book stalls that are worth a look. New stock for me. Candy floss and duck races and guess the weight of the marrow for you. It'll be . . . educational. You can win me something in the shooting gallery. I'm sure the reading room could do with a stuffed plush giraffe."

"I've never actually trained with a weapon." Michael followed Finn back downstairs, feeling bemused but already a great deal happier. "I might disappoint you."

"You missed my sarcasm there?" Finn had drawn humour back on like armour, like Michael's stoic calm. He appreciated it. "If you do win an enormous stuffed toy, you should feel free to keep it all to yourself. I'll simply enjoy your prowess. I'm driving, by the way."

The morning sunlight only broadened as they drove through wooded valleys where trout streams glistened, up onto the high moor and then down again into the next valley over. Michael's dark mood had lifted, and the purr of Finn's MG engine and the occasional brush of the man's shoulder against his felt raw and intense in a way he couldn't completely attribute to too little sleep and too much coffee.

Farnham was a little grey town around a little grey church. The Kings Arms pub faced the village fish pond, where a couple of keen anglers sat hunched over their rods. Between the church and the pub spread the village green, smooth enough for cricket in the warmer weather and now occupied by a score or so of trestle tables, ice cream and kebab vans, a hog roast, and a marquee. Finn and Michael arrived so early the stallholders were still setting out bunting, and the hog roast had not yet begun to sizzle.

"Business first." Finn dragged Michael into the marquee and up to one of the larger stalls, where a rotund lady with bottle-glass spectacles blinked at them both in half recognition.

"Dorothy, my love, my sweet. What have you got for me today?"

Dorothy rolled her eyes at Michael, who smirked back. "See for yourself," she said, indicating the spread of books on the table, and the pile of plastic crates behind her that held hundreds of others. "And in the meantime your friend will . . .?"

Finn raised his eyebrows at Michael as though astonished at the idea that he might need occupying, but he reached out and snagged a copy of *Kraken* by China Miéville and pressed it into Michael's hands. "Have you read this one?"

"No." Michael turned it over to read the blurb. He preferred action/adventure to be honest, but this looked weird enough to take his mind off his own troubles.

"There we go, then. I will browse through Dorothy's stall, and then move on to . . . is Rob here today?"

"Mm-hmm. And Steven."

"And then move on to Rob and Steven, hoping for bargains that they are undoubtedly too savvy to afford me. And Michael will get himself a second breakfast, read his book in the sunshine, and accompany me into the garden of delights once I'm done."

It proved a good plan. Michael found a bench in full sunshine, began the book, stretched out to get more comfortable, and nodded off. By the time he awoke, Finn had finished his wheeler-dealing and locked his purchases in the boot of the car. They spent the afternoon going round the rest of the stalls together, barbequed pork rolls in hand. They drank mulled wine and sampled homemade fudge and salted liquorice—which was both bizarre and moreish but sent them into the beer tent with a powerful thirst.

If he'd been asked to guess, earlier, how Finn would take to an event like this, Michael would have imagined the man disapproving, in some elitist, superior, cynical way. But the reality was far from that. Finn rarely stopped smiling, picking up the handcrafted knickknacks to feel their quality, laughingly losing a pound on the hoopla stall, and making Michael squirm by sampling every bottle of wine there was to sample without buying a single one.

There was alas no shooting range, but Michael made up for it by winning a bottle of shampoo and an egg cosy on the tombola and pressing them earnestly into Finn's hands.

The laugh he got as a result stopped the day for him, held him suspended in a timeless moment surrounded by trees and rustling flags, bright against the bright-blue sky, and Finn's face brighter, open for once, with the sunlight picking out his freckles and being put to shame by his warmth.

Michael tried to shake the revelation off, but it wouldn't budge— the crisis point when something that had been tipping in his chest finally reached the point of no return and fell. He closed his hands tighter over Finn's and held on until the man was looking at him properly, a little startled, a little vulnerable, pushed out of comfort and into intimacy. Then he used the grip to pull Finn in and kiss him properly, nipping Finn's upper lip between his own.

For a hot, glorious second Finn kissed back, but when Michael stepped in to close the distance between them, he set a hand on Michael's chest and pushed him back, his mouth still soft and his eyes wary. "Not in public. This isn't London."

"Okay." But it *wasn't*. Michael needed to strip Finn out of those clothes, to know what he felt like underneath, to touch him everywhere and fold all the pain and grief and uncertainty into his refuge, to be held and healed. "Is there somewhere private we can go?"

"Keen, are we?" Finn gave him a stronger version of his smug, teasing expression from the kitchen and waved an admonishing finger in his face. "Uh-uh. I want to poke around the church here. It's Anglo-Saxon, apparently. And then I expect dinner, which you will pay for because I don't go out with cheapskates. And then you'll prove to me that you can keep your hands to yourself on the drive home, because you're a big guy and I don't want a big guy with no self-control."

He put his hand back on Michael's chest, in between the open flaps of his jacket and his shirt, right where there was only a thin layer of soft cotton between his skin and Michael's. Michael's heart thundered beneath his palm, but he took a deep breath, ignored his tingling lips and the ache of pleasure in his cock, and said, "Yeah. Okay. Wise policy there. I can see that."

Finn's approval was laced with ruthlessness. He dropped his hand to Michael's belt and tugged him in, closing the distance with the swagger of a lion tamer putting his head in the lion's mouth, daring it to disobey. With the small part of Michael's mind still capable of rational thought, it occurred to him that Finn had put himself very firmly in charge, and oh God. *Oh God*. He liked that.

The rest of the day passed in snatches. The cool of a little church, Finn's hands moving in expressive curves as he said something Michael didn't catch about a faded triptych and a knot of carving about an arched stone door. Beautiful hands; clever, expressive fingers. They climbed to the bell tower, and he stood too close to Finn at the balustrade—Finn looking out on the yellow-leaved trees below, Michael closing his eyes and feeling the warmth of Finn's body through two layers of clothes, trying to imagine what it would be like when there were none.

Dinner in the pub, then they drove back in the dark, a big harvest moon shining ivory pale on the horizon.

"Why did you leave the Met?" Finn asked, ever so slightly too casually as Michael shifted to keep his knee from accidentally brushing against Finn's thigh.

They'd had more wine with dinner, enough to break Michael open and jimmy the locks he held tight around his soul. He put his head in his hands and let the flick flick flick of the streetlights shuttle past like prayer beads. "One too many failures," he slurred. "One too many people I couldn't protect. You get tired, you know? You get tired of it all being on you. You get tired of watching people get hurt and being able to do nothing."

Finn looked at him in surprise as if he had expected something else and then slowly reached over and put a hand on his knee, squeezing in a touch that should have felt like lust but felt like absolution instead.

The moment the bookshop door closed behind them, Michael was driving Finn up against it, crushing him into the uneven planks with his weight, compressing his chest and making it hard to gasp a deep breath. Oh, but the man was a tank, and he liked that. He spread his legs so that Michael could drive one thigh between them, press upwards and take him onto tiptoe, his own weight forcing his cock against Michael's leg. The security chain of the door pressed into his back, and when he wriggled it dug into his spine with a harsh-edged pressure that made him arch closer into Michael's grasp.

Michael had one hand in his hair, fingers tangled at the nape of his neck, pulling hard to bend Finn's head back, expose his throat. He leaned down to get those sensuous lips of his on Finn's neck, lick his way across Finn's collarbone, and suck hard at the pulse that hammered like a war drum under his skin.

"Mmm," said Finn, forgetting that he'd ever had doubts about this and scrabbling to try to haul Michael's coat off so he could get at those shoulders he had so admired. "Good, but . . ."

Always a problem with the big guys, in his experience—the responsible ones at least. They were just too scared of their own strength, scared of doing harm, of hurting him. But he liked a little hurt. "Bite."

"Mmm?" Michael had his hand up under Finn's jumper, undoing the buttons of his shirt and slipping inside. Calluses on his fingers dragged harsh and delicious over Finn's skin, licked rough as the tongue of a cat over his nipples and made him lift the other leg from the floor and wrap it around Michael's waist.

"Bite me."

Michael shifted his grip, slid both hands under the waistband of Finn's trousers, and cupped them around his arse, pulling him in closer, sending a flush of desire through him so strong it curled his hair. For a moment, Michael looked down on him in clear concern, and then he bent his head back to the bruise he had made on Finn's throat, and suckling it into his mouth, he bit down on the already sensitive flesh.

"Ah!" said Finn. "Yes."

He was going to say, *Not in the hall. Come on, have some class. I made the bed specially*, but Michael took all his weight on one arm—one arm!—and wound the other hand between their bodies to work at their clashing belt buckles and somehow it slipped his mind. Finn managed to push the coat far enough down Michael's arms that Michael could shake it off onto the floor. He immediately got to work on the shirts, pulling Michael's T-shirt out from his belt, hauling it over his head, taking the overshirt with it.

And oh yes. Michael's shoulders were everything he'd promised himself. He stroked the strength of them with appreciative fingers. And that powerful chest, heavy with muscle. He wanted to rub himself all over it; instead, he sunk his hands into Michael's black curly hair and tugged to make him let go of the little wound on Finn's throat, force him to look up so that Finn could take possession of his soft mouth and remind him who was in control.

"Let me down. Not in the hall."

Michael gave his arse a regretful squeeze and put him down. As soon as Finn had both feet beneath him, he headed for the stairs, pulling off his jumper and shirt as he went, feeling Michael's fingertips skim down his spine as he followed. He dropped his trousers in the kitchen, made it to the bedroom only in boxers just in time to lay Tom's picture facedown by the bedside so that Tom wouldn't have to see.

Sitting on the edge of the bed, he managed to dispose of his socks before he raised his eyes and saw Michael standing irresolutely in the doorway, looking at the face-down photo.

He too had lost his trousers somewhere in the house, but hadn't managed the sock gap with as much grace as Finn, and was watching Finn with the raw fear and vulnerability appropriate to a man Finn now remembered had never been with another guy.

"Who is he?" Michael nodded at the portrait.

"He was my partner." Finn folded back his gold silk coverlet, raised his hips, and wriggled his boxers off, throwing them to land on top of the socks. "He died five years ago. I'm thinking that if he's watching now, we should give him a show he can enjoy even in the afterlife."

Michael swallowed, came slowly forwards, his mouth half-open and a subtle shake working its way through the muscles of his arms.

"Come on." Finn took pity on him, held out both hands, and drew him down to lie beside him. He covered them both with warmth and leaned in to kiss Michael's mouth again and to run his tongue along the inside of his upper lip, while he closed his hand around the man's prick and stroked smooth and slow. Michael's hands clenched hard on his hips as he gave a growl of pleasure deep in his chest.

"Hold me down," Finn instructed, wanting all Michael's strength, all his bruising physical power. Wanting it to do what he told it to do. "Make it so I can't move."

Michael rolled on top of him, gathered both his wrists into one hand and pinned them above his head. Finn tugged at the grip, trying to pull them out, and couldn't budge them an inch. "Yes!" The helplessness hit kinks he'd barely known he'd had. "That's it. I want to be pierced and pinned like a butterfly to a board. Break me. Make me scream."

They were both slick with pre-cum, their cocks trapped together between their bellies. When Michael thrust tentatively against him, Finn stopped talking, wrapped himself around the larger man and held on tight, feeling dark delicious bliss and abandon and ruthless angry need coil through his body from his toes to the roots of his hair. "I want you in me. I want you in me. I want you to split me apart with your prick and hurt me."

"No." Terror in Michael's eyes again, and he stopped, damn it, cutting off the mounting pleasure like snapped elastic. "No, don't ask. I don't want . . ."

Belatedly, Finn remembered the man was fragile—fragile and a great deal more gentle than he looked. He rushed to make things right before Michael bolted. "Hey." He still couldn't move his arms, but he arched up and caught Michael's mouth in a tender, thorough kiss. "Shhh. It's okay. It's fine. You ever done anal before?"

His calm seemed to catch. Michael smiled ruefully and nodded. "My wife enjoyed it. I'm guessing it's much the same with a man."

Finn relaxed—freak-out averted—and nodded to the drawer by the bed where he kept lube and condoms. "How about you suit up and suit yourself then? We'll work up to pain another day."

"Okay." Michael smiled and leaned on his elbow to rummage in the drawer, tear open a condom packet with his teeth, and kneel to put it on. A position that gave Finn a great chance to ogle what he had in store for him. Like the man himself, it was not particularly long, but it was thick. He reached down and stroked himself in anticipation. He was definitely going to need to be ready for this, definitely going to feel it in the morning, and that was the very best thing.

He turned his hand up so Michael could fill it with lube and slicked himself, enjoying the silky glide of his own hand, getting himself loose and relaxed and ready. "Get on with it, then."

Michael laughed. "You're such a control freak." He dipped his dripping fingers between Finn's cheeks, dragging them over his hole, pressing lightly, too lightly for Finn's tastes, infuriatingly careful.

"You need it. Or you'd never get anything done. For crying out loud." Finn tried to arch up, press himself onto the blunt, teasing fingers, but Michael pinned his hips with the other hand, held him immobile. He rolled his head on the pillow, unconsciously offering his throat in surrender. "Please, you're going to kill me. Get on with it."

Michael relented, pushed a finger in and slid that restraining hand over until it was cradling Finn's balls. Between the deep delicious ache of penetration and the warm vulnerability of being cradled in a fist that could geld him if it closed tight, Finn struggled to concentrate on the educational value of the moment. "Feel around. Here's a key difference. There's a bump."

Michael looked at him like he half-resented being told what to do, but he got one arm under Finn's backside and lifted it for a better angle, sliding his lubed middle finger in exploratory curves. He hit the spot. Finn's mouth fell open, he closed his eyes, and clutched at his hair. "There. You want to do that again."

"So I'm gathering." Michael sounded relaxed now, amused and confident. He pushed a second finger in, leaning forwards at the same time to rub his slightly bristled cheek over the head of Finn's cock. It was rough and unexpected and sore; Finn gave a strangled cry, reached down, grabbed Michael's hair, and made him do it again.

He hit the prostate at the same time, and fierce stars exploded in all the cavities of Finn's body. "Enough prep," he gasped. "Just fucking do it. Then get up here so I can kiss you."

"So demanding." Michael drew back, kissed the inside of his knee gently, and then positioned himself, the touch of the blunt head of his cock against Finn's arsehole oddly tender before it began to drive inside, forcing him wide open, spreading him with a stretch that added a wire-thin intensity of pain to his pleasure. He bit down hard on his own lip to hold back the whine of wanton need and wound his legs around Michael's strong back, trying to open himself even more.

Michael's weight came forwards, blanketing him again, pressing the air out of his lungs with a force that left him feeling as though the man was everywhere inside him, filling even the hollow of his chest. He offered his throat again and the bruise there, but Michael captured his lip instead and bit where Finn had bitten, making his mouth ache and throb, swollen with blood.

Michael moved then, his thrusts long and slow, rocking them together, Finn gone liquid in his arms, utterly surrendered to the feel of his cock sliding over his prostate, the regular bursts of escalating bliss. He tangled his hands in Michael's hair and just held on, rocked and anchored and speared on that strength that was greater than his, that had no better purpose than to give him everything in the world that he could possibly want.

It built and built, slow and velvety and deep and soft, until he couldn't bear it any longer. "Please, please. Oh God! Please!" He struggled under the relentless weight, trying to speed the pace, to finally get off, his muscles clenched tight and straining, his balls aching, and his grazed prick bruised with need. Too much gentleness, nothing to focus on, nothing to bring it to a crisis point and let it snap.

Michael licked across the mark on his throat with a dark, approving growl. Then he bit so hard he almost broke the skin, and at the same time raked his fingernails across Finn's nipples, digging in deep.

Finn's world flew apart in an electric storm. He screamed and came hard, feeling Michael follow him over, a hard thrust and a burst of warmth inside. "You're perfect," he gasped, as Michael settled his damp forehead into Finn's neck and held on through the shudders of his own orgasm. "Oh God, you're perfect."

"Beautiful boy," Michael mumbled, not taking his face out from where it was tucked into Finn's neck. He rolled them both onto their sides, pulling out while at the same time he snugged Finn closer, wrapping both arms around him as tight as they would go, like he could meld them into one person. Like he was trying to hide inside Finn's skin. "Beautiful, beautiful boy."

Michael was shuddering and overwrought, so Finn didn't mention the fact that Finn was, both in fact and in temperament, clearly the grown-up in this relationship. He just found a towel while Michael dealt with the condom, wiped them both down, and then dragged Michael firmly back into his bed. Petting the man's hair, he drifted in the warmth of postcoital bliss, savouring the safety of the big body enfolding him and the wordless animal comfort of being held. After so long. After so long alone, it was . . .

He had not quite found the right word for it before he fell asleep. In the morning, he woke to implacable kisses and another round of gently overbearing sex spiced with small and welcome cruelties. The continuing question of finding the vocabulary to sum this new development up utterly slipped his mind. As did all his problems and troubles, put on hold by the magic of phenomenal sex.

CHAPTER
TEN

"**O**ut." Finn braced a hand on Michael's chest and shoved him towards the door. He let himself be nudged back a step, grinning. "Get out."

"My life as a sex toy," Michael grumbled. "You only want me for the nights."

"Too right." Another shove, and Finn echoed his grin a little fiercer. "Some of us have to work, you know."

He didn't want to go, and he wasn't going to pretend that he did, but he could see Finn's point. They'd pushed it as it was, with another round of sex and mutual showering, and a breakfast together in Finn's scattered, colourful little kitchen, watched by the half-restored face of Pegasus, where they had managed less eating than kissing.

It wouldn't last. They were both too old for the kind of heedless marathons of new-partner sex, the *don't come out of the bedroom for three days except to eat toast and bathe* weekends he remembered from his youth. But that didn't mean he wouldn't have appreciated spending the day as well as the night.

"I'm serious." A note of exasperation entered Finn's tone. Michael caved immediately.

"I know. I'm going." He caught Finn's shoving hand and used it to pull the man into his arms and kiss him properly, just to tide him over. "Can I come back this evening?"

"Can I stop you?"

Michael was fairly sure this was a joke, decided it was worth saying anyway. "Yeah, of course. You tell me not to, and I won't."

He hadn't quite worked out exactly where Finn stood on the whole question of who was in charge—hadn't expected him to yield with such abandoned sweetness when they made love. But this question was a no-brainer; he absolutely had the right to end it whenever he wanted, though Michael really hoped he would not.

"And that's why you can." Finn smiled at him, reaching up to turn down the collar of his coat and smooth it evenly over his shoulders. Louise used to do that too, and it brought a lump to his throat to be tidied up by Finn's quick, clever hands. It felt like love.

But Finn looked pensive afterwards, his eyes downcast.

"You okay?"

"It's been a while," he said, "since I had someone to fuss over. It just . . ." He gave a rueful laugh. "Brought back memories."

"For me too."

They stood smiling at one another for a little while, Finn's hands clasped in Michael's while the textures of their lives ran together around them. Then Michael stirred, pulled away, and opened the door. "This evening, then."

"This evening."

Everything became bittersweet when you were old enough, Michael thought as he ventured out into a blustery October morning. And maybe better for it—bittersweet like chocolate, or a subtle aged wine. But there was no denying that the top notes of today were all joy.

The trees, in their little squares of earth that formed an avenue along the street, tossed their golden heads in the wind, and russet leaves floated like confetti over the bike stands and bins. The bakers had their door open and the scent of newly baked bread joined the coffee from the cafés and the pungent floral scents of LUSH in a maelstrom of sensation. And Michael breathed it in like elixir, feeling strong.

Out here, away from London, away from the sinkhole into which the dirt of the country emptied, there really was still something clean to enjoy. When you turned the stones here, you found urchins and sea horses—beautiful things. You found extraordinary, capable, clever, funny, offbeat, generous people like his neighbours and, of course, like Finn.

Like Finn, who thought he was perfect, and who made him want to be perfect to prove him right.

Well, then, there were things he could do today that would give back to the world some of the joy it had given him. He swung by the local DIY shop, cut some spare keys and bought white paint and brushes. In the charity shop next door, he found a fake Moroccan rug that would just fit into the narrowboat's tiny living space, its blue-and-red pattern making the mismatched bedding and curtains look like they were planned that way.

He spent the morning painting the boat throughout, with his headphones in and a prog-rock mix cycling through Led Zeppelin, Hawkwind, and Motörhead, stopping him from thinking too much. It was done by lunchtime. He opened all the doors, windows, and portholes to let the paint stink out and stood in the stern, hands on his hips, admiring the affect and feeling accomplished.

It was, though he said it himself, pretty damn good. Austere, perhaps, but bare and empty and bright in a way that felt calming, that made the space feel like it was bigger on the inside, like you could lie here on the darkest of days and not feel trapped.

Maybe he could bring Finn here, instead of ever subjecting the man to the house again. They could go up the river—long lazy days filled with the sound and movement of water, fishing or sunbathing or just watching the banks go by. And at night they could cuddle up close on the not-quite-double bed and experiment with this whole pleasure-and-pain thing that Finn had going on.

Except . . . He folded his arms and sighed, letting the daydream go. He'd already made himself a promise for how to use this boat. He'd have to make a new one for Finn. Maybe make it with him—add more bookshelves, maybe some carvings, leather bench seats . . . gargoyles around the waterspouts? Something less generic than this. Unique as Finn himself.

It was a measure of how much better he felt that the prospect sounded exciting rather than simply exhausting. Committing himself to it, he washed and dried an old takeaway coffee cup with a lid, wrote a note saying, "I'm in the house, the boat is empty," and folded it into the cup. He dropped the hatch key in after it and fastened the lid on tight, sellotaping over the drinking hole.

Then he left the boat to air, and climbed back into the hulk. It hadn't rained for three or four days, and the inside was drier than before. There were still no signs the girl had come back. Wedging the coffee cup into the edge of her sleeping platform, above the green scum line that indicated the highest water mark, he knelt in the arched darkness for a moment and addressed a God he was afraid to believe in anymore.

"If she needs it, let her think to come here. Let her come here and find it. Let her be safe."

Of course he'd prayed the same thing for others. He'd prayed the same thing for Stacey and look how much good that had done. But maybe Trowchester was a place where God listened. Maybe Finn had turned his luck around. When he flashed back for the nth time that morning to the visceral memory of Finn giving up, giving everything up to him in utter abandon, he didn't see how it could be otherwise. Finn restored his faith in everything, in God and man, in the earth and the sky and even in himself.

Buoyed by the first flush of infatuation or love, depending on whether his cynical or romantic side was in the driving seat at the time, Michael braved being upstairs in the house for long enough to haul the futon out of the guest bedroom, heave and slide it downstairs, and assemble it like a sofa in the stripped living room. This looked like a war zone still, but most of its memories had ended up outside in the skip, and he had already proved to himself that he could sleep here if necessary.

He dropped a sleeping bag and pillow on the futon out of a Boy Scout notion of being prepared, but it was with the lightness in his stomach and the tingle in his lips of a man who expected something better. Making a bed, spreading out a sleeping bag on top of it, just brought back memories of last night, anticipation for more. He yearned not only for sex but for arms around him, to fall asleep wrapped in a tangle of limbs, Finn sleeping heavy and relaxed against his chest, breathing a wash of hot and cold air into his neck.

With the minimum done for survival in the house, he decided not to risk his good mood by staying inside. If he was to build a boat for Finn, something they could call theirs—the first fruits, maybe, of a newly shared existence—then he should get started before winter put the kybosh on everything.

He spent a productive afternoon in the workshop, cleaning it of years of neglect, sweeping away the spiders and the nest of hedgehogs who had made a home under some of the piled timber. With the aid of his laptop, he figured out the fuse box and restored power to the sockets and the lathe and the circular saw. By the time it began to get dark, he'd begun to scale up the plans Finn had sold him, transferring the shapes onto thin plywood templates, which he would use to cut out the structural timbers of the boat—keel, ribs, gunwales—the rudder, cabin, and all.

Straightening up from slotting together the first few shapes, he discovered that the light outside had faded to blue, that the small of his back felt as though it were stuffed with knuckles, and two of the blisters on his hands had popped, so that he was leaving bloodstains wherever he worked. Time to call it a day. He smiled up at the early moon, his good mood only getting better. Time to get some food to keep his strength up for tonight, and to make himself presentable. While he didn't suppose Finn would mind too much that he'd forgotten to shave, he suspected the guy drew the line at hair full of dusty spiderwebs, and old grease and graphite under the nails.

Once he was clean, and with his blisters plastered, he heated an individual lasagne and opened his laptop to check his emails. The rental firm managing his flat had finished subdividing it and found tenants already, so he could expect an income at the end of the month. A bank he did not have an account with was asking him to reenter his personal details, and two different people were apparently so concerned about the size of his penis they were offering him pills to enlarge it. It was very pleasant indeed to switch his usual mental response of *Who the hell cares?* to *Actually my partner likes it as it is*, and he felt altogether smug as he scraped the last of the meat and tomato sauce out of the silver foil with his spoon.

As if to complete a great day, the Skype alarm flashed up. He folded down the empty lasagne container and stuffed it in the bin, cradled the laptop in one arm, and hit Answer as he settled onto the comparative comfort of the futon.

"Hey, Jenny. Great to see you."

"You too," she said, looking like a bad clone of herself—slightly twitchy and with the hair all wrong. She'd always had problems with it being too long, too thick, and too slippery to control. Twisted up in a bun, it slithered out. Her ponytails were too thick for an elastic band to go round enough times to be tight. And yes, he'd joked about her getting it all chopped off, but now that she had, he wasn't sure he liked it. There was something terribly vulnerable, brutal even, about the short pixie cut that had replaced it.

"I like the hair."

She flashed a smile. "You mean you hate it, but you don't have enough of a death wish to say so."

"Pretty much. Your idea?"

Jenny rolled her eyes. "DS Egmont's. At least, he finally came out and told me he thought it looked unprofessional long. He's been in such a mood since you left that I thought I'd better take the hint."

He felt a twinge of automatic empathy. "Things not going well at the station?"

"Oh, it's shit."

And it was accompanied by an unexpected surge of lightness. Not his problem anymore. Egmont getting pissy, demands of overtime, heckling from the cells, being attacked in the corridors, jockeying for promotion, all of that was behind him too.

He was designing a boat for Finn. Good hard work for what he hoped would be an appreciative audience, and he didn't have to wade in any of that shit anymore. It was the first time he'd felt good about leaving. Maybe it showed, because Jenny's litany of complaint wound down into silence.

"Makes you glad you're out of it?"

"Yeah," he admitted, shamefacedly. "Sorry."

"No problem." She leaned back, stretching, the webcam giving him a good picture of her little flat behind her, chrysanthemums in a blue jug on the windowsill, and rooftops beyond. "I looked up your guy, by the way."

Oh shit. He'd forgotten that he'd asked. He shifted on the uncomfortably thin mattress of the futon that didn't quite pad the slats beneath and washed his palms across his face. Could he tell her he'd changed his mind and he didn't want to know? *Did* he want to know?

"It's good news, right? On the level, honest businessman, unknown to the police?"

Her look of sympathy gutted him. "Oh, Michael, you haven't fallen for the guy? You were supposed to wait until I checked him out. I went as fast as I could."

All of his new hope drained away. It became so hard to breathe, he was convinced there was actually something physically wrong with him. He hunched forwards over the pressure in his chest. "You sure you looked up the right bloke? I mean, Fintan Hulme, could you get a more common name? There must be hundreds of them."

She laughed dutifully at the joke, but didn't allow him to get away with it. "Well, this one was a high-class fence in Marylebone. His name came up in connection with numerous thefts from public buildings, art galleries, and private collectors. Charged and bailed on thirteenth August 2009, but the case was dropped for lack of evidence."

He took that and gripped it like a lifeline. "So maybe he was innocent."

"More like clever. One of those cases where everyone *knows* it was him, you just can't find evidence that will hold up in court. He left London soon after the dismissal, five years ago, and dropped off our radar. He was known to deal in all kinds of goods, but he specialised in antiquarian books." She gave him a soft-eyed sympathetic look that made him want to break something. "Sound like your guy?"

My guy, he thought, putting his elbows on his knees and bowing his face into his hands. "Yeah. Yes. It does."

CHAPTER
ELEVEN

Finn had been waiting, too wired to read or drink or do anything but pace his apartment and sit and stand at random for an hour. When the knock at the door finally came, it relieved a building pressure of conviction that something had gone wrong. Thank God, it hadn't. Michael was not now lying dead in his house of some sledgehammer-induced accident, or wired up on machines in the hospital because he had not been looking the right way when he crossed the road . . .

And oh God, what an old woman Finn was, to be sure. It was just that he had expected the man two hours ago, and been waiting for a phone call at least ever since to explain why he was so late.

But it was fine, here he was in person. Hopefully with a bottle of wine and an explanation, or at the very least a great deal of guilt to be taken advantage of.

Finn removed his reading glasses from where he had shoved them up onto his head like a hairband, put them on the mantle instead. Then he took a quick look at himself in the mirror by the door, raking a hand through his fringe to give it that artistically dishevelled look. He considered taking his tie off, and then he considered all the fun they could have with it on, and simply loosened it a little, to avoid being too formal.

Well, he would never be love's young dream again, but neither was Michael. They would have to make do.

Just the anticipation had him skipping down the stairs like a spring lamb. He threw the door wide, beaming, so convinced he would see Michael there that he couldn't comprehend what had hammered him in the chest and sent him reeling back to land on his arse in the corridor, until he was scrabbling to get up.

"What the fuck?"

The door *snick*ed shut and for a moment in the dim of the corridor all he was aware of was that there were two shapes and neither of them was Michael's. Two dark figures in hooded coats, their cowls pulled down around their faces. Both tall, both skinny, one carrying something in the crook of its elbow.

"If you'd only—"

"Welcomed us like that—"

"Last time. We wouldn't be—"

"Having this little tiff."

Benny loped forwards on his long legs and put down a foot in Finn's stomach, stopping him from getting up. Lisa made a gesture he couldn't parse, at first, and then the *clunk* and the two round gun barrels that had levered up into place added themselves together in his mind, and he saw with disbelief that she was aiming a double-barrelled shotgun at him.

Michael. Now would be a good time to turn up. Where's a fucking cop when you need one?

He raised his hands, rather stereotypically, and attempted a calm, reasonable tone of voice. "Lisa, Benny? Look there's no need for all this cops and robbers nonsense. We're not in an episode of *The Bill*. Let's talk this out like reasonable adults. What can I do for you?"

Lisa gave her compatriot an encouraging nod. Benny leaned down to grab Finn's wrists. He pulled them away, but she made a jerking movement with the end of the gun that called his attention to the fact that he didn't want to provoke her.

Finn let Benny twist his arms behind his back and wrench him to his feet. He scarcely felt the pain of being manhandled, his mind too busy with imagining what it would feel like to have a slug of lead penetrate your bones at a hundred miles an hour. What kind of damage did a gun like that do anyway? Would it make a neat, survivable hole, or would it blow out the back of his spine?

"This is why I didn't want to deal with you two in the first place," he said, something wild in him getting in between reason and the desire to survive. "I prefer to have civilised customers, and you two give Neanderthals a bad name."

"Go ahead and insult us."

"See how that works out for you."

Benny hauled him into the Jules Verne room, named after the clockwork model of the time machine that stood on a plinth in its centre. The thought of Pegasus, still half-wingless upstairs, of Lisa's soulless vandalism, of the possibility of the same fate befalling this jewel of creativity—he forgot about the gun and kicked back hard, jamming his heel into Benny's shin.

Benny reacted by jerking both of his arms so high his shoulders almost ground out of their sockets. He wasn't even aware it was him screaming until the sound tapered off and the agony subsided enough for him to tell his throat was raw. Some fear tried to worm its way through his anger, but it failed. The big kids used to do this to him in the playground. He fucking despised them then, and he despised them still.

"Did I hurt your tender feelings? Well, I'm sorry, but this is not going to persuade me to ever do business with you again."

Benny took a set of white cable ties from his pocket and snapped one around Finn's wrists. Then he kicked out the back of Finn's knees and collapsed him to the ground, securing his ankles with another.

"You hurt our rep," said Lisa, her pasty face still shadowed by her hood, but her pink-gloved hands pulled his books off the shelves and piled them up like kindling at her feet. "People think you can defy us, then they think they can too, so—"

"Nothing personal, but—" Benny kicked him in the kidneys and then put a foot on his wrists to keep him from getting back up.

Lisa tilted her head to give Finn a manic-pixie-girl smile. Shifting the gun back to her elbow, she took a box of matches from her pocket, lit one, and then let it drop into the pile of books.

"Bye."

No.

The flame caught in dry paper as of course it would, spread from leaf to leaf with eager voracity, pausing to really get its teeth into the leather-bound end boards before moving on to the next book, and the next.

"You fucking barbarians! I'll fucking have you!"

Lisa was already backing towards the door. The foot on Finn's wrists went away, but only to return as a kick to the back of his head that burst the world apart in a red rose. He barely followed the sound of retreating footsteps as everything went momentarily grey.

The inside of his nose stung when he next possessed conscious thought. His nose stung and his eyes watered. His raw throat burned, and the air he breathed caught at his lungs like a cigarette. He coughed hard a couple of times, but it didn't help, nor could he blink the grey mist out of his eyes. Truth was that the air was grey, grey with smoke, and the heat on the soles of his feet was making his shoes blister and melt.

He rolled onto his stomach and then to his knees. Pressing his forehead against a bookshelf gave him the leverage to straighten up, still with his hands locked behind his back and his ankles strapped tight together. In the centre of the room the pile of books burnt more strongly than ever, flames crackling over it, shooting up to lick and blacken the ceiling, creeping across the matting towards further bookshelves.

He tried to wipe his streaming nose on his shoulder, couldn't reach, while he thought. There was a Break Glass Here fire alarm and sprinkler system point in the hall, which he could not break without his hands free. If he tried to hop there, the flames would reach the bookshelves long before he had it activated. Besides, he wasn't keen on the idea of flooding his shop with water. Scarcely less damaging to the books than fire would be.

Lisa had not thought through the shape of the bonfire. If he could smother the flames on the carpet, there was a good chance it would burn itself out without spreading, leaving only a scar on the floor and ceiling. But how to suppress the fire on the carpet without the sprinklers, while he was equally unable to run for the fire blanket in the kitchen as for the fire alarm?

Paint bubbled on the ceiling overhead. His hair was smoking and his face tightening painfully in the heat. It hurt; it hurt to go closer, but maybe he could . . . He hopped towards the blaze, to the narrow avenue between shelves and bonfire over which a questing tendril of flame had begun to nose. Biting his lip, partly against pain, partly against the realisation that this was a truly awful idea, he stamped on the little blaze. Heat boiled through the melted rubber of his soles and scorched his feet.

He yelled in agony and jumped away, his shoulder colliding with the shelves, barely managing to hold himself upright. Now he was terrified—terrified of falling forwards into the flames, unable to pick himself up again, rolling in them face-first with his hair and his clothes going up like tinder and the rest of him like a wet log, taking far too long to die.

And yes, he couldn't stamp out the flame again. But even if he did make it to the sprinkler control valve, he couldn't operate it without his hands.

He sent up a quick mental apology to the maker of the clockwork and rammed it with his shoulder, tipping it onto the floor. It shattered in a burst of gears and springs. Carefully kneeling down he groped behind him for a shard of the display case. He cut his fingers twice before he had it angled up between his wrists and could push it forwards against the floor until the sharp edge sliced through his bonds. After which it was easier to cut the tie around his ankles.

Dropping the bloodstained glass into the ruin of his room, he sprinted for the fire suppression system, fumbled it with shaky fingers until only the single room was selected, and turned the sprinklers on. He stood out in the corridor while a wall of wet white smoke rolled through the house, choking him. The fire hissed like a basilisk, and for a moment he thought it grew stronger, leaping up all yellow-gold among the streaks of falling grey. He could see it, the water, hitting the books, flooding the shelves, staining bindings, unmaking the paper, soaking into the glue of the spines, crinkling the pages, and he didn't know whether to cough or to cry.

He thought the siren outside was his imagination—a wail of grief appropriate for the death of a whole room of his books—until the front door burst open again, rammed into the wall, and he found himself standing, shaking, hyperventilating, grabbed by the shoulders by an unexpected fireman.

"What the—?" he said, looking a long way up at a fresh-faced black child with buzz-cut hair. "I didn't call for you."

"Next door saw the smoke and called us in."

He noticed that he was putting no weight on his feet—the child was holding him up. Also berating him in a manner he resented. "You should have got out, sir. You could have been hurt. You should have got out first, and let us deal with this."

"It would have—" He squirmed to be put down, but the moment his feet touched the ground he buckled—his shoes were still melted, still hot. The fireman slung him unceremoniously across his back and carried him out. Which was frankly a great deal more pleasant as a fantasy than as a reality. He had not counted on being soot-stained and bleeding and weeping so hard that his nose ran, when he conjured up such an event in his dreams. "It would have spread and damaged my shop."

The man set him down on the step of the fire engine and looked at his bleeding hands and his melted shoes. "Better than dying, sir. As we tell everyone that tries to be a hero, providing they're still alive to hear it. How'd you cut your hands?"

Finn scarcely had control over himself—it was over, and because it was over, he was safe to finally feel all those things he had held away from himself for so long. He wrapped his arms around himself in a comforting hug, incidentally hiding the cuts and the bruised wrists from the gaze of authority, and shuddered under waves of fear and fury, silently mourning, and considered his options.

A little farther down the road, an ambulance drew up to the pavement and parked. The emergency services were all in each other's pockets. If he told this nice fireman how he'd cut his hands, the nice fireman would get the police involved. And it was none of their fucking business. They could stay out of it.

They had better stay out of it. They had better not start looking into the business of the abbot's psalter. They had better not, please God.

And where the fuck was Michael? Why hadn't he come running like the white knight he was supposed to be? Had they—his blood turned to ice—had they got to him first?

Belatedly he remembered he had been asked a question. "I, ah, hurt them on the fire alarm. It had a break-glass cover, and I didn't have anything to break the glass with except my hands."

Would Lisa and Benny know about Michael? He fumbled his phone out of his pocket, slippery though his fingers were with still-seeping blood, hit the number, and it went to the answering machine.

The pair of them weren't known for their research. Would they know Michael was someone Finn cared about?

Paramedics came over. Between them and the fireman, Finn found himself coerced to sit in the ambulance, to have his hands and feet bandaged and his breathing monitored for smoke damage.

"I think we'd better take you in," the paramedic said. "Just overnight. I don't like the look of your breathing. You may be in danger of going into shock."

It snapped him back to his own concerns with a vengeance. "I can't just leave the place like this! I have to get back in, save the books that can be saved before the water damage is irreparable. I'm not in shock, I—"

His friendly fireman leaned in through the ambulance's open doors, looking grimmer and older and considerably more concerned. "I'm going to have to tell the police that in my opinion this fire was deliberately set. They'll have to come and look it over. No cleaning up until that's done and signed off. You're best out of it, mate. Honestly."

Finn raised a hand to his head but couldn't close his bandaged fingers enough to pull his hair in frustration. Fucking officious do-gooders. Fucking interfering neighbours, trying to *help* when he had everything under control. Why couldn't they all leave well enough alone? He tried not to think of the police station, the police cells, the cold, stolid, respectable disdain of a society that didn't actually care if he lived or died so long as he obeyed the rules. The police were coming here with their questions? Then maybe he did want to be somewhere else.

He hit redial on his phone. It went to voice mail again. "Michael. If you were going to come by this evening, don't. I've had a trifling little emergency—nothing to be concerned about but . . ." Maybe there was something to be said for the idea that he was in shock. He couldn't think how to end that sentence. He let it go. "But let me know that you're all right, okay? Phone me back. I . . ." All his words were slithering away. "I worry."

He gave up and allowed himself to be strapped in for the journey to the hospital, trying to calm himself down with reason. After all, Lisa and Benny would have said something, the odious creatures. If they had hurt Michael as a way of hurting Finn, they would have had every reason to tell him and none to keep it silent.

Michael was probably fine.

He was certainly fine.

Why the hell wasn't he answering his phone?

CHAPTER
TWELVE

A hammering at the door dragged Michael back to consciousness. He wormed a hand out of the sleeping bag and groped for his watch. 7 a.m. And he'd finally crashed at five. The walls still swung around him, pulsing in and out of focus, because he had not yet slept off the drink.

But whoever was at the door did not give a fuck about his hangover or his sleeping habits. They were not going away, and they were not toning it down. "What? Wait!" he growled, unzipping himself and rolling out of the bag onto the still-gritty floor. His stomach lurched as he stood, and his brains swirled in his skull like water around a plughole.

He found the keys inside his shoe and fumbled the deadlock open, twisted the Yale lock, and swung the door ajar. The two policemen on the other side gave him identical stares. He could feel them taking in the scruff of beard, the sweat- and dust-stained T-shirt in which he'd slept, the bleary gaze, the scent of booze, and the bandaged hands. He knew exactly what they were thinking because he would have thought it too.

"Mr. Michael May?" The senior one recovered first, his politeness underlining his disdain. He was a fine figure of a man, well over six feet tall, athletic, with clean-cut features and the kind of polished-silver hair normally reserved for movie actors. He looked down on Michael quite literally as he moved in, trying to force an entrance by mere politeness. "I'm Constable Shipton, this is Constable Lane. May we come in?"

"Sure." Michael moved away from the door and picked up his trousers from the floor, hastily pulling them on while the police officers sized up the state of his house and drew what were undoubtedly correct conclusions. "What can I do for you?"

He didn't like this. The police were his people, his clan. They were everything he had aspired to all his life, the family he had chosen. To have them turn up at his house like this—to have them look at him the way they were looking at him now—dropped the floor out of his universe.

I'm on your side. I'm one of you.

"Are you acquainted with a Mr. Fintan Hulme of the Bibliophile Bookshop, 43 High Street?"

Michael swallowed nausea and rage. Sat down on his futon bed, letting them stand over him. It was a mistake, drawing their eyes to the half-empty bottle of whiskey and the tin mug next to it.

Fuck.

"I am."

"You are in fact Mr. Hulme's boyfriend." It wasn't a question so much as a condemnation. Oh, there was nothing unprofessional in the man's expression, movie-star perfect as it was, a kind of bland, dispassionate curiosity, but the contempt flowed off him like a liquid and closed over Michael's bent head.

Was he Finn's boyfriend? He wasn't sure. *I slept with him once* wasn't going to go down better. "I don't know," he admitted, wrong-footed and on the defensive, capable of admiring the officer's interrogation technique and being appalled by it at the same time.

"You don't know?"

This time the second man actually laughed, a polite little scoffing noise as he opened the door to the hall and looked upstairs, where torn-up carpet and torn-down wallpaper clogged the landing. Michael's disappointment and betrayal last night had been channelled into finally getting everything out of his parents' bedroom.

There had been only one thing of hers that his father had not already sold—a tiny glass unicorn Michael had bought on a school trip to Venice. He'd found it under the carpet, under the bed, hidden under a loose floorboard, its legs and horn broken. That had been what started him drinking, and once he had started, there hadn't seemed to be a good time to stop before he passed out.

He took the mug into the kitchen, filled it with water, and drank carefully, trying to dilute the dizziness and the despair. Why'd he ever thought that moving back here would make things better? Things were shit *everywhere*. Everywhere in the world.

He put the kettle on. "You want coffee?"

PC Silver Screen gave him another jolt of condescension. "I would just like you to answer my questions, please, sir. Are you intimate with Mr. Hulme?"

"It's hard to say," Michael tried again, aware that it sounded like he was being evasive when actually he was telling the absolute truth. He put a spoon of instant granules in a mug while he wrestled with a better way of putting it. "I only just moved into town, only just met him. I, uh . . ." The kettle boiled. He poured the hot water, then sipped scalding coffee in the hopes it would sharpen him up enough to get some kind of handle on this conversation. "I like him. A lot, actually. But I wouldn't say I really know him."

"How about these people?" Shipton passed him a photo of a hard-core-looking couple, a tall man and a woman with a gaze like a fist.

His stomach settled enough to risk a larger mouthful of coffee and let him turn his head in search of the Paracetamol he'd bought yesterday for his hands. "I don't know them."

"They were seen yesterday coming out of Mr. Hulme's premises. Can you tell me what his relationship is with them?"

It pissed him off, the clear assumption that he was lying. "I have never seen them before, so I have no idea."

"You can't say what they were doing in his shop last night?"

"No, I can't." Michael realised with a shock that he was glaring, leaning forwards into Shipton's personal space, and that his hands were clenched so tight the blisters were bleeding again.

"How about this man?" Another photo, this time of a man he almost recognised. Seen once on a file brought over from another division, maybe.

"What's this about?" he asked, rather than say so. They had to have looked him up, they must know he was an ex-cop. He really didn't want to drag all that into this conversation, have them accuse him of being a quitter or a coward or a traitor.

"Since you're new in the area—" Shipton gave him a falsely avuncular smile, one cop to the other "—you may not know that these charming young people are wanted in connection with the burglaries of several stately homes around here, over a period of several months, including Harcombe House itself. Now we find them consorting with a known fence in our patch, with whom you have also been consorting. It would be remiss of us not to look into how much you know about that."

"I don't know anything about it!" Michael's head hurt, and his heart hurt too, dropped straight out of hope into condemnation. He should have known. He should have known that anything that seemed so good was too good to be true.

Shipton exchanged a glance with Lane, who had been notably absent for the past five minutes, no doubt checking the upstairs for stolen goods. Lane shook his head minutely, and Shipton dialled back the aggression only to replace it with extra quantities of disgusted pity, as he took Michael out of the mental category of *villain* and put him into that of *dupe*. He swept a dismissive gaze over the wreck of Michael's house and life.

"Well, then, you can consider this a warning, sir. It's easy to be taken in by these charming types, but you heed my advice and have nothing further to do with Mr. Fintan Hulme. Ignorance is no excuse in court, after all. And now you don't even have that."

After they finished questioning him, Michael followed them out into the garden to watch them leave, uniformed in their high-visibility squad car. By that time, it was half seven and the Lis would all be awake, maybe watching out of their windows. Michael didn't care. He didn't care that his respectable neighbours now had every reason to look at him askance. He didn't care about the aspersions cast on his good name and his honour and his honesty.

He didn't fucking care, all right.

In the absence of something to punch in the front garden, he staggered back inside, made it to the bathroom in time to throw up wretchedly in the toilet, tile floor cold against his knees and his eyes streaming from acid and misery. When he'd finished purging the alcohol, he rested his forehead against the ceramic tiles of the wall, let the early-morning chill pierce through him and bring the kind of peace that snow brought with it.

Carefully, he gathered himself together again. He didn't care. He took off gritty, shameful clothes and soaked himself pink in the shower. He didn't care.

Avoiding meeting his own eyes in the mirror, he shaved and brushed his teeth and tried to slick his too-long curls down into something professional, as though he could somehow reset the whole interview with the police, restart it with himself as he was when he was prepared and armoured and ready to look normal and competent and . . .

Except he didn't fucking care, all right?

He forced down half a bowl of cornflakes and another cup of coffee. The headache receded to a dull throb between his eyes, but his hands wouldn't stop shaking. He told himself that he'd had a narrow escape. That he should do as Shipton suggested. He should write Finn off. Get himself together, make that boat and sell it. Plough the money back into a new business, concentrate on good, hard work and his good neighbours, ask them, maybe, to introduce him to other friends. Keep his head down and his nose clean, and get away from this stumble as fast as he possibly could.

He tried laughing, but the sound of it made the hairs on the back of his neck stand up. Dressed in clean clothes, he shifted his phone out of the pocket of his dirty jeans, turned it on, and saw that he had missed a half a dozen calls. Four of them from Finn.

Boats wouldn't build themselves. He sank back onto the futon, looking at the little shining screen. Sooner or later his savings would run out, and he should have something big to sell by then because not even the rent on a London flat would keep the wolf from the door forever. He should be the sensible grown-up he knew he was and delete the messages unheard. He should make the break, right now, while disillusionment and anger would still make it easy.

Of course he didn't. "Michael." Finn's faint Irish accent made the name sound exotic, made Michael's limbic system sit up and beg, flushing him with memories of how it had sounded gasped out in bliss. "I have a trifling emergency. If you're thinking of coming over, don't."

He stabbed the recording off, anger joining the unwanted arousal. Don't come over? Why? Because Finn's accomplices had turned up unexpectedly, and he couldn't risk having an ex-cop around. Why the hell? Why the hell had Finn led him on the way he had if he'd known, as he must have known, that Michael was the enemy? Had he done it deliberately to undermine Michael's reputation with the local force?

Or just to mess with Michael's obviously vulnerable heart because it was there and he could?

Earlier in his career, he might have thought that picking up his keys, putting on a coat and scarf, carefully locking the door behind him, indicated calm premeditation. The fact was he did them without thinking, found himself outside, halfway to Finn's without any conscious intention of going there at all. Something seethed in him, making his breathing hard and his steps long and easy. His hands were too tightly clenched to shake, but he could feel the vibration nevertheless, inside his bone marrow, inside his blood, reverberating in his brain with a thin shrill.

The door was open. Burst open, in fact, the lock splintered. Someone else had come in here in a fury. It didn't surprise him. Finn was a lying, twisted little bastard. If he'd played with Michael, it stood to reason he'd play with others too—others less reasonable. He slapped the door aside, stormed through the passage down into the shop.

Black marks streaked along the ceiling, and the place smelled of tar and ash. Pegasus's empty plinth mocked him—Finn had lied about what happened to the sculpture. He had lied obviously, lied with abandon, lied like it was an Olympic sport. And Michael, Michael who knew *exactly* what it was like growing up in the snares of a man who was deceitful just because it was fun, had still somehow found it endearing.

He was such a fool. He was such a fucking loser. He deserved every iota of this misery.

Down and to the left, the burned smell strengthening, he followed the marks on the ceiling, the stench. His feet squelched on the coconut matting. He turned the corner, and there Finn was, in the centre of a black star whose tendrils crawled out over the floor, over the bookshelves, over the ceiling like some kind of obvious metaphor of evil.

Finn glanced up as Michael came in, and Michael's fury missed a step. Finn looked so lonely there, so slight and undefended and sad. The green eyes raised to Michael's angry gaze were so peridot, like willow leaves. If they had lit with pleasure to see him, he might still have smiled back. Something in him very much wanted to engulf Finn in his arms and bury his face in Finn's neck and hold on tight until it all went away.

If Finn had seemed at all receptive to that . . .

But Finn didn't. He raised his chin and narrowed his reddened eyes and said, "Where the fuck have you been, then?"

And Michael had had just about enough of this shit for one lifetime, thank you very much.

CHAPTER
THIRTEEN

Finn debouched himself from a taxi at a godforsaken hour in the morning in front of his shop. His feet were not as bad as he'd initially feared, only tight feeling, stinging, and stiff, but he had not slept, despite being forcibly pinned to a hospital bed all night. Partly this was because who could? Surrounded by six other burn victims, all tossing and groaning in their sleep. Surrounded by nurses who walked briskly through the wards, wheeling carts full of things that clattered, and who congregated in the corners to whisper in scarcely lowered voices. Who could sleep through that?

Even when he had slipped into a doze, he found himself being woken every two hours to have his breathing checked, to reassure everyone that his lungs hadn't been cooked from within by residual heat, or eaten away by the acidic residue of the smoke. Imagining that had naturally led him to be afflicted by phantom chest pain all night long.

And while he lay, not sleeping due to this onslaught of irritants, he could not help but picture the police in his poor flat. He was fairly certain he no longer had anything incriminating or illegal on hand. The supplies he used for falsifying provenance on objects without it could be readily explained away as supplies he needed to create books like the one in the window. Other than those, everything was aboveboard and paid for.

It didn't mean he liked the idea of the plod rooting through everything with their cold eyes and their cold hands. Lumbering up and down his stairs, opening his cupboards and fingering his things. Looking at his pictures of Tom and raising their eyebrows at one another because these days they couldn't get away with the full-blown sneer.

They'd fixed a hasp with a padlock over the front door to secure it after the fire brigade had smashed in the lock. He hobbled gingerly

ALEX BEECROFT

in through the back garden, where he kept a crowbar in the shed and
levered the hasp away, more out of principle than rational thought.
After he'd done it, he regretted it, but he hadn't been able to bear the
thought of having the police's lock on his front door—a lock for which
he didn't have the key. No one locked his door against him, damn it.

He would phone a locksmith as soon as the shops opened. Until
then, he could lock the flat upstairs and put up with a few early tourists
wandering in out of the cold.

They hadn't let him shower at the hospital, and his clothes were
still full of ash. He headed up to get clean and to eat something.
His insides felt TARDIS-like, cavernous, bigger and emptier than
anything his skin should be capable of containing.

He wasn't liking this business of being an honest man so far. But
fuck them. Fuck them all, if they thought they could bully him out
of it.

Bathing and dressing in clean clothes did a little to alleviate his
mood, but not even eating bacon and eggs, toast and marmalade, and
coffee did anything to fill the hollow inside him, where everything
that he was had drawn itself deep inside, retreated, squeezing itself
together in a singularity of soul so buried he couldn't tell if he was
angry or sad or calm.

The sun had risen and was lancing through the bookshop windows
when he ventured back downstairs again to see the damage. The open
front door framed a yellow tree in front of the bakers' steamy red-
painted windows and the nodding purple violas in their hanging
baskets. It was also cleansing some of the smell of char and heartbreak.

He walked through each room telling himself it wasn't so bad. In
most it was almost true. A lick of paint would spruce up the ceilings
where the smoke had left a brown, carcinogenic stain. Only the two
rooms directly connected to the Jules Verne room needed their carpet
pulled up and replaced where dirty ash-grey water had soaked from
one room to the next.

The arch into the final room proved difficult to walk through.
He stopped in its liminal embrace, with his hand on the coving, and
closed his eyes, while flames leaped in his imagination, his cut hands
stung, and his eyelids tightened as though they were still burning.

Was he afraid? God damn it. No one was going to make him afraid in his own fucking house. Yes, very well, he could admit it had been a little scary at the time, but it was over now, and he had survived. He was not going to be the kind of idiot who allowed himself to get intimidated after the fact.

Straightening his back, opening his eyes, he walked into the disaster area. Glass squeaked under his new shoes, but the floor was already almost dry. The scar left by the fire, when he studied it with determined optimism, resembled a giant kraken with tentacles reaching from one side of the room to the other. It didn't seem to have done any structural damage. Perhaps when he redecorated, he could make a feature of it. Call it a portal. Put the horror stories in its epicentre as though they were crawling out of the very pit of Hell?

He'd have to do something like that. He approached the nearest bookshelf like a mourner approaching a corpse. He'd have to, because the books that had been in here before were as good as pulp. It was as he thought—the water had destroyed them as thoroughly as the fire. Some of them would have to be shovelled out.

Bending, he picked up a gear from the ruined automaton whose casing had saved his life. Fire and terror boiled out of it and up his arm. He dropped it and recoiled, shaking and panting and academically intrigued. That was what a flashback felt like, was it? Well, it was interesting to experience once, but it had better not happen again because he was really not— He tried to get ahold of his breathing, slow it down, slow down his racing thoughts and heart. He was really not—

A distant crash as the door was shoved open. Was that Kevin? He hoped it was Kevin. He wanted someone to make him coffee and to clean out this mess and to dust the ash from the other rooms so he could pretend in ninety percent of the shop that nothing had happened at all. Kevin was young and resilient and not at all sensitive, and the boy's cheerful obliviousness would be a comfort at the moment.

Still at the heart of his destroyed sanctuary, Finn turned and waited to be rescued.

The footfalls in the passage were heavier than Kevin's. They had a rhythm and a cadence that made the compressed thing in Finn's chest unfurl a little, hopeful and relieved and pathetic.

There was a worrying base note of doglike devotion to his reaction, something in him hoping to be swept up in strong arms and comforted, to be told how brave he was, and to sit down while Michael sorted everything out. To be told it would be all right now, and he should not worry.

Finn despised that part of himself and despised Michael for provoking it. Hard on the heels of the joy came the deferred anger of a night of unanswered phone calls, a night spent alone in terror, when it should have been spent together.

"Where the fuck have you been, then?" he asked, before he'd even processed Michael's glower of fury. He wanted the man to stop, back off, look guilty, so that Finn could shove him and yell at him. Now that the blue touch paper had been set alight, his whole soul was going up in starbursts of anger, shaking him, seeking a convenient target, and Michael would do very well.

They came together like a car crash. Michael strode up to him, with his craggy face stonelike with anger, grabbed him by the elbows, and shook him, pushing him backwards. He stumbled in astonishment and betrayal. "What the fuck is the matter with you?"

"Why didn't you tell me you were a fucking con?"

Finn tried to get his footing back, scrambling for reason under the unexpected onslaught. Too much to feel, lit up as he was by glorious explosive rage and disbelief.

He dug his heels in, but he might as easily have stopped a tank with his bare hands. Michael drove him across the shop and smacked him into the wall. The shock of pain across his shoulders and down his back transmuted into a kind of savage joy, and oh, this was actually every bit as sexy as he had imagined when he first saw Michael, and he first suspected the violence seething under the man's kicked-puppy exterior.

"Oh yes," he laughed, high on a blend of fury and defiance and lust—with, beneath it, just that little tint of relief at having Michael's hands on him again, just that little delicious anticipation of being made to surrender. But he wasn't going to make it easy, and he wasn't going to give in. "Oh yes, because I knew how reasonably you'd react."

"You should have told me."

"Yeah, because sleeping with me somehow grants you the right to know everything about me? You're the fucking enemy, Michael.

Ex-Met? Why wouldn't I want to screw you over, literally? Why wouldn't I have been *laughing* inside, knowing you thought I actually cared?"

The anger had taken control of his tongue. He was saying things now just to hurt, his wrists still pinned against the wall by Michael's grip, his chest compressed by Michael's weight, and all of him on fire to win this fight any way he could because this was a fight he could win, this was an enemy he could hurt. Lisa and Benny weren't there, so Michael got to bear the brunt of his anger with them because Michael could take it.

Because he trusted Michael to take it and not give back any more than Finn could take in return. Because Michael was safe, safe to attack, safe to hurt, safe to kick and gouge and destroy.

"You . . ." Michael's grip tightened until the bones of Finn's wrists ground together, but his eyes had gone wide and his mouth slack with shock. "You . . . The whole thing? You were laughing at me the whole time?"

Oh, that had gone home, all right. Finn grinned in the man's face, hoping— He didn't know what he was hoping for. Maybe for a slap, maybe for Michael to lean forwards and bite him on the mouth, pushing in closer, forcing his thigh between Finn's legs, pinning him. He would struggle, of course, but he wouldn't stand a chance against Michael's strength, and there would be vicious, painful, hard-core sex that would scour all this anger out of them both and let them start again clean.

"Why wouldn't I?" He craned forwards and closed his teeth around Michael's earlobe, pulling, just to give him the idea if he didn't already have it. "When you walked in here so sad, so pathetic, practically begging to be taken advantage of. Don't tell me you really thought it meant something?"

They stood in the moment before detonation, locked together, breathless, with its potential beating on Finn's skin like a heat, both of them panting hard. Michael's head bent and his breathing was rough with a growl Finn could feel through his chest. *Come on,* he thought, anticipating having all the man's strength unleashed upon him, *punish me. You know you want to.* "Please."

But the explosion never happened. Michael raised his head and gave him a look of devastation, sharp enough, cold enough to cut through Finn's fey mood like ice water in the face.

Michael let go, stepped back, still transfixed by him as though he were seeing something alien, something horrifying. "It did to me."

Another moment of incomprehension, and then Michael turned on his heel and walked away, leaving Finn's wrists bruised and his skin cold. Leaving him alone against the wall, shaky with adrenaline and arousal, angry and turned on and abandoned all at once. What? What had just happened?

He levered himself away from the wall and clutched at his hair, still panting. That had not gone the way he had expected it to go at all. What was Michael playing at? He couldn't just storm in here and threaten and say four words and leave like that? Could he?

They had to talk about it. After—after the angry sex—they had to talk. Unless. Oh God. The gorgeous, fiery, floating rage turned by degrees into miserable frustration and then into dread. Unless that's what Michael thought Finn had been doing all along. Unless the bone-headed, muscle-bound idiot thought Finn had meant it.

He couldn't, could he? He would know. He *must* know that what Finn had said he had said for effect, to provoke him, to play with him, He must know, surely, that it wasn't true?

He turned and leaned on the wall, doubled over, panting, as he gathered himself together out of the cloud of incandescent gas he had become. When most of him was scraped inside his skin, he lurched out of the front door, in the hopes of seeing Michael's retreating back, to shout after him, "I didn't mean it, come back."

He wasn't there of course. Well, wasn't that the start of another wonderful day? Fecking idiot. Weren't they such morons, though, himself and Michael both?

CHAPTER
FOURTEEN

Michael honestly thought he was going mad. He couldn't . . . He stormed home barely able to feel the pavements under his feet. He couldn't connect one thought to another. He was better off. Better off without the lying little bastard. Better off to have found out about this now before he got sucked into some vortex of crime, better now he could finish it and—

His chest ached, and his vision was white around the edges, too much shallow frantic breathing, too much fight-or-flight response with nowhere to go. God, he'd almost . . . he'd almost lost it altogether and punched the guy, and he was not, he was not the kind of man who hit the people he slept with.

He couldn't stop the breathing—the rapid, shallow panting breaths that came like sobbing—and he needed to calm down. He needed to calm the fuck down and think, because something wasn't adding up here, but he was too wound up to work out what it was.

The edges of town passed like a blur. Coots scattered from their nests as he reached the bridle path along the river and sped along it, breaking into a jog and then a run in an attempt to burn off some of the energy, the anger, the panic. He was really starting to get scared now. What the hell was happening to him? Even when he'd attacked Watkins he hadn't felt this unhinged, this out of control.

It was all a lie. Fucking Finn, who had seemed to be his lifeline, who had pulled him out of the water, only to push him back in and hold his head under until he drowned. How could anyone do that? How could the gentle, whimsical man he thought he'd met be someone who picked up guys deliberately to break their hearts?

He couldn't— He couldn't believe it. He couldn't.

Fishermen along the water's edge looked away as he passed, seeing his face. Even the swans on the stream took off in a long laboured effortful stepping up the yellow morning sky. His house came into view too rapidly, closed like a castle over its secrets, grey and stony and unwelcoming.

What he couldn't do was go back there to think. He needed a refuge, somewhere calm, somewhere he could breathe out this panic and not just finish the rest of the whiskey and down some sleeping pills. He was a fucking adult. He would get a handle on this and figure it out and turn it around and win, and going anywhere near his father's ghost would not help until after that process was done.

He slowed to a stop where the chain-link fence marked the official bottom of his garden, the house to his left, the narrowboat to his right. It was a no-brainer. He hauled the keys out of his pocket, unlocked the boat, and went to ground inside. A quiet day up the river, that would sort him out. The sound of water, the shadow of trees, and time to think.

He still couldn't breathe. *It's okay. It's okay, you've been running. You've got to expect . . .*

He had to expect the sobbing? He had to expect the shakes? The feeling that he was falling apart, like he could barely, barely hold himself together anymore?

The hatch slammed behind him as he came down into the boat's small galley. The stink of paint was cut with the smell of piss and rotten leaves. After the clear light of the golden morning outside, even the white-painted interior was dark to him for a moment, and his mind was too torn apart to register what he was seeing before the tiller bar smashed into the side of his face and knocked him to his knees.

It was the best thing that had happened to him all day. Instantly all of the disparate pieces of himself drew back together, sharp and ready for a fight. Something dark and stinking tried to push past him to get to the door. He surged to his feet, shoulder-checked it in the stomach, lifting it off its feet and throwing it three feet down the boat to land sprawled on the tiny sofa. It rolled and leaped up again, still with the iron pole in its hands, and came for him, yelling, "No, no, no! Fuck you, no!"

It was the homeless girl.

"Wait," he said, teetering for one moment as a whole thing, as a glass after being dropped, just before it hits the floor. God damn it! She had trusted him and come here for shelter, and now she thought...

And then he broke. He crossed his arms over his face and let her hit him, the smack of the iron rod against the long bones of his forearms breathtaking. "I'm sorry," he choked out, buckling to his knees. "I didn't know you were here. I swear! I just wanted, just once, for something to go right."

"No!" she shouted again. He locked his hands over his head and huddled, drawn in to himself like a weeping child. As though the posture had set it off—finally given it permission to become what it had really been all along—his grating breaths turned into sobs. His storm of shredded emotions settled on rain.

She hit him one more time, across the back, but he was curled into himself, oblivious, and it registered as less of an agony than what he carried in his heart.

He must have been a pathetic sight. What felt like a long time later, she put the tiller bar down with a clang. The ammonia scent of her came closer and then small hands closed around his wrists and pulled.

"Are you all right? Did I hurt you?"

He uncurled a little, raised his head, and focused his streaming eyes on her face. She was so young, with two round chicken pox scars on her cheekbone and eyes the colour of newly split slate. She looked at him like she didn't know what she was seeing, which was fair enough because he didn't think he'd ever seen a grown man cry as abjectly and pathetically as this either.

"I'm sorry," he said, wiping his nose on his sleeve and drying his eyes with the other cuff. "It's been a shit year. Not your fault. Are you all right?"

She moved away a few steps, far enough so she could pick up the bar again, but she had stopped trying to force her way past him. Stopped trying to run. Hunkered down with both her feet under her. Bare feet—her worn sneakers visible beneath the bed in the distant bow.

"You said I could sleep here."

"Yeah." The crying seemed to have let off some of the pressure. There was space in his skull now, the mad kaleidoscope of broken feelings slowing to something he might have a chance to control. "And I meant it. I just didn't know you'd taken me up on it."

"I can leave."

"No. No, it's good." The part of him that had wanted to hit something, the anger that had been as red and swollen as a blister, had also been drained off. Looking at her, wary, cautious but unafraid of him, he'd never been more grateful for that. He tried a smile, and though it was a little watery, it didn't feel strange. "Let me show you how to work the water pump for the shower and the sink. I'll bring in some wood for the heater, and maybe some food and clothes, and then I'll leave you be."

She clutched the tiller bar with both hands. "You want something for this. You must. I'm not going to—"

"No, hey." He held his hands out in surrender. "I don't. Look, my name's Michael. I'm . . . I used to be a policeman. I worked in the missing persons unit. I tracked down lost kids, and so many of them . . ."

He had to pause to get a handle on his breathing again, his chin trying to tremble with all the years of grief he'd laughed off with black humour while he was still at work. "So many of them I couldn't save. If I want something for this, that's all—I want to know I got it right, just once. Okay? I'm not going to do anything you don't want. You want to go, you go, I won't stop you, but you're welcome to stay."

Another long moment during which she looked down on him, like a wild thing deciding whether it was safe to come closer, to accept an offering of food. Then she put the tiller bar down by her feet and said, "Sarah."

He was pretty sure that wasn't her real name, but it made him smile up at her nevertheless, hugely relieved. "Hi, Sarah. It's good to meet you."

Slowly he raised himself to his feet. She backed up a little but didn't go for her weapon, and that made him smile too. She peered from a distance as he got the water pump going and demonstrated the shower, her filthy hands clutching at her grimy clothes as though she simultaneously hated them and was afraid to emerge from their shelter. He guessed they made pretty effective armour, given the fact that he would want to put on rubber gloves to handle them. Even her dirt was a defence.

"I'll go see about some other clothes," he said again, happy to have something uncomplicated to do, something that overwrote all the miserable business of his life with useful urgency. "I don't have anything your size. How do you feel about meeting another teenager? My neighbour's child is about your size. They might have something you could borrow."

"'They'?" she said, her hands now fiddling with her hood as though she wanted to raise it, to hide, but was making the effort to trust him with her face.

"Yeah, Tai's . . . um . . ." What was the correct word? He wasn't really familiar with today's terminology, and in his day there hadn't been a term for it at all. "Genderqueer? Neutrois? They're kind of neither one thing nor the other."

Sarah twisted her fingers in her messy greasy hair. "And their parents still love them?"

Shit. Would she ever stop making him cry? He bit the inside of his cheek to keep himself together. "Yeah. They're good people, the Lis. They're sure to want to help."

"You can't tell them," she said, her hands now tugging at her collar, always clenching and twisting somewhere over herself, like she could pull her skin off and be someone else. "About finding me on the streets. You have to tell them I'm your niece or something, or they're going to think it's dodgy, and they're going to tell social services."

"I can't just go around lying to people," he protested, slightly horrified at the thought.

And she bristled, stooping down to reach for her shoes. "You can. You have to. I mean *you* get to be honest because everyone always believes you, because you're an adult and you're a man and you're the law, so what fucking reason have you got to lie? It all works out your way anyway. But when everyone's against you, you tell them whatever works, because they wouldn't listen to the truth anyway."

It had the ring of bitter experience behind it. When he thought about how small he'd felt, how accused and how disbelieved by the police when they visited, he could almost see what she meant. If the as out to get you, dealing with it honestly might just be the thing as standing up to get punched.

Adopting a niece sounded like a hell of a responsibility. Something he really hadn't bargained on when he'd offered her a shelter, but she had a point. If it became widely known he had a sixteen-year-old runaway on his property? Well, people would draw conclusions and things could get ugly fast. Not to mention that his niece would have a respectable address and persona, would have job opportunities and a chance to establish herself in society that a nameless homeless girl would not.

A niece. For all intents and purposes a daughter. Wow. He was not in a good mental place to be taking on something like that. But the alternative was to—what? Turn her back out again? Shove her into a government system she was terrified of? That was never going to happen. He reconsidered.

"All right. How about this. I'll go and buy you some clothes, so you can get changed first, and then we'll introduce you to the Lis as my niece. I think you'd like Tai, and Mrs. Li's always looking for someone to help her clean out the boats, so you could maybe pick up a job there if you wanted."

"And pay you rent," she said, eagerly, as though paying him rent would be a fail-safe way of fending off any unwanted advances. It twisted his heart, reminded him that she really was so very young.

He smiled, for her sake. "Yeah, pay for your food and fuel and rent, so you're properly independent. It doesn't have to happen all at once, but that's the long-term plan, okay?"

This time she did tug her hood up, disappearing into the shadow, her little mouth twisted with ferocity and her thin wrists raised, covering her face. He dropped his gaze to the floor, knowing anguish when he saw it, praying that it was the anguish, the disbelief of someone who recognised hope after too long without.

He figured she needed to be alone with that, and backed away, coming out into the overcast grey weather of an autumnal noon as a changed man. Shutting the doors behind him, he set off back into town with new purpose and focus to his life, fairly sure that when the gains were balanced, she had rescued him, not the other way around.

The weather had worsened, and it was cold and damp, the leaves on the trees now thin and sad against the white sky. Long plumes of reeds hissed along the riverbanks, a sound as relaxing as the susurrus of the sea.

As he walked, he thought about lying—Sarah's assertion that sometimes the truth was a luxury the underclass could not afford. Like everything else in his life at the moment, it made him think of Finn.

Finn who surrounded himself with outrageous lies. Finn with his misdirection and evasion and downright deceit; Finn who loved words for their own sake, not necessarily caring if he meant what they said.

What made him think that Finn was telling the truth this time?

Michael always believed *I don't love you. I was just playing with you.* It had gone home like a bullet to the brain. But years of self-examination had taught him that he believed it too easily, that he sabotaged his relationships by expecting it. That that flaw in him was a neurosis left over from his father and only strengthened by his divorce.

He knew that Finn lied as easily as he breathed.

There was a distinct chance that Finn had not meant what he said.

Michael's pace slowed as he came off the bridle path, into the park from which a footpath led up into the streets of the town. With his mind clear of rage and misery, he found himself remembering details he had skipped over this morning.

Finn small and abandoned in the centre of a black star. A black star? Michael slowed to a halt, examining his memories. Smoke in the air, water underfoot, drenched books covered in ash and the black scar of newly doused fire on the bookshop ceiling and floor.

What the hell?

He knew he'd been preoccupied, but there was no excuse for missing the fact that there had been a fire at the bookshop. A fire in the heart of Finn's pride and joy, in the place that was almost an extension of his soul. He remembered now that the man's hands had been wrapped up, and his eyes smoke- and tear-reddened. God. Thank God Michael was no longer on the force. He deserved dismissal for not noticing these things before, for not connecting the dots.

There'd been a fire at the bookshop last night, when Michael's phone had been off, when he'd been drinking himself into a stupor

...ill thought of as betrayal. He'd been unavailable while
...living through some kind of terrifying near-death experience.
...wonder the man had greeted him with anger.

And instead of calmly trying to find out what had happened,
Michael had lost his temper. Finn had . . . Well, he still couldn't quite
work out what Finn had been trying to do. They'd both said the most
damaging things that had come into their heads, and things would
probably never be the same again between them.

Guilt pulled at him, tried to slow him down, suck him under into
suffocating despair. It was as hard to walk through as quicksand as he
pushed himself uphill towards the shops. Shit. He had not handled
that well.

Finn was still a villain though. That mattered, didn't it?

Or did it? After all, Michael was not a cop anymore, and Finn
knew it. Of the two of them, it was Finn who'd taken the biggest
chance, getting involved with the other side. Finn who risked being
grassed up or sent to jail. What did Michael risk by loving Finn?
Only disappointment and the loss of a reputation he probably didn't
deserve.

Michael bought two changes of girls' clothes in Primark, judging
the sizes by eye. The cashier looked askance at him, particularly when
she was ringing up the underwear. "My niece has come to stay," he told
her, and watched her face relax at the explanation. Now he was a liar
too, and probably on the wrong side of some child protection law he
wasn't aware of himself. "The airport still hasn't found her suitcase."

The bags seemed to burn his fingers as he stood outside, close
enough to the Bibliophile Bookshop to see the locksmith repairing
the door.

Finn had every right to be pissed off with him, and *he* was still
pissed off with Finn. He didn't know if he wanted to be involved with
some London fence. No, scratch that, he was pretty sure he didn't.
There were plenty of things he was willing to tolerate in a partner, but
a criminal career wasn't one of them.

He took out his phone nevertheless and dialled Finn's number.
It rang twice, was snatched up as if Finn had been waiting for it.
"Michael?"

He really wished he didn't have such a reaction just to his voice. Roughened by smoke though it was, it still set his heart pounding, dampened his hands, and made him feel warm all over. "Yeah. Look, I don't really know what happened this morning, but we should talk."

"I was thinking the same thing myself."

Finn made everything seem easier, more reasonable. Of course they would both want to talk. All intelligent life forms were agreed that was the only sensible course of action. Although he wished it wasn't the case, Michael felt the tension leave his body at Finn's words, and wished he could close his eyes and have that smooth Irish lilt close over him like a stream and lap him to sleep.

"Is now good?"

"It's not, really. I've got the book club lads round, and they're a prying nosy bunch of gobshites that wouldn't let us get a word in edgeways."

Michael wondered if he was being fobbed off for a moment, before the distant sound of cursing and laughter corroborated Finn's story. The guy had someone there with him. That was good.

"I'm sorry about the fire." He lowered his voice and whispered it as if the nosy lads were standing at his shoulder. "I'm sorry I didn't notice you'd had one. I was kind of wrapped up in my own concerns."

Finn laughed, and the sound relaxed Michael from the hair down. He had it bad if nothing more than standing here with Finn's voice on the phone made him feel so much better.

"You don't say," said Finn. "Look, I'll throw everyone out at 6 p.m. Come over at half past and we'll get this sorted out like grown-ups. I'm glad to know you're all right."

"I'm glad to know that you are too," Michael agreed, smiling, because yes, even if Finn was a villain, and even if this was over, he still really liked the guy. He still wished him well. "Don't do anything I wouldn't do in the meantime."

Finn laughed again, a little more naturally. "Darling, leave me space to breathe. You're far more of a stick in the mud than I could ever be."

Which was at least not any kind of lie.

"See you then." Michael couldn't keep the warmth from his voice or tamp down the pleased excitement at the thought, parts of him not at all troubled by questions of illegality, the rest of him troubled that he even had those parts.

"See you."

Considerably happier, Michael rang off and turned towards home, intending to take Sarah her jeans and jumpers and new shoes, to call on Tai and ask if they wanted to come over for a visit, and maybe to finally get some more work in on the new boat.

There was still a little over five hours until six thirty. Plenty of time to do everything else that needed to be done. Five and a half hours was frankly a lifetime.

CHAPTER
FIFTEEN

"**T**hat was him, wasn't it? Your mysterious lover?" Idris paused in his grimy task of levering the rolled-up carpet out of the door, bending it to try to fit it through the passage without smudging the paint so that it could be taken out to the back garden.

"Whatever gives you that idea?" Finn tucked his phone away with the sensation of being three stone lighter, the constricting bands of tension around his chest having loosened at Michael's call.

"Oh, that's a besotted smile." Idris gestured, the loose shapes of his hands seeming to describe something that was self-evident. He caught James's eye and gave a little jerk of the chin, inviting his opinion. "Wouldn't you say? That's the smile of a man who's in deep."

James—their local archaeologist—had taken a day off the digs at Wednesday Keep, Trowchester's Bronze Age hill fort, to lend his expertise with all things small and delicate. He tugged his reading glasses down and looked at Idris and Finn over the top of them. "I don't believe this invisible boyfriend of his even exists. I thought he was supposed to come to the book club? I note he never appeared."

He raised an eyebrow sceptically, turned back to the plinth where he was carefully sorting the gears of the automaton that he had earlier retrieved from where they were scattered around the room. The retrieval had taken him an hour, and the cataloguing another two, but he had just begun the process of fitting everything back together, and it was going like a charm—the benefits of the scientific method.

"I've seen him," Idris insisted.

"Well, you're the only one who has."

"Does my experience count for nothing, then? Am I such an unworthy witness?"

Finn tried to tuck his smile away as he finished wiping the residue of ash and water off the now-empty shelves. He'd rung everyone in the book club soon after breakfast. David and Peter had come over at once and put in two hours shovelling the worst damaged books into bin bags, while he took those he thought might be salvageable upstairs so he could work on them. At nine o'clock, they had gone off to their jobs, and Idris and James—both of whom were their own bosses and could take time off when it pleased them—had taken over.

The room was stripped and clean, even the flaky black soot scraped out of the scar in the ceiling. The floor beneath the carpet had proved to be tiled, and was blackened but otherwise unharmed. The shelves were intact, and altogether he was convinced it could have been a great deal worse.

After emptying the washing-up water down the drain, he returned it to the kitchen. Took a dose of Paracetamol and codeine for the pain in his hands and feet, thankful that they had come away so relatively unscathed. Made a pot of tea and brought it down on a tray with the cake Idris had brought.

His return only sparked the conversation again as though he had never been away. James had that philosophical twinkle in his eye that tended to presage a long discussion on authorial intent, and the statistical likelihood of whatever plot twist they were discussing. The look of a man who liked to argue logic just because it was there. "In the absence of Finn saying anything at all about this 'boyfriend' of his, there's nothing to prove Idris is not hallucinating the whole thing."

Finn turned the heating up, emptied the water from the dehumidifier he had brought from the basement, and smiled at them both.

"You can't just refuse to talk," Idris protested, drawn close by the responsibility of cutting the cake evenly. "Tell him. Tell him about your pocket-sized bear." He switched his attention to James, who had just fitted a copper disc on the back of the time machine and was checking to make sure it still rotated. "It's gorgeous. It's like they're specially scaled down for each other. The guy is Finn's height but built like a bulldozer. Handsome in a brutal sort of way. Alexander the Great was short, wasn't he? That's what the guy looks like—tiny, but hard-core."

"Are you casting aspersions on my altitude again?" Finn tried for lighthearted, but found he didn't quite have the resilience to laugh off short jokes at the moment. "I carry my inches somewhere else."

"Uh-uh." Idris waved a finger under his nose. "You don't get to deflect this even with well-phrased dick jokes. Tell the man I'm not making this up—that you have fire in your heart as well as in your buildings."

That was in such bad taste it startled a laugh out of Finn. "I'll tell him what I told you." Finn perched on the lower steps of the stepladder to pour the tea, and conceded the point—they were helping him put his life back together out of mere friendship. Perhaps they deserved to be included. "Which is that I don't know whether he's my lover or not."

"There's a simple enough test." James wound up the clockwork time machine and beamed with satisfaction when it began to whirr, good as new. "Did you sleep with him?"

Finn rolled his eyes and sighed gustily. "Yes."

"Well, then. And are you going to sleep with him again?"

Finn's cup clattered in its saucer. He put it down quickly, but not quick enough to avoid James's sharply sympathetic glance.

"Scared him off?" said the archaeologist, settling on one of the stools Finn had brought in to access the upper shelves. "I don't think any of us have failed to notice by now that you always recommend the BSDM novels. A bit too vanilla for you, is he? Not open-minded enough?"

"Good God." Finn glared at them both, Idris round faced and amused like an onlooker carved on a sexy temple fresco at Khajuraho, James infuriatingly perky under his spiky haircut. "You see. This is why I didn't want to discuss it. Can a man not keep his perversions to himself in this town? There's a reason they call it a 'private' life."

James seemed to realise that he'd gone too far. He spent a long time dissecting his slice of carrot cake as though he expected to find a Bronze Age burial in the centre of it.

"We ask because we're your friends," Idris said, closing a hand around Finn's wrist. "And because we can't help noticing that the thing that upset you most this morning was that someone wasn't answering their phone. When I put this—" he gestured at the bare, burnt room "—on one side, and him on the other, and I realise that he is more important to you than the burning of your books. Well, that's serious. All joking aside. That's serious, isn't it?"

Finn's head and hands and heart all still hurt. It had been a hard morning's work, and he was tired. He put his cake down and drew his stinging hands in to his chest to cradle and keep them warm. Maybe it *was* time he started being an honest man in other areas, not just his business but his private life too. Michael would approve.

"Yes, it's serious." He gave in, talking to his hands rather than having to watch their faces. "And yes, he's a lot more vanilla than I thought, but I think we could work that out, given time. It's just that he's an ex-cop and I'm . . . Before I came to Trowchester—well, I may have done some things that were not strictly legal, and he may have just found out about them."

In the terrible silence that followed, he died a couple of times, somehow not having thought that this confession might cost him his friends, realising it too late, only when the room filled with startled thought.

"But you're on the level now," James said carefully, the words weighted somewhere between a question and a statement.

"Yes." That came out a little too vehemently. Finn toned it down for the next sentence to improve believability. "I turned over a new leaf when I came here. That was *why* I came here—so I could leave it all behind."

"Well, then." Idris's response was also too much—too positive, too bright. "All you have to do is tell him so. He'll believe you. What kind of a lover wouldn't believe you? And it will be fine."

Finn pushed his plate away, the relief of hearing Michael's voice again fading, because it was clear enough that Idris already had doubts about what he was saying, and the man didn't know the worst of it— didn't know his contacts were pressuring him to go back, didn't know he'd already slipped.

In a way, the failed trial had drawn a line under his activities in London. There wasn't enough evidence to prove they had actually happened at all, and the trial, the accusations, the lawyers, being unable to be there for Tom . . . He'd been punished for them nevertheless and he felt clean of them.

But the abbot's psalter was new, and he could just feel it now—it was going to gnaw through the inside of everything like a worm in the apple until all he had left was a handful of rot.

Briggs wouldn't even have burned it. He would have found someone else to fence it for him. How could he have ever believed such a blatant lie? He was such an idiot.

And now it was too late, and everything was ruined. He'd lose Michael for sure. He'd be lucky if he even kept his friends.

"Yes," he said and tried to smile. "Of course he'll believe me. I'm such a reliable witness, after all."

They flinched, both of them, but they stayed, and he was grateful for that. "In the meantime, let's not be maudlin. Time to put some books back on these shelves."

"I'll be going home now, then, Mr. Hulme." Kevin put his head around the shower curtain that Finn had secured in the door between the damaged room and the rest of the shop. Like a trooper, Kevin had manned the cash register and kept the shop open while Finn and his friends worked to restore the Jules Verne room. The boy deserved a Christmas bonus, something in cash he didn't have to declare to the tax man—or his parents. Something just for himself.

"Thanks, Kevin," he said. "You've done a grand job today. I appreciate it."

Kevin reacted with a duck of blue hair, embarrassed, and grunted something unintelligible in return as he swept through the room and paused with his hand on the back door. "It's looking good."

Finn stretched the aches out of his back and regarded his work. A new coat of paint on the walls had made the place clean again. He had painted suckers and questing fingers onto the tendrils of scorching that rose over the ceiling and embedded two faceted red buttons into the centre of it that winked as you turned your head, very like shifting eyes. He'd painted flames around the burn marks on the floor and attempted a trompe l'oeil scene of a rift opening into Hell, from the centre of which a semiruined arch supported the shelves he had stocked with his horror and true crime volumes.

It wasn't the greatest work of art, but it gave the impression of being deliberate, as though he'd chosen it, as though it had not in any way been forced on him. That was the effect he'd been going for.

"Not so bad for a day's work," he agreed. "I think we can open the whole shop tomorrow."

"I know you don't want me to know what's going on." Kevin stuffed his hands in the belly pocket of his hoodie and shifted from foot to foot. "But someone did this, right? 'Cause you pissed someone off, somehow. Are they going to come back and do it again?"

There was another question he didn't want to think about. Curse inquisitive employees and nosy friends.

Benny and Lisa would almost certainly come back, bringing something they had stolen and wanted fenced. He would refuse them again and yes, they probably would do it again. Or worse.

"Don't worry about it," he said and opened the back door, pointedly. "We'll cross that bridge when we come to it."

"It something to do with your old patch? Because my dad knows some people. He could probably arrange to put the frighteners on whoever it is. Keep 'em away."

Oh yes, because it wasn't enough to put his own recovery on the line? He'd be damned if he'd lead Kevin back into the underworld. The boy was thinking of college, making something of himself. He was not dragging Kevin into any of this.

"Run along," he said, pressing one hand to his forehead, twirling the other dismissively. "I have everything perfectly in hand."

He locked the door behind Kevin, took another satisfying examination of the renewed room, and then went upstairs to make himself a coffee and a quick omelette. The book club boys had gone at half five and Kevin at six. There wasn't a lot of time to wait for Michael, but it made the most of itself, stretching like a rubber band, every second longer than the last.

It was raining outside, in long ruler-like streaks of cold grey water. A cheerless, miserable night, fully dark now. He looked out to see if he could distinguish the headlights of Michael's from any others—surely the man wouldn't walk here in this downpour—but he couldn't tell one set of lights from another as they rushed up and flicked past.

He would say, "I didn't ever mean to deceive you. I left that life behind, just like you left the force. We're new people now, and there's no reason we can't be new together. I'm sorry for what I said to you. I didn't mean that either. I wanted you to hurt me a little, and I thought it would give you an excuse. We should have discussed it beforehand, I know. Worked out safewords and all of that tedious business. I'm going to be more honest with you in the future. If we have a future, which I very much hope we do."

If one was going to quibble about details, it would be one of the largest lies he'd ever told, because he didn't intend to tell Michael anything about the abbot's psalter. Considering how off the rails he'd gone over a record that was unproven five years ago, he would utterly lose his shit over anything more recent, and Finn didn't think he could deal with that right now, when he had so many other things to fret about.

The sound of a vehicle drawing to a halt by the front door drew him out of his thoughts. A rougher, deeper sound than he had expected. He peered through the window again and saw headlights high off the ground, the boxy shape of a farmer's Land Rover. Disappointment did not have time to strike, as a second set of lights pulled up across the street. That was the purr of a large car. He couldn't tell one car from another particularly in this light, but it seemed roughly the right shape for Michael's Volvo, and it backed so carefully into one of the marked parking bays that it had to be driven by someone who respected the rules far more than was healthy.

He closed the curtain with a sick sense of anticipation and worry and an irrepressible hope, and bundled himself down the stairway posthaste to get the door open so Michael had to spend as little time as humanly possible outside in that rain.

The bite of cold, and then a tall figure streaming with water shouldered its way inside.

Oh, fuck, he thought, having a moment of intense déjà vu as the person came smack up into his face and grabbed him by the arms. Not Benny, not Lisa. Overwhelming scent of wet wool and sheep dip and dung. Another figure in the door, and the security light he'd had the locksmith install this morning finally flicked on, showed him a farmer, flat capped, tweed jacketed, with dirt-covered wellington boots and a shotgun cradled in the crook of his arm.

"What the hell is this?" he demanded, his voice rising into the upper octaves as the first man got a better grip on him and dragged him out into the night. "What's this about? Who the hell are you?"

Water hit him in the face, soaked his hair and his indoor clothes. The second man opened the back door of the Land Rover and together they tried to force Finn into it. He got his feet braced against the metal step, and struggling with all his might, twisted to look over at what he still thought was Michael's car. "Help me! Michael, help!"

The second farmer, the one with the shotgun, followed Finn's gaze. He was outlined in Michael's headlights, one hand on the barrel of his gun, its stock still tucked into his elbow. He tilted his head, considering, and then he slid two cartridges into the barrel and snapped the gun closed. Finn's heart stopped as he took aim.

Abruptly, Michael's headlights snapped out. Darkness fell like a stunning blow, beneath which they could just hear the note of an engine driving away. By the time Finn's eyes adapted, Michael's car wasn't there at all.

He's left! He's gone and left! The thought stole the strength from Finn's legs. They buckled, and his captor pushed him into the back of the Land Rover and locked a metal door on him. He was left crouched in a dog cage, fingers through the bars, trying to shake it apart, as the two farmers climbed in the front and the Land Rover lurched and rattled away to God alone knew where.

What the fuck? What the ever loving fuck was going on now?

CHAPTER
SIXTEEN

Finn shook the cage again, well aware that he was probably not capable of doing more damage to it than a couple of healthy sheepdogs. Was this what being an honest man required for everyone or was it just him? Because he hadn't appreciated the sheer level of heroism involved.

"You all right back there, son?" The man in the passenger seat twisted round to look at him. Oncoming headlights washed tidally over a weather-beaten face beneath a close-cropped silver beard. Kindly, Finn would have said, though perhaps with a hint of implacability in the set of the mouth. This was the man who had aimed a weapon at Michael, scared him away.

"What do you think?" Finn demanded. "I'm wet and cramped and confused and extraordinarily pissed off, and I have not the faintest idea what I've done to deserve this."

"Ah, well." The man gave him a philosophical smile, wriggled on the seat to get a hand in his pocket and then reached out to thread a hip flask through one of the holes in Finn's cage. "I can't tell you that. Have a nip of this, and you'll feel better."

Finn took the flask in astonishment, and as he did so his captor fiddled with the dashboard, turning the heating up. "Be warmer in a moment. You just sit tight, and we'll be there in no time."

"We'll be where?" Unscrewing the top of the flask, Finn sniffed warily. It certainly smelled like an uncomplicated whiskey. Ancient Grouse, maybe. He wasn't confident of his own ability to smell poison or tranquillizer—or God knows, truth drugs—under the homely scent of spirits, but what would be the point of drugging him now, when he was already so firmly under their control?

"You'll see."

He took a sip. It tasted like whiskey too, tracing fire down his throat and warming his cold belly. After five minutes in which he continued not to be poisoned, he took a larger gulp and passed it back. This was probably the least alarming kidnapping he could have imagined, and with that realisation, his fight-or-fight-harder response tamped down enough to let him think.

Dog hairs were mulched into the muddy carpet on which he knelt. The smell of the Landie was the smell of the countryside—earth and petrol and dung. This wasn't some hastily disguised getaway vehicle. He was pretty certain the guys looked like farmers because they were. And that was probably a good thing, because it meant that while they were ruthless to poachers and rabbits, they were probably not accustomed to being hit men for criminal gangs.

That made sense of the civility, but when had he ever done anything to annoy the sons of the sod? He'd always regarded the countryside as picturesque but largely irrelevant to a life spent cherishing art and knowledge for its own sake.

As he calmed down, his thoughts turned back to Michael—how cleverly and how nonchalantly Michael had got himself out of danger. The guy had been a cop in London, where the criminals had guns and the police were armed with sticks. Finn's first panicked belief that Michael had been frightened off didn't stand to reason.

Probably, possibly, Michael had simply circled round the block to avoid being fired on, and had picked up the Land Rover's trail as it left. If that was so, he might be following them right now. At the other end of this, when they stopped, Finn needed to be alert for any attempts Michael might make to get him out of there.

Or he could be delusional. After all, Michael had retired, burnt out, with his mental health as stable as a set of swings. It was also entirely possible that he had seen the gun, panicked, and gone off somewhere to have a flashback in private. The guy had been entirely useless and disappointing during the fire. Why should he break that streak now?

Finn tried peering through the back window to see if they were being followed, but in the darkness he could only see the car directly behind. That was not Michael's. He tried telling himself that Michael would not be foolish enough to be that obvious in how he followed them, and while it was a good argument, it didn't soothe Finn's nagging feeling that he was on his own again, that no one was looking out for him and no one ever would.

Past the ring road and away into fields split by dry stone walls, then dense woodland on both sides of the road and a wall on his right topped by stone pineapples. The Landie turned through an archway spanned by wrought iron, with a lamp hanging in the centre of it, dimly illuminating a series of signs advertising the Bonfire Night fireworks display on the weekend just past, a Christmas Craft Fair yet to come.

The Landie's wheels *sssh*ed over gravel and thumped into potholes as the road beneath them became a track through rolling meadows. Rain clouds drew aside for long enough to let through a chilly silver sliver of moonlight, in which he glimpsed a distant herd of deer that went bounding away from the sound of their wheels.

"This is Harcombe House," he said, mostly to himself. Seat of the Harcombe family, lords of the manor of Trowchester since the Norman conquest. "I come to the car boot sale here every third weekend of the month."

"That's right." The driver took his cloth cap off and wiped a hand over his bald patch. In happier circumstances he would have made a fine Father Christmas, with his bushy beard and his air of well-fed conviviality, though Finn had not forgotten the strength of his grasp, probably honed by holding down bulls for slaughter. "It's a good place to buy tools on the cheap."

"Oh no, they're crap," the whiskey-proffering bloke commented. "Chinese stuff. Lasts maybe half the winter, and then you have to throw it away."

"You know." Finn's knees ached, and he had a storm inside him threatening to break out, but he managed a light pleasant tone nevertheless. "You don't seem like the kind of people who would normally go in for kidnapping."

"Ah, it's not my métier," Whiskey agreed. "But when you live in the tied cottages, it's expected you'll do the odd little favour as part of the rent."

"You don't seem the hardened villain we were led to expect either," Driver chipped in, as he passed the stable block and the private chapel, swung round the red-brick Tudor wing of the stately home and parked by a small entrance in the larger, L-shaped Georgian side. "But you still can't go round burgling people's houses, even if they are as rich as Croesus."

"I didn't—"

"Well, you've got to say that, haven't you?" Driver waved a hand as though he were batting a wasp aside. "But don't waste your breath on us. It's not our business. We don't want to know. Isn't that right?"

Whiskey opened his door and climbed down, retrieving his gun on the way. He unlocked the back door, then stood carefully outside lunging distance, with the gun trained on Finn while his partner unlatched the cage. "That's right," he smiled like a lovable grandfather. "Strictly pick up and retrieval. Out you come."

Finn had to admire their style. They made Benny and Lisa's hard-man tactics look vulgar.

Now would be a good time for . . . He thought he saw movement, and his heart rate and mood spiked in fierce joy as he glanced back up the drive to confirm it. But no, there were no headlights, no one out there in the dark ready to ram into Whiskey and give Finn the chance to run. Michael had not come.

Disappointment stole his strength. He clambered stiffly out of the dog cage and let Driver haul him through the small servants' door to whatever fresh annoyance awaited him inside.

It was clearly the kitchen door, opening onto a low-ceilinged vaulted passage entombed in hundreds of years' worth of cream-coloured paint. They passed roped-off show pantries and kitchens, decked out in period features and inhabited by mannequins dressed as Victorian butlers and Georgian dairy maids. The cutesy country history of it raised Finn's hackles, as one who came from a country where people in houses like this had all but exterminated his relatives.

They would have called it that too—extermination, thinking of the Irish in their bogs as pests to be exploited or slaughtered at will. Now their livelihoods depended on opening their houses to be a fun day out for the plebs, and it still hadn't stopped them. They were still forcing their tenants to do their dirty work, still oppressing the likes of him.

He tipped his chin a little higher as if he was looking down his nose at the owners of this house for the past twenty generations.

Then his escorts pressed him up a final servants' stair and out into the mansion's great entrance hall.

It had a marble floor in shades of red and cream and green. The central staircase swept up from it, magnificent and curly like the horns of a goat. The walls were lined with portraits of puffy-faced, stern-looking folk who all appeared to disapprove of him. An ugly bunch, and not even the work of a decent portrait artist among them. But he approved of the vases that stood on the rococo tables along the walls, roped off. They were worth something, late period Tang dynasty if he wasn't mistaken.

In fact they looked suspiciously like the vase Benny had tried to sell to him. He hissed in annoyance at the thought. Bloody Benny and Lisa, when would they stop getting in his hair?

"Here we go, then," said Whiskey behind him, as Driver opened a door on the second floor and ushered Finn inside with a tug on his elbow. He caught a quick eyeful of Italian stucco work on the ceiling and William Morris wallpaper—probably the genuine article, considering how it had faded. A large white fireplace surrounded by optimistic fire screens held a small and sullen fire.

He was dragged in front of a Chippendale desk and parked there while his two companions touched the peaks of their caps simultaneously, in an old, old gesture of respect that made Finn's skin crawl.

The woman behind the desk smiled coolly up at him. She had the same sort of careful hair as the queen, apparently casually upswept but actually a work of intense art that would survive hurricanes. It was darker than the queen's, and she was a younger woman, hale and hearty and big-boned under her designer jacket. Her mohair jumper was pale lavender, accessorised with three rows of flawless pearls like moons on a string.

"Mr. Hulme." She rose automatically as if to shake his hand, revealing a matching Carven skirt, all very expensive and understated and sure of herself. He reached out for a handshake, and she snubbed him, drawing back with a horrified expression as if his fingers were dipped in shit. "I have a bone to pick with you. Let's go for a little walk."

Since he had no choice—the shotgun at his back a persuasive argument for obedience—he followed her out, down the corridor, across a landing (where a nice Caravaggio hung above a Queen Anne table covered in flowers), through a maze of small rooms and into an old wing, into the library.

He could tell at once from the bindings that whatever ancestor of hers had kitted this place out had ordered his books by the yard, more interested in the status of owning a library than the actual content of the books. The place was as regimented as a soldiers' dormitory.

The first long room terminated in a turret, a little magical cylinder of stone, white painted, with a window seat set into the tiny mullioned window, and an oak display case in its centre. Picturesquely but somewhat unwisely, his guards entered the room before him, and stood on either side of the window like pilasters, trying to pretend they were somewhere else. The empty space at Finn's back beckoned him.

"Do you see this?" The lady of the manor encompassed the display case with both hands, leaning down over it.

The glass-fronted case had been padlocked in three places. He could still see the scars where the hasps had been gouged out by some kind of crowbar.

"On the night of the thirteenth of October we had a break-in. The thieves took a number of paltry items of silverware—some candlesticks, a commemorative plate—and this book."

It was the right size. The velvet cushion in the case had a dimple just the right size. Finn went cold and then hot all over with enlightenment. This was the psalter's home? This was where Briggs had stolen it from? Scarcely ten miles from his shop? What kind of amateur tried to fence an instantly recognisable item in the town it was stolen from?

He gave an artfully unconcerned shrug. "I didn't take it."

She gave him the mild look of a woman who doesn't need to raise her voice to be instantly obeyed. "That's not my concern, but you are going to get it back for me, or failing that you're going to tell the police where they can find it so that they can retrieve it themselves."

Oh, and he hated being told what to do by some hoity-toity English aristocrat, who'd probably built her wealth on the starvation of his people, whose family had probably sat back and laughed as the Irish rotted alongside their crops in the famine.

"Look at that now." He waved a hand at the case, buckled down as it was. "You left it lying wide open in sunlight. Did you not care you were fading the ink and destroying the vellum? Did you ever read it? Did you give one thought to it at all before it was taken from you? Do you care now, beyond the fact that it's yours?"

She raised her perfectly shaped eyebrows in astonishment at being spoken to in this tone of voice, and Finn lost it at the condescension, lost it for long enough to speak the truth. Perhaps he had a death wish. Perhaps he just wanted to get this off his chest. "Yes, they brought it to me. The ones who took it from you. They put it in my hands like a baby. I didn't know who it belonged to. They didn't tell me that. But they said they would burn it."

He was shouting now, pacing and gesticulating as it all came out, his emphasis swamped in the big rooms, provoking only the smallest of smiles from her. "They said they would *burn it!*" he hissed again, because she clearly wasn't getting it. "It was a thousand years old. Unknown, a discovery beyond price. It belonged in a museum, where they could scan it and preserve it. Where scholars could read it and learn from it and share that knowledge with the whole world."

"And that's where it is, is it?" she interrupted his rant effortlessly, her voice scarcely raised but pregnant with authority. "You donated it to a museum?"

He hated that she felt so damn secure on the moral high ground there. *It's fine for you to be so smug with your own private army.* "And if I did? Would you go in, guns blazing, and get it back?"

"While I admire your passion for the past," she said graciously, "the book is *mine*. It was donated to my ancestors by the abbot himself in exchange for twelve hides of land for his hunt. Whether I choose to share it or to bury it under the floorboards, it belongs to my family. It is mine to keep or to destroy, mine to hand down. It's the principle, you see. People do not steal from the Harcombes and get away with it. It is my job as the head of the family to make sure that tradition continues. Now you can tell me where my book is, or I will—"

Yeah, this would be terribly frightening two centuries ago. Right now, Finn had had enough. "You'll do what? You can't keep me here and torture me until you get it out of me. That's false imprisonment, and I suspect your good gentlemen here won't stand for that. My boyfriend sure as hell won't, and he's barely hanging on to his sanity at the moment as it is. You don't want to get on his bad side, believe me."

Empty bluster and bravado. It was a wonderful thing.

"So yes, this was a lovely chat, and it's nice to know the provenance of the book I *saved from the fire*, but I am walking out of this mausoleum right now, and there is not a thing you can do to stop me."

He took a step back, turned. The lads by the window stirred as if waking up, their honest faces confused. Lady Muck's expression creased into bemusement too, as though she couldn't believe he would be so rude as to break off the conversation before she was finished. He considered the relative merits of a dignified walk away weighed against running as fast as humanly possible. Dignity would be nice, but— He took off like a rocket down the bouncy wooden floor of the ancient library.

A click behind him made his back prickle all over—the sound of a shotgun being armed. He wouldn't outrun that, but he didn't really believe that Whiskey would shoot him, and he was going to stake his life on that belief.

He poured every ounce of his strength, of his terror, into running, the soles of his poor blistered feet on fire again with pain. Behind him, heavy footfalls broke into a jog and then a run in pursuit, but he was faster. And no shot came. The library door took a lifetime to reach and then suddenly it was there. He burst through into a pink-striped room he didn't actually remember, slammed the door behind him, and looked round for something to slow his pursuers.

Yes. When visitors came round, the doors were wedged open and one of the wedges was visible beneath the overstuffed pink velvet couch. Cupids, painted on the ceiling, smiled down vapidly on him as he darted forwards and grabbed it, kicked it firmly into place, pinning the library door closed.

The burly lads would break it down soon enough—probably go through the hinges if they put their minds to it—but it bought him time. And frankly he needed time because he didn't remember which of the three doors that opened off this room they'd come in by.

The first thud and shudder came at the barred door as he was peeking through the one opposite. No, fairly sure he would have noticed a piano and a harp as he was forced to edge around them. Next. He thought he'd have registered the heavy gold bullion on the curtains, if he'd come this way before, but could he really be sure?

The library door boomed against its frame, making the chandelier tinkle above him. Through the third door he could see, yes, the Queen Anne table. He ran through, hearing a wooden crack behind him.

No time for this! Jogging again, he chose the next door at random, pelted through a succession of grotesquely overdone bed and sitting rooms, skidded out onto a little landing on the left of which was, dear God, steps down into a hollowed-out cavern of a room in which stood a nineteenth-century shower of the sort that had a water tank on top that needed to be filled by manservants as you bathed.

Well, he definitely would have remembered that, had he come this way before. It was official—he was lost.

"Fuck."

Another door opened from this landing-cum-shower room, debouched into a more conventional bathroom, if convention ran to Italian marble nymphs and gold fittings. He got the hell out of that as fast as possible, found himself in a dressing room-cum-wardrobe, equipped with heavy Tudor chests of drawers and an early-twentieth-century ironing board next to a hearth full of flat irons.

Another door, another bedroom, and he was seriously sick of the opulence and the ostentatious, unnecessary overspending by now. But this last door brought him onto the main stairwell, within sight of the overblown front doors.

He leaped down the stairs like a mountain goat and sprinted with renewed strength towards the way out. Only a statue of Zeus stood in his way, aiming a thunderbolt at an inoffensive flagstone, and he'd dare the wrath of stone gods any day. Grinning, he sped towards the exit.

And Driver stepped into his path. Finn skidded to a halt rather than run into the man's arms, couldn't see at first where he'd come from, but then a hidden panel, painted to look like the wall, swung open and Lady Harcombe stepped through, followed by Whiskey, still cradling the shotgun he didn't have the ice in his soul to use.

"You can't keep me here." Finn held his hands up in surrender and tried backing innocently towards the door. Whiskey might not shoot him, but he was not going to bet the man wouldn't pin him like a rogue sheep and think nothing of it. "You can't just abduct me and keep me against my will. I have rights."

Lady Harcombe was hardmouthed as a warhorse. "Yes, you have rights," she said, still poisonously courteous. "But I have more. Enough of this nonsense. Gentlemen, grab him. We will continue this conversation in the cellar."

Driver lunged for him. Finn ducked under the grabbing hand and made a run for the doors, reaching up for the enormous wrought iron rings with both hands. It took all his strength to turn one. He threw himself forwards to drive the door open. It shuddered slightly but didn't move. Locked.

Oh fuck. He turned, set his back to the oak and watched the two men approach, out of ideas as to what to do now. Very, very nearly out of strength.

"I don't think so."

A shadow detached itself from behind the plinth on which Zeus's perfectly shaped feet were planted. Black trousers, black duffle coat with the hood drawn down and the face shadowed, but Finn would have recognised everything about the guy from stature and posture and the way he walked, even if the rough, wolfish growl of a voice hadn't started up his fainting heart like a triple espresso in the morning.

Michael got between Finn and the oncoming bully boys, most of his attention on them, his head turned only slightly towards Finn as he spoke. "The wicket gate's unlocked. My car is outside. Get in. I'll deal with this."

Finn laughed, utterly delighted to be proved wrong. To think he'd given up hope that a rescue would ever happen. "I'm not leaving you here while I cower in the car. What do you think I am?"

"I think you're an idiot." Michael turned his attention fully on the two men in front of him, and the woman in charge, standing poised behind them with her hands folded across her stomach and a disapproving expression.

"Let me guess, you're the mad boyfriend."

Finn opened the wicket gate. Idiot was fair enough—of course no one would unlock the monstrous portal if they could get through a normal-sized opening in the side of it. Leaving it open, he returned to Michael's side in time to see him smile.

The smile made him shiver. Cold, humourless, a smile that said *I'm three seconds from tearing out your throat with my teeth.* He could see it strike fear into the farmers. They didn't step back, but they looked like they desperately wanted to.

"That's right. Nice to know he's been talking about me."

Lady Harcombe raised her chin and met Michael's eyes. Then she blanched like she wished she hadn't.

"You know what I hate?" Michael took a step forwards, crowding into Whiskey's personal space. Whiskey's eyes widened, and as he struggled not to step back, Michael reached out and casually took the gun from his hand.

"I hate people who put other people in cellars. I hate people who kidnap defenceless fucking innocents and don't let them go. Are you that kind of people?"

Whiskey gave a nervous laugh, and Finn actually felt sorry for the guy. He seemed like a decent bloke who had not bargained for this. "No. No, we're really not. So can I have my . . ."

He reached out imploringly, as though he expected Michael to apologise and give him his gun back. Michael's smile grew a shade warmer, even as he cracked the gun open and pocketed the cartridges.

"Huh. Yeah. Well, maybe you're not. And maybe you'd better go home right now and consider the choices you almost made."

Finn had to give Lady Harcombe points for style. She had recovered her mocking smile and was tapping a foot on the floor with an air of being so done with this idiocy. "I can assure you that your boyfriend is far from innocent."

"And what are you? Batman? You don't get to take the law into your own hands just because you live in the big house."

"No," she smiled. "I get to take the law into my own hands because I am the local magistrate, and in this manor I decide what is a crime and what is not."

Driver and Whiskey shifted nervously on the marble floor, exchanging a sidelong look, like a team of draft horses deciding they've had enough for the day and stopping dead in the road. He wondered if Michael had noticed it, but of course the guy had, trained as he was to read body language as a matter of survival.

"Finn. Get in the car and get it running." Michael backed off, letting the situation defuse itself. There was still a troll-like brutality about the set of his face that said he would rather be barrelling in there, taking them both down, breaking some bones. But he wasn't going to give in to it unless he had to, and it seemed like Finn's captors didn't want to make him have to.

"We're leaving. I'll drop the shotgun in the road as we drive away, but this conversation is over."

"For now." Lady Harcombe nodded and watched them go.

CHAPTER
SEVENTEEN

"**S**eems like you've got a lot to talk to me about," said Michael as they turned onto the main road and were safely lost among the other moving lights. Something inside him was purring with the satisfaction of a job well done, and it was a sensation he hadn't had for years. He almost didn't recognise it. All the turmoil over the last few weeks, the digging and the turning up of stuff, must have freed a few good things along with the bad.

He sighed deeply and let the wariness leave him. Glancing over to the passenger's seat brought a view of Finn leaning against the window with his eyes closed. The man looked shattered, innocent and delicate, with the light of oncoming vehicles turning his pale eyelashes platinum, washing out his colourless lips and faded cheeks, highlighting the deep shadows under his eyes. He'd obviously been out in the rain earlier this evening. His hair was darkened with it, and his shoulders soaked.

"Are you okay?" Michael decided to leave the interrogation until they got home. He fished a Tracker bar out of his coat pocket—they were Jenny's favourite, and he hadn't got out of the habit of carrying them yet. He handed it over and turned the heat up to maximum.

Finn opened his eyes to frown at the chocolate-covered thing in his hand as though he wasn't sure how it related to him. Michael took his hand off the gear lever for long enough to push the food towards Finn's mouth. "Eat it. Sugar—it's good for the shock."

That raised a very weary smile. Finn's mossy eyes in their bruised sockets slid sideways to regard him with fond amusement. "Muesli coated in chocolate. Someone can't make up their mind."

But he opened it and took a bite, then a larger one, and wolfed the rest down on the third.

"I didn't think you were coming for me." He kept on smiling, but his gaze returned to the window. "When you drove away. I thought everything was over between us. That you'd decided I was too much trouble."

Michael turned over all the things he could say, should say. *We might well be over* being the chief and hardest one of all. No, not until Finn was in his own home, washed, fed, and warm.

"Well, you're certainly that. Doesn't mean I'm going to swan off in the middle of a kidnapping and leave you. I just wanted to make sure that guy with the shotgun didn't take out one of the wheels so I couldn't follow you. And it was difficult coming down that drive on your tail without being spotted. I had to wait for them to get a long way ahead and then roll down quietly with my lights out."

He came off the ring road, swinging onto Jasper Avenue, where the superstores and garden centres clustered around the outside of the Roman wall. Through the gate, and as always it felt like the air had changed, like they'd come in from the cold, as the style of the buildings switched abruptly from modern bunkers to Georgian chic.

"I guess you don't have any reason to think I'd come through for you, after the fire," he said, the satisfaction of heroism dimming as he remembered how he'd failed. "You going to tell me about that too?"

"Honesty is the best policy?" Finn pulled his feet up onto the seat, laid his cheek on his knees, and closed his eyes, and it occurred to Michael that Finn really wasn't faking his exhaustion, wasn't quite as tough as he seemed. Or he might just have reached the limit of his tolerance for bearing with arson and armed abduction. Who could blame him if he had?

"Don't go to sleep," he warned. "We'll be there in a minute, and you'll feel like shit if I have to wake you up after you've been asleep."

"Mmm."

He shook the man by his slender shoulder. "I mean it."

"Gobshite."

Laughing, Michael pulled up outside the bookshop and parked. He pushed the hair off Finn's forehead and stroked his face with the back of his hand, continuing the caress across his cheekbone and down to the gilt bristles on his chin. "Wakey, wakey."

"Bastard."

He got out, opened Finn's door, and shoved his hands in the man's damp pockets, looking for his keys. Finn grinned at him, not entirely with it. Michael unlocked the shop, pocketed the keys, and lifted Finn out of his seat, carrying him indoors bridal style. Finn lolled his head against Michael's shoulder, shut his eye, and smiled.

It was the sweetest thing. Michael hadn't had time or inclination to try to figure out Finn's odd combination of sex and viciousness, but this cuddly version, quiet and trusting and utterly relaxed in his arms was something he was going to miss. He smiled down as Finn looked up at him with sleepy affection, settled the guy on the couch, and went to run a bath.

Finn held up his arms imploringly when the bath was ready. "Carry me?"

"You're not injured anywhere? You looked like you were walking well enough before I stepped in."

Finn sighed. "My feet hurt, but that's not the point. I want you to carry me. You do it so well. So easily. It's very affecting—makes me want to forgive you for everything."

Well, that made for an easy enough absolution. Michael went to his knees beside the sofa so that he could undo the knot of Finn's tie, unbutton his rain-soaked shirt, and pull all the layers of damp clothing off at once.

"I dream of you ripping me out of those," Finn said, still worryingly undefensive, softer and more straightforward than Michael was used to from him. "But this will do for a start."

"You want me to ruin your clothes?" Michael removed Finn's shoes and socks, peeled the clinging trousers down his legs, taking a moment to admire his body—not quite boyish, but lithe and slender, just muscular enough for beauty. He should never really have thought that anything this lovely could belong to him.

Tenderly he pushed his arm beneath Finn's knees, wound the other around his back, and lifted him. Finn snuggled into the embrace like a child, and it made him wish the walk to the bathroom wasn't so short. He lowered him into the hot water reluctantly, helping Finn hook his bandaged feet over the side to keep them dry, smiling as Finn closed his eyes and sighed with bliss.

"I want you to tear my clothes off me," Finn murmured, his voice somnolent with pleasure. "As you hold me down. While I'm squirming and laughing and trying to get away, and bursting out of my skin with excitement. You're so . . ." He opened an eye and focused it on Michael, his mouth still smiling but his gaze serious. "Strong. Angry. Overwhelming. I don't think you've made your peace with that part of yourself, but I love it. I want to help you let it out in a way that'll make us both happy."

Abruptly, Michael had to look away, press his fist against his mouth to stop himself making a noise of anguish. He hated the anger. He hated it. He'd worked so hard all his life to keep a lid on it, loathed himself every time it came out. It had lost him his job and his self-respect, and he despised himself for it. He didn't know what to do about finding someone who accepted it. Who loved him for it.

"You're a ridiculous man, Fintan Hulme," he said in a thick voice, crouching by the side of the bath in a cloud of steam that smelled of samphire and cinnamon. "But I think I love you."

"Oh, we're in trouble now." Finn smiled back. "For I think I might return the sentiment. What will we do, the pair of us?"

What Michael wanted to do was peel off his own clothes and get in the bath with him, wrap himself entirely around those narrow limbs and hide his face in Finn's shoulder. That was somewhat counterproductive if this was still going to have to be good-bye. He rubbed his hands over his face, shoved his cuffs further up his arms to keep them dry, and as he did, Finn reached out and brushed his fingertips lightly over the purple welts that stood up along his forearms where Sarah had smacked him with the tiller bar.

"Acushla," whispered Finn, the warmth in his voice deepening into concern. "You're hurt."

The bruises throbbed a little, but he'd put some ibuprofen gel on, and they were no problem really. "It's nothing." Guilty and embarrassed, he tugged his sleeves back down again to cover them. "A misunderstanding. I'm fine. I'm not the issue here. I want to find out what's been going on with you." He traced the path of a water droplet down the slope of Finn's arm. "My partner in the Met tells me you're a fence. What made you decide it was a good idea to go out with an ex-cop?"

"This—" Finn's tone sharpened, leaving him sounding more alert, more like himself "—is not a conversation I can have naked. There are pyjamas in the chest of drawers in my bedroom. Top drawer. Get me some?"

Michael had risen to his feet before it occurred to him that he should not still be taking orders from Finn. He had a bizarre flash of mythology, the thought that if he was a fucking animal at times, maybe together, with Finn's controlling hand on the reins, they could be a centaur.

If they could only get past this whole crime thing. If only. How he wished . . .

He ducked his head and went to find the pj's, and to make them both a cup of tea. A few minutes later found them curled up together on the couch, Finn still boneless and warm against Michael's chest, a handwoven woollen throw wrapped around them both, mugs of tea in hand. The curtains were drawn and the room seemed a million miles from anywhere, a whole world of its own.

"So," Michael tried again, "are you a fence?"

"What's it to you?"

He should probably be happy that Finn's evasiveness was returning. It meant he was feeling better, more like himself. It was also as irritating as hell. He put his tea down on the floor, dug his fingers into Finn's shoulders, and shook him to make him pay attention. He didn't want to have to say this, but he saw no alternative, no way to overstep this fundamental line.

"I'm not getting involved with a criminal. I'm not going to end up your bodyguard or your hit man. Apparently I've already made an enemy of the laird, and if she's doing something illegal, then she needs to watch herself, but I don't—"

"Oh, give over." Finn's voice was sharp, but he rested his cheek against Michael's biceps and closed his eyes. "I'm not a fence anymore. I'm an ex-villain, just like you're an ex-cop. You can shag me as much as you like without it troubling your conscience in the slightest."

Michael's arms tightened around Finn almost by themselves. Inside, potent forces of hope and yearning and ground-in despair tried to fight it out, bare-knuckled. He squeezed his eyes shut and buried his face in Finn's neck, breathing in the scent of him, acutely aware of how his lips grazed smooth skin.

"I wish to hell I could believe you. But if that's the case, then why would the local magistrate abduct you in the middle of the night? Why would someone set fire to your shop?"

He wished he hadn't spoken, hadn't felt forced to think these things. Wished he could just let it go and for once do the thing that would make him happy. But that had never been who he was. Maybe he wasn't the world's brightest or quickest mind, but he observed stuff and thought and made connections, and he couldn't make that process stop just because the connections ripped his heart out and stamped on it.

"Something dodgy is going on, and you're right in the middle of it. So yeah, I wish I could believe you. But I don't."

CHAPTER
EIGHTEEN

"**W**ell, that's *your* problem isn't it?" Finn said without thinking. It came out, as so many wild and fanciful things came out, partly as a big *fuck you* to the world, partly because the truth was so terrifying. When you told the truth, people knew how you really felt, and then they used that information to hurt you. Their jabs were always so much less accurate if they didn't know what they were aiming for.

"Yeah." Michael's voice hardened. His body tensed all around Finn, making him uncomfortable to sprawl on, and his arms loosened. He hadn't moved, but he was suddenly very far away. "That's my problem. So what's it going to be? Am I important enough to you to tell me what's really going on? I'm going to find out anyway, because I'm going to look into it now, but you can choose to trust me or not. If you don't, this is over too."

He tried to shove Finn off his lap, already leaving. Finn clutched at his hair, torn between two different instincts. He couldn't tell Michael about the psalter. He couldn't, because then Michael would leave. But if he told him a lie, he would also leave.

"Don't!"

Michael resisted for a moment, effortlessly stronger in that way that made Finn a little fuzzy inside. Finn twisted to gaze up into his face and found him looking down, his hazel eyes both fond and frightened. It occurred to Finn reluctantly that the guy was not in the best mental shape at the moment, that this conversation must be as hard for him as it was for Finn. Could he trust him? Did he dare?

Well, it seemed he had nothing extra to lose by trying it. If Michael was going anyway, no matter what he did, he could at least try to be kind to the poor dumb sod in the end.

"Don't go. I'll talk." The phrase put him in mind of film noir, let him smile involuntarily and say, "Your interrogation technique is unusual. I'm not sure if I'd appreciate it from anyone else."

"Huh." Michael shook him again, in what he thought was a combination of amusement and annoyance. "Yeah, let's not get distracted. What's going on, Finn?"

"The evening after you came in the shop the first time," Finn started, quickly so as to get it all out before his soul revolted from the bare nonfiction of it, "I had a visit from an old associate I thought I'd left behind in London."

Very well, there was the hook. Now some backstory. "You have to understand that the trial—you know about the trial, five years ago?"

"Mm-hmm." Michael rested his forehead on Finn's shoulder, as though his thoughts were too heavy to hold up.

"It scared me to death. And it prevented me from being there when Tom died. I couldn't hold him, couldn't tell him how much I loved him at the end. I was fucking devastated, Michael; you've no idea. I was unmade. Everything, everything was unmade without him in it . . ."

His throat closed. The sobs piled up in his lungs and made his breastbone ache. Tears leaked out of the corners of his eyes, and he closed the door on those memories and put his back to it to keep it shut.

"It was the end for me. The end of everything. I was finished, changed. I wanted to be someone else. So I decided to leave town, turn over a new leaf, and go straight." He scoffed. "At least in that respect."

He turned his head so he could rest his cheek against Michael's black curls and closed his eyes. Michael smelled of safety and warmth and some horrible orange-and-ginger shampoo that Finn was going to wean him off if he ever got the chance.

"And though I say it myself"—he recovered a lighthearted tone—"I did very well. I doubt if I'll ever be rich, but the bookshop is supporting me and keeping young Kevin out of the kind of trouble his family would otherwise get him into." Strange, but still true: "I'm a pillar of the gay community in Trowchester. And happy."

When he thought back to the time before Michael, to dinners shared with ghosts and vagrants, to the empty upstairs and the empty bed, talking to himself or switching the radio on so his silences could be filled with a friendly voice, *happy* seemed an exaggeration.

"Or *content*, at least. Then Briggs showed up, and he had a book to sell me. A priceless thing. Do you know the Lindisfarne Gospels?"

Michael looked up, startled and interested. Of course he knew them, Finn rebuked himself. A man who knew how to treat an ancient manuscript couldn't help but know of them.

"Yeah."

"This was like that. Similar antiquity and beauty. Briggs said he would burn it if I didn't buy it, and I couldn't risk that. So I told myself 'one last time.' I bought it from him, and I sold it on to a collector I know of who treats her books impeccably. I told myself I was rescuing it, and I was, I think. At least it will be safe where it is."

"So you fell off the wagon." Michael's voice was dark, disappointed, but he didn't repeat the attempt to leave.

Finn breathed out slowly. Well, this was good. No immediate abandonment, and the rest of the story was an improvement.

"What about the fire?"

"Briggs obviously went away and told everyone else where I was and that I was back in business." Finn's turn to tense up, let anger and annoyance pierce the atmosphere of warm shared confidences that had spread like the mingled heat of their bodies from everywhere they touched.

In response, Michael raised a hand to comb his fingers gently through Finn's hair in a soft, petting stroke that made him want to purr like a cat. He stretched lazily, relishing the rub of his back against Michael's chest, and settled again, hackles lowered.

"A couple of lowlifes called Benny and Lisa turned up with a vase they'd liberated from somewhere, and tried to sell it to me. I had already realised the lapse was a mistake I didn't intend to repeat, so I turned them away. They didn't take kindly to that. Hence broken Pegasus followed by burnt bookshop. And that, children, is the end of our tale. Now who can tell us the moral of the story?"

The end of our tale. As they did so often, his words came back to mock him, flippant, light little words circling above a pit of dread. This time when Michael slid Finn forwards, moved to sit up, Finn didn't stop him. They detangled themselves, ended sitting side by side, while Michael planted his elbows on his knees and lowered his face into his hands.

"There's no need for you to be so sad," Finn told him, leaning forwards to put a palm gently down between Michael's shoulder blades, because he'd somehow got to the stage where he needed to be touching Michael in order to feel fully himself. "I'm miserable enough for us both. I thought we had a good thing here. But if you can't live with it, I'm not going to try to force you."

Michael lowered one hand and turned his face so he could look at Finn from the corner of one of his beautiful dark-lashed eyes. "Did you turn them down for me?"

Finn gave a hollow laugh to cover his confusion about where this remark was coming from. "Don't flatter yourself."

"I mean it." Michael sat up fully, took both of Finn's hands in his and pressed them with fierce strength, moving some of the ache that had been in Finn's heart away to his fingers. He wasn't sure what Michael was self-destructing about this time, but it didn't seem to be the rejection Finn had expected. "Did they burn your shop because of me?"

"Oh, bless your guilty conscience." Finn had to laugh. "No. I turned them down because I don't want to be sucked back into that life. I'm an honest man now, and I'll be buggered if I let those weaselly little bastards bully me out of my new life. I did it for me, Michael. I would have done it even if you hadn't been here."

Michael hung his head, his eyes screwed closed and a crease between his brows so deep it might have been put there by an axe. Finn freed his hands and bracketed Michael's face with them, hurting for him—this sad Rottweiler of a man. "So don't fret now, darling. If you have to go, go with my blessings. You don't owe me anything."

See how fast he slipped back into lying. What he wanted to say was *Don't go! Fuck you if you go. I want you to stay!* He wanted to find some words that would put the desperation and the need in his own heart out there to change the world and make Michael stay.

But he hadn't even finished the thought in the privacy of his own mind when Michael made a strangled noise halfway between sob and laugh and lunged forwards to wind both arms around Finn. He pulled Finn in so close he had to scramble into Michael's lap and lock his legs around Michael's waist to keep from being bent like a bow. Crushed against the wall of muscle that was Michael May, he was not going to complain.

This close, he could feel Michael's semihysterical laughter in his own bones. He let his head fall into the hollow of Michael's shoulder and rubbed silent circles on the man's back.

Gradually, Michael's ragged breathing smoothed out into peace. They softened into relaxation against one another again, as Finn's desolation rose like a fog and wisped away. His body hummed with satisfaction, telling him that this was where he wanted to be. More than anything, this was where he wanted to be for the rest of his life.

"We'll tell the police." Michael was saying some things that might have disturbed him more if he hadn't just found his Valhalla. "They'll deal with Benny and Lisa for you. Tell them who you sold the book to; they can restore it to its owner, and then it's all over. It's all over and you're in the clear forevermore."

"Until the next 'old friend' turns up on the doorstep." Finn got a hand under Michael's T-shirt, pushed the material up, exposing the soft skin over the hard muscle of Michael's belly, flanks, and pecs. Sitting in this position, prick to prick with the other man, he was rapidly losing the will for further debate.

"And I'll be here to punch them in the teeth for you." Michael gave Finn's old, well-washed, semitransparent pyjama top a critical examination, and flashed a grin Finn had never seen before but wanted very much to see again. He took hold of Finn's collar and ripped through the buttonholes in one long, tearing yank.

Finn's breath stopped. He looked up in astonishment as all rational thought fled in the face of a wave of pure *yes*. "Oh God!" There were things he had to say about Michael's plan—caveats, fears—but Michael had already taken him by the hair and bent his head back and was biting him. Not hard enough to draw blood, but enough so the sharp pain and the slow sucking ache that followed convinced him he had far more important things to be concentrating on right now.

Yes, yes, oh God. It could all wait.

"Bed?" he managed, as Michael snapped the waistband of his trousers and shoved his hands inside to cup Finn's arse and pull him even closer.

Michael pressed him back against the sofa cushions. "I was thinking 'couch.'"

CHAPTER
NINETEEN

Finn woke slowly, warm and more relaxed than he could remember being for years. His body glowed with satisfaction, and the hinterland of slumber was like lying on clouds saturated in sunshine. He was tucked up against Michael's back, with an arm under the man's neck and the other around his waist, hand resting on his belly, feeling the slow rise and fall of his breathing. He opened his eyes to a shock of dark curly hair and the nape of Michael's neck, which he kissed.

"Are you awake?"

"Hmm." Michael stretched, turned over. "I am now."

He had quite a range of smiles that Finn had never seen before. Last night's had been roguish, sexy. This was sweet and perhaps a little shy. *You should smile more*, Finn thought. *It suits you. I'll get working on that.*

"Good morning. What time is it?"

Finn extricated an arm from the refuge of the bedclothes and picked up the alarm clock to peer at it. Dim light behind the curtains at this time of year said it was later in the morning than it should have been. "Oh fuck," he said. "I forgot to set it last night. It's half eight already and the shop has to be open at nine."

Michael pulled him in close to land a gentle kiss on the most tender of his love bites. Although sore, he found himself amenable to the thought of fitting a quickie into the half hour he had to make himself presentable and fed, but Michael rolled away even as he was reaching for him. "You shower, I'll make breakfast. No problem."

It was probably for the best, given that sitting on the edge of the bed was uncomfortable. "Can you cook?" he asked, not bothering to restrain a fierce smile at the memories of being well used. "You don't seem the sort."

"What does that even mean?" Michael climbed back into yesterday's clothes. "Is this some kind of gender stereotyping bullshit you're pulling on me? I make a mean plate of bacon and eggs."

Finn located his dressing gown on the sitting room floor, hung it on the back of the bedroom door, and walked to the shower nude. There was no point now in being coy. "Maybe I'll keep you after all."

With November, the golden days of autumn had finally given way to heavy overcast skies and lightless days that dragged through as if underwater, but today the electric light in the bathroom seemed enough to dispel the gloom. He turned the radio on and sang along to Studio Killers with great self-satisfaction as the burst of water against his back flushed his skin pink.

A day without shaving would do him no harm. He dried himself, cleaned his teeth, and wandered out in search of clothes. Something comfortable seemed called for. Michael had made a game effort at giving him some of the pain he liked alongside his pleasure, and he wanted something soft on his scratches. A brushed-cotton shirt, moleskin trousers, and a nice Aran sweater would do the trick, with a cravat to hide the purpling of his throat.

Quarter of an hour later, he was sitting at the kitchen table with a cup of coffee at his hand as Michael put down a plate of bacon and eggs and hot buttered toast in front of him.

"I could get used to this." He smiled up at Michael, who had sadly lost his smile in favour of a more common look of worried guilt.

Michael sat down with his own plate but didn't eat. "Are you all right this morning? I know you were enjoying yourself, but I didn't hurt you for real?"

"You're the one who's ridiculous." Finn leaned in to kiss the man on his overly earnest cheek. "But you're very sweet. I'm fine." He wasn't sure if it would seem too clingy, too much like demanding commitment to ask, but he had the feeling Michael wouldn't mind either of those things. "You can check me out tonight and salve my wounds, if you like?"

Michael relaxed. "Sure." He ate his toast, and every so often the little shy smile would break over his face as they finished breakfast in silence.

Finn waited until he was ushering Michael out of the door to venture, "You should bring some essentials with you. Toothbrush, changes of underwear. That kind of thing."

"I will." Michael broke into a grin, picked him up off his feet, and kissed him properly, then walked away into the morning drizzle with a light step. Finn watched him go until the low clouds swallowed him, then he turned all the lights on in the bookshop, and bit his lip against the urge to whistle. Moving things in. *Moving things in.* This was getting serious!

Kevin arrived soon after, took one look at him, and said, "Oh well, we know what you were doing last night. How about a raise?"

He was tempted to give the boy what he asked just for his cheek, but bought them both lunch instead, when the time came.

The day managed to be perfect without being anything much out of the ordinary, and though his legs and heels were burning by the end of it, from preferring not to sit down, the fact gave him the same pleasing glow as the knowledge that everyone who saw him could tell at once that they should envy him.

He ushered the last customer out on the dot of five. Switching off the lights in the shop, he went out to leave a thermos of hot chocolate and a covered plate of sandwiches and cake for his ghost, feeling guilty that he had completely forgotten to put out food last night, and when he returned, there was a hard *rat-tat-tat* at the knocker, and Michael was standing outside.

Finn's smile fell from his face because Michael had brought two policemen with him. The fuzzy warmth in which he'd spent the day froze in an instant of betrayal, and Finn ground to a halt in the doorway, as if Michael had shot him with a freeze ray.

"Finn?" Michael stepped forwards and took his arm, turning him around and marching him inside. "You okay? I did say we should tell them what's been going on. You agreed, remember?"

"I didn't agree!" The filth closed the door behind themselves, a young black woman with a keen expression and an older jowly fellow who looked like a restaurant candle—one of those ones that had been artfully melted. "I don't want them in my house. I don't want to talk to them. I don't know how you could have . . ."

He wanted to be angry, angry in a brisk, joyous way that led to fighting and making up, but instead he felt only a kind of sick dismay. "You distracted me. I didn't agree to anything."

Finn had many faults, but being unfair was not one of them. If he cast his mind back, he could see how Michael could have interpreted his assertion of going straight as an assertion of being willing to cooperate with the police. He had been too busy at the time to correct Michael's assumptions.

"You should have fucking talked to me about this. You can't just spring the filth on me like a 'congratulations, you're in a relationship' present."

"To be fair, sir," said the WPC, "we were planning to come round today anyway to investigate the fire brigade's reports of arson at these premises."

"Your, um, partner said you had some information on some burglaries in the area," said the man. "Are we to presume that you don't want to cooperate with us anymore? Because we can take you in anyway if we think there's cause."

"Never. I'm never fucking opening this door ever again outside office hours. Nothing good ever comes of it." Well, there went Finn's good mood, skewered and dead on the floor. He acceded to the inevitable, grudgingly. "I suppose you'd better come upstairs."

The police took the seats at the kitchen table, leaving Michael to lean against the wall by the fridge, and Finn to make tea. He put down a pot on the table. Let the coppers pour for themselves. When they had done so, Michael brought a mug over to Finn and stood in front of him like a dog that knows it's been bad. He took Finn's hands, bowed his head.

"I honestly thought you'd agreed. I'm sorry."

And despite everything, Finn couldn't keep up a decent level of resentment towards Michael today. He didn't want his puppy to be sad. It was that nauseating.

"I suppose I did. Or I would have, given time to think about it. Like she said, I'd an idea they were coming anyway."

Stiffly, against his own reluctance, he leaned by the cooker and cleared his throat. They had been politely pretending not to listen. They stopped that at once and gave him matching attentive looks.

"I suppose I do wish to cooperate. At any rate, I'd be glad to help you catch the terrible twins. Benny and Lisa burnt my books. They deserve whatever's coming to them."

"I'm glad to hear it." Melted-man smiled, drawing his face up and taking ten years off his age for a few seconds. "I'm PC Davis, by the way and this is WPC Clarke, and we're here to help you with that. But first of all, we understand you know where to find a certain valuable book, stolen from Lady Harcombe's collection on the night of the thirteenth of October?"

That was the rub, wasn't it? He'd always had good relations with his customers, felt a certain kinship to the few other people who appreciated beautiful things enough to risk reputation and safety for them. He'd hoped to get out of the business without burning all those bridges, making enemies of all those less than scrupulous people.

He pressed the heels of both hands into his eye sockets, felt Michael come close and slip arms around his waist, taking some of his weight, saying nothing, just being confident that he would do the right thing.

Michael's respect on one hand, Dr. Whinnery's on the other. Was it really much of a contest? Whinnery's unhappy books recurred to him, drenched in blue light, unread, hoarded like jewels that would never be worn. At least Lady Harcombe shared a single page of hers with the general public. At least she would put it back in a library. And perhaps now she'd felt the lash of his tongue, she might consider keeping it better, scanning it for posterity and the peasants.

The abbot himself would surely want her to have it, kin down a long line of blood to the man who valued it enough to give away part of his estate for it. Finn rested his head against Michael's throat and sighed in surrender. "It's at 1358 Colstone House, Canary Wharf, in a hidden vault that opens out of the living room wall, with a fingerprint and a retinal scanner. I saw it there when I visited her recently. She showed it to me to make me jealous."

He allowed himself an inner smirk at a believable explanation for having seen the book that did not implicate him in having sold it to her in the first place.

"All right." WPC Clarke was keying the number in on her mobile. "Let me phone this in and then we'll set up some surveillance cameras to try to catch your Benny and Lisa the next time they try to sell you something."

That was a better thought. He was really very fucking ready to get some revenge on those toerags for trying to force him into something he didn't want to do. "Should I actually buy it? I mean, better to get them on 'selling stolen goods' than 'attempting to,' right?"

Davis's smile was obviously taking considerable effort to maintain. His face was trembling. "I think that might be best for many reasons, sir. Better not to risk another incident like—"

A knock on the door. He was starting to recognise it now, the pattern of three quick raps and two long. His heart hit the roof of his mouth and his trepidation abandoned him in favour of the thrill of the hunt. "I think that's them."

"So." Davis took stock of the situation. "No surveillance cameras. We'll have to make do with mobile phones. Is there somewhere WPC Clarke and myself can hide that will also allow us a good view of the transaction? Ideally you should keep them in a lighted room, allowing us to watch from the dark."

"We can do that." Finn discovered that cooperating with the police could be rather fun after all. "I always keep them downstairs. If I take them into the main room of the bookshop, where the till is, there'll be open doors on either side onto dark rooms—that way you can get different camera angles, which will make it harder to say you faked the footage at the trial."

"You think of everything." Clarke gave him an approving smile as she followed him silently down the stairs, but it didn't do nearly as much for him as Michael's look of pride.

"I'll stay up here until you've got them in the book room." Michael's brisk tone contrasted with the warmth in his eyes. "Then I'll come down and see if I can get a third angle from the hall. I'll be right outside if you need reinforcements. Good luck."

It was a real buddy-cop moment. Their eyes locked, and Finn felt like he'd finally found someone who would walk through explosions in slow motion for him. "Thanks."

He waited until they were all hidden. The knocking at the door had become louder, more relentless by then, and from the sound Benny was pounding on it with something heavy.

"What!" Finn shouted through the letter box. "What the fuck do you want this time?"

It had the desired effect—the battering stopped, and Lisa's high-pitched voice called sweetly, "Let us in or we break down the door."

"You burned my books, you fucking skanks. You nearly fucking burned me with them."

"Yeah, well, maybe you realise now—"

"What a bad idea it is—"

"To tell us no."

"So fucking open the door, or else."

It was quite possible this entire conversation had been caught on the discreet CCTV camera that monitored the front of the crystal and massage shop next door. Finn judged that not much more could be gained by stalling them any longer, so he turned his key in the deadlock, *snick*ed the Yale lock open, and stood well back.

"It's open."

His poor front door! Benny kicked it in, it bounced off the wall, and Lisa walked inside like a Russian mafia boss. She had exchanged her hoodie for a pure-white fake fur coat, and wore bright-red lipstick, like the spilled blood in the tale of Snow White. Finn glanced down. She had not yet succumbed to the lure of high heels—still practical enough to appreciate a shoe in which it was easy to run away—but he thought it was only a matter of time.

Benny by contrast was shabbier than ever in a quilted skiing coat from which the stuffing was beginning to leak.

"All right." Finn gave them both a practised long-suffering sigh, while the soles of his feet thrilled with pain, and his hands stung, "Come in here and say what you've got to say." He snapped the light on in the main room and led them inside, to where the pedestal once occupied by Pegasus was piled high with wrinkled water-damaged volumes on sale for 50 pence each.

"What's to say?" Lisa smiled at the evidence of damage. "We said it all—"

"Last time."

"So what we want now is to have you—"

"Have a look at this."

Benny unwrapped the parcel beneath his arm from its bin bags. White marble, a sculpture of a veiled woman carrying a water jug and leaning on a wall, its heavy square base marked with smears of torn bin bag and paint from his door.

"You fucking philistines! Did you just use a Cesare Lapini as a battering ram? I swear it's the utter lack of beauty in your souls that vexes me most about you, burning my bookshop notwithstanding."

Benny made a gesture as though he intended to drive the sculpture into Finn's stomach. "Yeah, well, we can always do that again if you don't—"

"Shut up and tell us what it's worth."

Rebecca at the well. Finn estimated he could sell it on for a bargain price of £10,000 to an eager collector who knew it would be worth £20,000 from an honest source. He sucked his breath in through his teeth, enjoying himself. "Well, he's an underappreciated genius, in my opinion. You know that the art world has fads, yes? Artists fall in and out of favour, and sadly Lapini is out at the moment. I'll give you £500 for it as an investment, in case he comes back in."

"You're having a laugh." Lisa looked around for something to destroy, but the bookshelves were nailed down, and he hadn't yet found a replacement piece of art for the centrepiece of this room. "Should have thought the fire would have taught you—"

"To deal with us straight."

"Two thousand."

"I am dealing with you straight." Finn tried not to smile at the whopping lie, but he appreciated the irony of it inwardly. "If you want me to still be in business next time you need me, you have to give me a fair price. "Seven fifty."

Lisa stepped out of the way, to allow Benny to get up in Finn's face, looming over him too close in an obvious display of physical threat.

"Thousand five hundred and—"

"We don't hurt you."

This close, Benny stank of cigarettes and weed, and something chemical, sweet like pear drops. Glue, maybe. Lisa's sharp little dark eyes were giving him the creeps. He wanted them both out of his shop and his life for good, hoped his team were getting everything they needed, because it was time for this to be over.

"Oh, very well." He stepped back, palms raised in surrender, and went for the till. "Look, I have about three hundred in here in cash. I'll give you a cheque for the rest. You know I'm good for it."

Benny had stood the Lapini up on the cash desk as Finn counted notes into Lisa's hand. Now he took it away again.

"We don't take cheques."

"Strictly cash only."

Lisa folded the notes from the till and tucked them in her pocket. "We'll come back tomorrow. You give us the rest of the money, we give you the statue then, yeah?"

Performance-wise it was probably not ideal, but he didn't have a thousand pounds in cash hanging around so it would have to do. "All right. And after that, I don't want to see you again. Just leave me alone, okay?"

"Until the next time."

Lisa headed for the door, but Michael stepped out of the corridor and blocked it just as Davis and Clarke emerged from the darkness of their own hidey-holes. Lisa gave a cry of rage, turned, and tried to claw Finn's eyes out, but Michael got her by the back of the collar and lifted her away. In a brief, economic flurry of movements, he had her in a lock, her shoulders immobilised, his forearm across the back of her neck, forcing her head forwards and down.

Benny made a break for the back door, but Clarke got there ahead of him. He went for the WPC's throat, she caught hold of his coat, threw herself backwards, and using his own forward momentum tossed him over her head. He landed all in one piece, flat on his back, and as he was struggling to pull his astonished thoughts together, she slipped a baton under his arm and carried out the same hold on him as Michael used.

"You fucking cunt!" Lisa yelled at Finn, as Michael handed her off to Davis for him to read her rights to her. "What the fuck is this? We're going to take you down, you fucking traitor."

Finn found himself trembling, trembling but satisfied, like he'd just crossed the line at the marathon, was ready to collapse at the strain, but also ready to accept some well-earned congratulations. "I warned you both. I told you I'm an honest man. What did you expect?"

"Right, then." Davis's voice shared the satisfaction. "Let's get you two in the car, shall we?"

When they had gone, the room was suddenly too silent and empty to stand in it alone. He and Michael came together like they were sharing one thought. Finn wound his arms around Michael's shoulders, leaned his forehead against Michael's cheekbone and held on to the man who was becoming his anchor in a treacherously changeable world.

"Did we do it, now? Is that it, over and we're done?"

Michael rested a warm and supportive hand at the small of his back and carded the other through his hair. He sighed. "I wish it was that easy, but—"

Davis came back through the door and grabbed Finn's wrist where it lay over Michael's shoulder, tugging the two of them apart. "Mr. Fintan Hulme," he said, with no intonation of regret at all, the bastard. "I am arresting you for receiving stolen goods."

"Wait!" It was making him bloody seasick, this being thrown from glory to dread until he had no more emotion left in him. "That was a setup, we agreed—"

"To whit," Davis interrupted, "one book, ancient, belonging to Lady Mary Harcombe of Harcombe House. You do not have to say anything, but . . ."

Of course. They must have phoned the plods in London, who had gone to Martina Whinnery to get the book back. She would have told them who she had bought it from, would have protested that she thought he had come by it honestly, would have shown them the documents of provenance, on the bonded paper he had in his study, and his handwriting, and his pens, because he had been out of the business long enough to have forgotten—in his rush to get the thing out of his house—to disguise all of those things.

He pushed himself away from Michael in horror. Arrested! He'd said never again. Never again would he go through this. And now Michael had brought these people into his very house.

Michael made a grab for his arm, trying not to let him get away. "Finn, it'll be fine. There are extenuating circumstances. And assisting with the capture of two burglars will go in your favour. You're an honest man now, Finn. That's what it means. You trust the law to get it right."

Trust, eh? he thought bitterly as he was squeezed into the police car alongside his tormentors. No, he was having no truck with it. Look what had happened when he tried—he had trusted Michael, and Michael had led him into the snare.

CHAPTER
TWENTY

Michael drove to the police station on the police car's tail, with Finn's parting look rolling around his mind, crashing into the sides of his consciousness like a loose cannon on the deck of a sailing ship. He tried not to let it run him over too often. Of course the guy felt betrayed right now. Of course he did. Who wouldn't? But there would be time for him to think, and when they had secured a solicitor and taken statements, Michael could take him home and make it up to him.

By the time he had found somewhere to park the car, Finn and the others had passed through into the secure unit and were nowhere in view. Michael identified himself to the duty officer, registered his availability to give a statement and intention to bail Finn out as soon as it became possible, found a vending machine from which he could get a cup of coffee, and sat down among the other undesirables in the waiting room.

It was a new experience for him to see a station from this side of the desk. Fewer smiles greeted him. The officers who passed by did not look at him, busy and distracted by more important matters. He felt itchy and out of sorts, wanting to explain to everyone that this was home for him, that he was one of them, wanting them to stop treating him like an unwelcome stranger.

But it wasn't home, not anymore. Finn's little flat was home. Or perhaps Finn himself, because he had no particular affection for the rooms themselves.

He phoned Jenny and spent a quarter of an hour apologising to her for only phoning when he needed something, but could she possibly recommend a good solicitor in the area?

"Right," she laughed. "So I can see you took my advice and stayed away from your beau."

"I'm helping him go straight."

"I'm sure there's a joke in there somewhere," she said, tapping away at a keyboard in the distance. "Right, here's the phone number of the most successful firm of defence solicitors in your area. But you seriously owe me bed and breakfast over the Christmas break for this."

O . . . kay. He really should get the house sorted out. "It's a deal. I hadn't thought about Christmas yet, but it would be fantastic to see you again. You can meet him, see what you think for yourself."

"You sound better," she conceded. "Whatever else he is, he's obviously good for you. Take care, Michael."

"You too." He smiled at her down the phone, pointless though that was. "Thanks for this, and see you soon."

The solicitors' office was indeed reassuringly efficient when he called it next. They promised to send someone along directly to advise Finn while he was being questioned and charged. After which, Michael was called upon to give a statement of his own, detailing what he knew of Finn's dealings with Benny and Lisa, his movements on the night of the fire and the day after.

Since he'd still been in London, vouched for by the Metropolitan police on the night of the Harcombe burglary, they didn't ask him about that, and he did not volunteer any information about storming Harcombe house to free the magistrate's captive.

It was an awkward interview. He was unfamiliar with how to react on this side of the deal, and his interrogator was evidently not quite sure whether he was a suspect or a colleague. He tried to get a glimpse of the cells as he walked out, but could see only a shut door. Finn would be all right. The guy kept his cool in front of armed robbers. He'd be fine in an inoffensive box, with toilet breaks and tea breaks and someone to talk to.

He was sitting back down in the waiting room, wondering if he could draw that copy of *The Independent* out from beneath a sleeping baby's pram-wheel without waking the infant up, when Lady Harcombe arrived. She was ushered to the desk by two constables with the pomp appropriate to her rank.

Michael ducked his head, hoping she wouldn't spot him as she leaned her forearms on the desk and said, "Sergeant. I received a phone call saying you have something of mine?"

"We do indeed, ma'am." The desk sergeant bent to unlock the strongbox by his feet and drew out a small, carved Indian box. "We need you to identify this."

"My book!" she exclaimed, opening the casket lid and taking out an object wrapped in what looked like one of Finn's silk handkerchiefs. She unwrapped a corner of an oxblood-red leather-covered book.

Michael craned forwards to see the marvellous thing that had caused so much trouble, and she spotted the movement and turned. This time he didn't have his hood on. He felt her examine his lower face, his mouth and chin, and his coat. Her eyes narrowed.

"You!"

Their gazes held as they engaged in a silent contest of wills. *I could have you arrested for breaking and entering*, hers seemed to say.

He hoped his replied, *In which case I'd have you done for kidnapping.*

She seemed to read something in it at least, smiling and turning back to the desk. "I presume this will be needed as evidence?"

"That's right, ma'am. But you can have it back straight after the trial."

"Excellent. Well, good work, Lionel. Jolly good work."

He knew she would come over at once. He moved his gloves and hat from the seat next to him so she could sit, but she chose to stand, looking down on him like a distant queen over a troublesome serf. Today she wore a camel coat and tall tan boots and a fur stole made of thousands of jaunty little rabbit fur balls. Her dark-brown hair was in an informal bun and it made her look younger, maybe even younger than him.

"Do I presume wrongly that you had something to do with this?"

"It was Finn's idea, ma'am." He stretched the truth a little, but not so far that it broke. "He said the abbot would have wanted his book to come back to you. He told the police where they could find it, and the woman who bought it from him shopped him in revenge. He's in the cells now, being charged."

"Well." She raised her eyebrows at him in a gesture that seemed to indicate a kind of sceptical but pleased astonishment. "He would have done better to tell me when I asked."

Michael agreed, but he could see how Finn's pride might have bridled at that. "He's a good man, your ladyship, and he's been trying his hardest to be an honest man, but he has a very strong, defiant personality. He doesn't react well to threats. He calmed down when I got him home and—"

"And you changed his mind."

"I might have helped a little."

She smiled, steely and very much in control, but benevolent with it. "You are obviously better acquainted with the man than I am. And you'd swear that he's honest?"

"He's in the cells right now because he made an attempt to do the right thing. Because he trusts me, and I trust the British justice system."

Maybe there was something to Finn's assertion that anger wasn't all bad. Michael could feel it simmering under the surface of this sentence—anger for everything that he was putting Finn through in order to be finally free—powering his conviction.

Lady Harcombe raised her eyebrows again. A slightly different tilt to them that seemed to express amusement and tolerance for his naïve beliefs. "Well, what a refreshing view, and all too rare these days. I look forward to seeing you again, Mr. May."

What did *that* mean, from the local magistrate? She thought he was an idiot for trusting the law because she *was* the law, and she was also the person who had been about to imprison Finn in her basement.

His heart sank. He trusted the criminal justice system in general, true. But how far did he trust her in particular? Hell. And why hadn't he thought of that beforehand?

After another two hours, Finn was charged with the crime, and Michael was able to bail him out. He emerged from the secure unit looking small. Though he was shorter than Michael's five foot eight, and slight with it, he had never seemed anything but a giant among men before, coming into a room like an electrical storm and instantly becoming its centre.

Now he seemed faded and weary, as though the cells had sucked out his uniqueness, turned him into a statistic. Michael rose abruptly, instinctively, as he came through the door and was at his elbow in three steps, trying to touch him, pass on some of his own vitality to replace what had been stolen.

Finn pulled his arm away, glancing at him sideways with eyes green as deep water. "I'm not talking to you."

"Right." Michael passed him the coat and scarf he had brought with him. "You just sit in the car and say nothing, then, while I drive you home."

"I'm taking a taxi."

Louise had left him, saying he spent too much time at his job, and that even when he was home, he was not truly with her. There were nights he still woke confused from dreams of her and reached out, expecting to touch her hair, feel the lash of her temper for disturbing her sleep.

It wasn't hard to believe that Finn too might simply have had enough of him, might want his peace and space more than he wanted Michael. Michael bit the inside of his cheek and worried it between his teeth to take his mind off the despair of that thought.

He sighed. "Look, throw me out later, okay? I'm here, I stood bail for you, you don't need to pay for a taxi when I'll take you home for free. And if you want me to piss off after that, it's fine; I'll go. Just, just let's not argue here, all right, in front of everyone."

He half expected Finn to run with that—take it as a challenge and stage the biggest shouting match the station had ever seen. It would have been embarrassing but reassuring at the same time—showing that Finn retained his fire, his defiance, and his love for the theatrical. Instead Finn just shrugged the coat on, hugged himself, hands knotted in the ends of his scarf. "All right."

"The hearing's in a week," Michael offered, tentatively, as they turned down Jasper Street. "That's really fast. Lady Harcombe must really want her book back."

Silence. Finn rested his head on the window and watched the city go by.

"It's not going to be that bad," Michael tried again. "Didn't the solicitor tell you? You have no previous convictions. You turned yourself in. If you plead guilty, they'll go easy on you because you didn't jerk them around. You assisted the police in a different matter. It's a first offence. You'll get a suspended sentence at the very most."

He thought this overture too would be ignored, but as they waited for a car to pull out of the residents-only parking spaces to allow them in, Finn turned his head a millimetre. "They won't send me to prison?"

Michael laughed before the horror hit him. "God, no. D'you think I would have risked you being sent to jail? This was about getting it all out from under you so you could have a fresh start with nothing hanging over your head. A clear conscience and a record that said you'd paid for what you'd done, and it couldn't ever be used against you again."

Finn turned another millimetre towards him. "But she has it in for me, that woman, she'll—"

"She's just a magistrate. If you plead guilty, she will have to refer you to the Crown Court for sentencing, and that will leave you being sentenced by a judge who doesn't know you at all. That's how it works. You were never looking at a custodial sentence, or I wouldn't have persuaded you to give yourself up. You are not going to go to jail, I swear it."

It didn't bear thinking of, Finn in jail, with his off-kilter sense of style and his not-quite-camp delivery, tiny and blond and pretty as he was. But now that Finn had put the thought into his mind, he couldn't quite shake it off. Sometimes judges did decide to come down harsh on something in what felt like a whim. And what if Lady Harcombe had friends in the Crown Court? What if she only had to tip the Crown Court judges the wink, and they too would do exactly what she said?

He stopped the car, covered his face so that he could pretend in the darkness of his fingers that he didn't actually exist, that he couldn't be here to continually make these bad decisions.

What if by some fluke or corruption it did happen? Would Finn ever make it out again as the lighthearted, strangely innocent person that he was? Had Michael done everything in his life to avoid it and still become the kind of man who tormented and broke anyone more defenceless or weaker than himself?

"Good," said Finn beside him. "That's good. I didn't like to think you'd do that to me. I suppose a suspended sentence is not too bad, and then it'll be well and truly over, and I can relax."

Trying not to let Finn see his sudden doubts, Michael raised his head to smile at him. The animation, the dynamo glow that suffused Finn's presence, had begun to show again beneath his face, filling the car with relief, and Michael couldn't . . . It was . . . He just couldn't bring himself to poison it with his infernal doubts.

"Yeah." He leaned over to open Finn's door for him. Though Finn was clearly capable of doing it by himself, the guy—even in this subdued form—had a movie-star quality that made Michael want to wait on him hand and foot. "Yeah. It's going to be no big deal. I'm sure of it."

Finn let him stay after all, and he was in combination so grateful not to have been kicked out and so guilty-worried about the upcoming trial, he may have taken the protectiveness a little far.

"You're fucking smothering me," Finn said as he drove him back out of the door two days later. "Every time I bloody turn around, there you are." He pushed Michael in the chest, making him take two steps back. "Don't take this the wrong way, because I know you're concerned about me, and that's sweet, but I don't need you around here constantly. Go and do some Michael things. Stop bothering me."

He stood on the doorstep in another grey, chilly, autumnal day and wanted to be able to smile. If Louise had only wanted him to stop bothering her sometimes, they might still be together, paradoxical though that sounded. It was one more reason why he desperately didn't want this to end, as prison would surely end it.

Finn seemed to have taken Michael's reassurance as gospel truth, and was almost back to his old self, though sharper and with less patience. But in return Michael had picked up Finn's fear, and he didn't know how to put it down.

"Okay," he said slowly, retreating another step with his hands up. "But this has been a shit couple of days, and we're both on edge. So can I just check that you mean 'get out of my hair for a few hours and come back this evening,' and not 'piss off, I never want to see you again'?"

Finn's brave face was like his outfit, a little more conservative than usual, the colours paler, the vibrancy dimmed. Michael was beginning to think he hadn't really stopped worrying at all. He was just determined not to show it anymore.

Finn managed a strained smile. "I have forgiven you, you know. Subject to unexpected incarceration. I knew what I was getting into, taking on an ex-cop."

"So that means...?"

"Yes, yes. It means come back this evening, you idiot, and we can do the awkward-conversation-followed-by-desperate-sex thing again. But for now I need to work, so sod off."

ALEX BEECROFT

It was pleasant to get out of the tight confines of the flat, even if it meant walking down streets slippery with rotten leaves, desolate and quiet now the tourists were gone, half the shops shut up tight until the winter solstice. Michael left the car at Finn's and walked home, glad of the exercise and the peace. Simultaneously relieved and terrified that there were only four more days to go until the trial.

Awkward scarcely covered it. Michael was frightened and clingy; Finn was frightened and sarcastic. Michael wanted to wrap Finn up in silk sheets and worship him as if he were precious and breakable. Finn wanted to be hit. With copious self-restraint and a great deal of careful conversation, they were managing to hold it together, but the thought of the oncoming trial was already beginning to assume the shape of a relief, however it turned out.

Streaks of pale rain fell through the hanging streaks of reed feathers along the borders of the river. A curl of darker grey smoke rose from the chimney of a narrowboat he almost didn't recognise as his own. Hard to tell, with water in the face, but he didn't remember it having scarlet panels choked with golden roses, or blue hyacinths on its stern, or a cluster of black-enamelled watering cans on the roof, on which copper Daleks shot death rays of green ivy and a board proclaiming that these things were for sale.

He knocked at the stern door, now painted to resemble a set of theatre curtains. "Sarah? It's Michael. Can I come in?"

The door opened, but it was Tai on the other side, clutching their laptop to themself and giving him a sceptical look. "I suppose so."

Ducking through, he found the blank white canvas of the interior of the boat equally transformed, with tattoo-like birds and flowers on every wall, and one or two dinosaurs hiding amid the leaves.

"We didn't steal anything." Tai retreated backwards, not taking their eyes from Michael's face. "My father had some ends of paint cans left from when we painted the house, and I bought the varnish and the things to be decorated from my cleaning money."

Gone was the minimalist emptiness of the small sitting room from which Michael had thrown out everything that could be moved. Now the table was covered in paintpots, brushes, cleaning rags, and varnish. The starboard side of the floor was covered in unpainted wares—flowerpots and planters, watering cans, narrowboat storage

188

chests, and blackboards. The port side was cluttered with the same stuff, but beautifully, strikingly painted, in a style that combined traditional narrowboat motifs with pop culture in a way that even he could see would have the younger boaties geeking out.

He would never have recognised the girl sitting cross-legged on the bed, surrounded by books on the history of art, if it wasn't for the bare feet and the way he had to stand quite still for five minutes before she would raise her gaze off the bedclothes to meet his eye.

"Sarah?" Oddly enough she could have been his niece by resemblance, though some part of her ancestry must have been black. She had the May family curls, and the beauty that they tended to grow out of around age thirty and mourn forevermore.

She looked so much more vulnerable with her face washed and visible, wearing the bargain jeans and the fuzzy sweatshirt he'd bought her with the white stars, its hood lowered. He thought again about her absent parents who had thrown her out to live on the streets. *How could they? How could anyone?*

"Hi," she said, after she'd determined that he was not going to lunge forwards and grab her.

"Hi."

Tai seemed to regard this, rightly, as a cease-fire. They relaxed from their position in between Michael and Sarah. Michael only realised that he was seeing a gesture of protection—a knight getting between his lady and the monster, a mother getting between the threat and her child—when Tai dismissed him and dropped to the sitting room bench, sliding their laptop back on the table.

"You didn't say I couldn't," Sarah ventured, her voice small, as though she expected this to be the last straw, expected to be told to leave.

"I think it's great," he said. "Genuinely. In fact, when I get my new boat built, will you paint it for me? I'll pay you by the hour."

Tai had definitely appointed themself protector and guardian, possibly agent too. They poured a cup of tea and slid it over the table to Michael. "Well, we might be able to help you. It depends on how business is doing by then."

Michael wasn't a hundred percent sure whether to be charmed or unsettled. He'd only been away three days. When had all this happened? "Business?"

Tai swung the computer around to display the screen of an Etsy shop on which the newly painted goods were displayed.

"I paint things," said Sarah proudly, "and Tai helps me sell them, for ten percent of the profit."

"Yeah?" He brought his reading glasses out of his pocket and looked more closely at the screen. "And people are buying them?"

She looked worried that she had done something wrong, and he hurried to add, "That's wonderful!"

"We've already sold nine items and paid for the materials." Tai beamed with pride. "And traffic is increasing to the website all the time."

"They stop outside too," Sarah offered in a voice so quiet he wasn't sure he had heard it. "They see the notice on the top and berth nearby, and come over to buy cans or plant pots. I don't really like that, but they're mostly nice."

"I'll stay with you!" Tai offered fervently, their eyes wide with sincerity. And yes, Tai was a good kid, but they had to learn to back off a little.

"How d'you feel about dogs?" Michael asked Sarah as they exchanged a glance over Tai's head, him asking if the kid's enthusiasm was a problem. He got the impression that she thought she could handle it, was flattered rather than frightened. Good. But it didn't hurt to make sure.

"I'm thinking we could get you a terrier of some kind. Something small enough to live on board but fierce enough to go for people's ankles if they thought those people were making you unhappy."

"You can't keep giving me things!" She sounded distressed, but he had seen the moment before, the moment when she was a child again who desperately wanted a puppy.

"I wasn't going to," he trod carefully. "But rescue dogs are cheap. Tai or I could drive you to the nearest shelter to pick one up. And now you've got money of your own, you could buy one for yourself."

A smile. An honest-to-God, unrestrained, unambiguous childish smile. She looked away immediately afterwards as if to conceal it, but it was too late. He had seen, and his day was made.

CHAPTER
TWENTY-ONE

Michael had fallen asleep at four o'clock in the morning, after trying to match Finn's restless sleeplessness all night long. He didn't wake as Finn slid out of bed two hours later, having grown impatient with darkness and waiting and his own thoughts.

Finn slipped his feet into slippers and wrapped a dressing gown around himself, looking down at the barely visible lump in his bed that was his sleeping lover. It had been a shit week, and he had been bitter and difficult to live with, and here Michael still was, reliable, calm, and affectionate through it all.

He wanted to blame the guy for all of this, for shopping him to the police, for setting him up for this trial, for forcing him to face the consequences of his own actions. But the truth was that this, or something like this, was inevitable the moment he had opened his stupid mouth and confessed to Lady Harcombe in her library. It had slipped out on its own in a wave of self-righteousness, that perhaps meant he had begun to have the instincts of an honest man.

Michael wasn't to know that, of course, but with his background he would naturally assume the truth would come out sooner or later, would assume it was best to tell it yourself and have the world give you extra credit for owning up.

If Finn wanted to be honest about it, he had pretty much accepted this the moment he'd accepted Michael.

He reached down and pushed his fingers into Michael's thick shock of black hair. Michael nuzzled into the touch but didn't wake, worn out. Shagged out, more likely. *I hope you appreciate what I'm doing for you, darling.* Finn found himself smiling despite the nauseating twist of his nerves. *Because it doesn't get much more heroic than this.*

It didn't get much more heroic than leaving the man to sleep, when Finn would have appreciated the company. He opened the bedroom door as quietly as he could and tiptoed downstairs.

The garden was eerie in the predawn hush. Not a car on the street, only a flash of black movement at head height as a cat jumped from the back wall. The plate of shepherd's pie he'd put out this evening sat on the table with cold mashed potato gone runny with rain, and cat paw prints amongst the gravy.

For the second night running, his ghost had not appeared, abandoned him without a word of thanks. He hoped nothing terrible had happened to them, wondered if this was another case for the police. But what exactly could they do? He'd never seen the ghost's face, could not describe their clothes except for *dark*, knew no name, or circumstances, or age. Had lost any DNA traces in the dishwasher two nights ago.

Like an electric shock, it struck him that tonight he might not be here either. He might be inside. What was it like in there? Surely not as bad as American media would have you believe, with their jokes about dropped soap in the showers and their smug unstated assumptions that prisoners were getting what they deserved. Such things would not be allowed to go on in a British jail, with the assumption that the purpose of the institution was to rehabilitate rather than to punish.

He raised shaking hands and rubbed them over his face, his burning, gritty eyes. Not this again! Could he not even control the inside of his own mind. What was the point? What was the point of making himself sick with worry like this, when it would either happen, or it would not, and worry would do nothing to prevent it?

He felt like a dropped glass, only his willpower keeping the pieces from flying apart, holding time and ruin still by determination alone.

Thank God, it would be over today, and he could accept . . .

Snatching up the unwanted plate, he hurled it against the wall, where it smashed with a slap and a crash that wasn't satisfying enough. He picked up the seat by the table—wrought iron, almost too heavy for his shaking arms—and tossed that after, gouging holes in the ancient brickwork. A plant pot full of spring bulbs—it shattered and rained daffodils and soil all over him.

He couldn't accept it. He wouldn't accept it. He didn't want to go to jail.

A bigger planter, with a hebe in it. As he struggled to raise it off the ground, Michael's arms slipped around him and pulled him back into the warmth—a blazing warmth now that Finn was thoroughly chilled—of a sturdy body.

"Let me go! Let me go!" He kicked and struggled. Michael's grip eased instantly, letting him twist around and slap the man hard across the cheek. "I hate you. I fucking hate you. Why did you do this to me?"

No reaction. He didn't know what reaction he wanted, but indifference was definitely not it. Fucking dolt. Fucking immovable, unfeeling bastard. Finn balled his fist and threw a punch, anticipating the crunch and pain as bone met bone and he broke Michael's nose.

But Michael caught his fist in one hand, tugged and twisted, doing something Finn didn't quite follow, that ended with Michael behind him again, Finn's arm held firmly and tightly across his chest, trapping his other hand. Disarmed and defenceless except for his words.

"I hate you."

"I know." Michael bent his head, tucked his face into Finn's neck and held on, the way he did when they slept, when it was cold outside and he was afraid to wake. "I'm sorry."

They shook together in silence, wound tight, Michael's right hand still hard around Finn's wrist, his left spread wide on Finn's chest, over the heart, increasingly holding him up. Finn's legs gave way before his resolve not to cry, but that followed soon after. He hid his face in Michael's biceps and let the guy pick him up and take him back indoors.

"It's going to be okay," said Michael, patiently and unconvincingly as he sat Finn down at the window seat and kissed his eyes. "It's going to be fine. I promise. I'm sorry."

"You piece of shit. You've ruined my life."

Michael winced. His mouth tightened and turned down, his gaze fell to the floor, and his shoulders hunched as if crushed by a heavy weight, every line of him expressing a kind of mute, unbearable, animal misery. "I'm going to make you some breakfast."

He fought to get to his feet—Finn could see the struggle in the stiffness of his movements, as though his muscles had locked over terrible pain. And Finn hated him—hated that he cared about him too much to bear to watch him suffer like this. It wasn't fair. It *wasn't fair* that he had to be the magnanimous one, but if it came down to a choice between forgiving Michael or driving him away by doing this to him, forgiveness didn't seem so hard.

"I'm sorry," he managed, before Michael had entirely left the room. "I'm just scared. I didn't mean that."

"I'm scared too." Michael turned back slowly, looking wretched. "And it was true."

By eleven forty-five, when his case was called, Finn had moved through fear and raw, peeled pain into an exhausted acceptance. There was something very numbing about the institutional carpet of the courthouse, the heavy, old oak furniture, lacy with the gouged graffiti of earlier generations, the bustle of ushers and solicitors, policemen and witnesses. It was all very businesslike and boring.

Michael sat by his side with the expression of a man in hospital beside the bed of his injured wife, looking helpless and guilty and sad. Finn's resentment finally cracked at eleven thirty, with the knowledge that this might end up like the last time—he might lose the chance to tell Michael what he felt before it was too late.

So he nudged his shoulder against Michael's, looking studiously in the other direction as he did. "I've already forgiven you, you know. I'd have thrown you out much earlier if I was going to."

"You say that now, but—" Michael glanced warily around, arranged a coat between them and grasped Finn's hand under it, holding on tight. "If it does go bad, you're going to hate me."

Ridiculous, that Finn had to be the one giving comfort. But it had been this way with Tom too. Arguments were tricky things for both sides to win if no one ever gave way first. There was something terribly domestic about the small sacrifice of ego, of first place. Sure, sex was a fine thing, but a fight at the end of which the pair of you were more lovingly entangled than ever, that was closer to being one flesh, one soul, than anything else.

"Don't flatter yourself, there. I knew what I was getting into when I took you on. I think I always knew it was going to come to this."

The pressure of Michael's hand bent his bones, as Michael's face shuttered down on some intense emotion, maybe gladness, maybe anguish. "And you thought I was worth it?"

"I did so. And I do."

"Mr. Fintan Hulme?" the usher called, even as Mr. Todd, his solicitor arrived, looking inappropriately sunny in a pale suit and a yellow tie. Michael picked up the coat, but Finn didn't allow the man to let go of his hand, so they walked in to court together, under the gaze of the recorder and the prosecution solicitor and the magistrate high on her bench, looking untouchable in her blue cashmere suit. A single pendant diamond the size of a fingernail shone like an oncoming headlight in the hollow of her throat.

Two other magistrates sat with her, one on either side, both of them looking shifty and worried. "She got to them," he whispered, as he was forced to let Michael walk away to the public benches. "Look at them, they can't even look me in the eye. They're going to do whatever she wants."

"I'm sure you're imagining things, Mr. Hulme," Todd humoured him with a tolerant smile, spreading out his files on his own bench as they sat, waiting for Finn to be accused.

The prosecutor rose to read the charge. "Remember," Finn's solicitor whispered beneath the drone of his opponent's voice, "when he asks you how you plead, you're going to answer 'guilty.'"

"On this charge, Mr. Fintan Hulme, how do you plead? Guilty or not guilty?"

Finn stood up, opened his mouth, and Lady Harcombe made a stop gesture with a hand constellated with diamond rings. "A moment. Mr. Hulme, Mr. Todd. I would like to speak to you in camera."

Todd gathered all his papers together with a *harumph*, as though this was highly irregular. The magistrates rose, and Lady Harcombe led the way out of the court through a small side door. Finn and Todd followed.

For an inner sanctum, it was very disappointing. More scrubby wood panelling and threadbare carpet, a scuffed desk piled with cardboard folders, a single chair in which Lady Harcombe sat enthroned.

"You asked us here so you could gloat?" Finn allowed himself to be unwisely goaded by her little small smile. "It's not enough to get me jailed, you have to apply the personal touch first?"

"This kind of behaviour is not helping you, Mr. Hulme," Todd whispered urgently, trying to press down his thinning hair as if it too were being dangerously rebellious.

Lady Harcombe laughed. "Don't say that, Mr. Todd. I find it rather charming."

Pretentious, condescending, evil-minded witch.

"So utterly self-defeating. You don't even know what I'm about to say, Mr. Hulme."

"I'm sure you'll tell me soon enough."

He wasn't going to show her fear, that was for sure. He could survive this, and he would. He would come out and be done with it, ready to start a new life blameless as an angel with a man who was ready to stand by him however long it took.

Dear God, he already missed Michael's presence at his elbow, that sense of patient, silent support. Why would he not come back for that?

"I understand that I have you to thank for the retrieval of my book, Mr. Hulme?"

"That's right." *Much good it did me.*

"Mr. Hulme, please look at me when I'm speaking to you."

He did, if only to check that she'd really had the audacity to say such a thing. She must have done. She was smiling.

"We had an agreement, you and I." Pink lipstick, like an English rose, and a smile as cunning as any serpent's. "Did we not? You would help me get my book back, and I would let you go."

His mind took a wrong step and tripped up. Why would she say that? Where would that sentence take her that she could possibly want to go?

"You may have said as much," he ventured, trying to see how the agreement might harm him, but coming up empty.

"Well, then." She offered her outspread hands as though passing him something—a conclusion. "I strongly advise you to plead 'not guilty.'"

"So you can send me up for trial? So I forfeit any leniency I might get? So my punishment is worse?" What was she up to? Was she making absolutely certain he would go to jail? Was she really that devious?

"I saw your young man in the public seats." She toyed with a pen, turning it over and over, and stars danced from her hand to run along the walls. "Perhaps you could pass on a message to him from me?"

Finn inclined his head to signify that he was still hearing her words, even though they were not making a lot of sense.

"Tell him I am obliged to him. I was about to do something—" she took a lawyer's pause, as if hunting about for less incriminating language "—ill advised, that night. Something I might have found it difficult to live with afterwards. He prevented me, and I am grateful. For his sake as well as for yours, take my advice and plead 'not guilty.'"

Finn looked to his solicitor for an explanation, but Mr. Todd seemed as lost as he was. "Well, you're my legal counsel. Counsel me."

Todd tightened the knot of his tie. Loosened it again. "I'm bemused," he said at last, slowly. "But it's always been my experience that when a judge gives you a firm hint to do something, it's to your benefit to do so. I would therefore advise you to change your plea and enter 'not guilty' after all."

Back in court. It was now a little past noon, though the light through the high, paned windows was so grey it could have been dusk. Finn caught Michael's insistent glance—*What's going on?*—and answered it with an eye roll—*I don't know.*

Was he really going to risk his chance for leniency on the word of the woman who was responsible for him being here in the first place? He'd never been the most trusting of men, and it went against everything he was to lay his fate so gently in an enemy's hands.

But she owed Michael, she said. She owed him a clean conscience; she wanted to repay him. And maybe Finn wanted to help with that. He'd never managed any other thank-you to Michael for the rescue.

"To this charge, Mr. Fintan Hulme, how do you plead? Guilty or not guilty?"

He stood. The weight of the courtroom roof diffused through the grimy air and pressed on his back. He was the centre of attention, the hero of the play, given his three seconds in the spotlight. Why not do something startling with it, after all?

"Not guilty," he lied, firmly. He hoped convincingly.

Lady Harcombe smiled. Michael half rose from his seat, looking like he wanted to shake Finn till his teeth rattled.

"My colleagues and I have reviewed the evidence carefully, and we are agreed—" Shifty looks and surly mouths on either side of her. *Agreed* was obviously stretching it. *Coerced into keeping silent* might have been closer. "—that there is simply not enough evidence in this case to take a prosecution forward. Accordingly the case is dismissed as 'no case to answer,' and the defendant is released without a stain on his character. Mr. Hulme? You may go. And I hope never to see you here again."

He was too dazed, his expectations too undercut to react at first. Todd hustled him out of the courtroom before the prosecution lawyer could even start on the angry outburst that seemed to be brewing beneath his reddening face.

"Well, that went better than I envisaged." Todd allowed himself to be tugged over to Michael's side. "I suggest you two get out of here while the Lady of the Manor lays down the law to my opponent. I'll send my bill to you, shall I, Mr. May?"

"Do."

Finn hadn't asked himself where the solicitor had come from, assumed he was provided by the state. He made an attempt to pull himself together, floored still by generosity and good luck, only partially following the flow of life, with gaps in his concentration and his understanding.

Now Todd was over by the courtroom door, hissing in whispers with the prosecutor, obviously saying something placating by the tapping-down hand gestures. And gradually the sense of the morning cracked open like a seed in Finn's chest. It put out leaves of lightness through his arms and his legs so that he was buoyant. It pushed a stem of astonishment and joy and relief up his spine and flowered in his head into laughter.

"Did you hear that?" There was before him the most handsome man he had ever seen, with a touch of that Italianate bad boy thing that all the girls loved. A mature James Dean. Maybe a little too short in the leg for a movie idol, but close enough for Finn. He grabbed Michael by the biceps and allowed himself to be picked up and twirled for joy. "Did you hear it? Not a stain on my character."

Onlookers on dusty chairs lifted their gazes to him, resentful or bovine or happy for him according to their natures, as he dangled with his feet an inch off the floor in Michael's crushingly overjoyed embrace, and he cut off all the many things he meant to say until they were in private. *I love you. She did this for you—as a present. Look at you, you saved me again.* Those things weren't for these people to hear.

"Michael, acushla," he said instead, with the happiness shaking his voice, and the relief in his bones like warm water. "We're done here. Let's go home."

It was still only barely the afternoon when they reached the shop, but Finn locked the door behind them and left the Shut sign firmly in the window, sagging against Michael's sturdy frame as soon as the world was securely outside.

"It's over, then."

Michael slid an arm under his jacket, under his jumper, the heat of his palm cradling Finn's hip through the thin cotton of Finn's shirt. It felt real, solid again, as touches had not felt this past week.

"Should I go?"

The guy was a bundle of insecurities, but Finn had known that from the moment he first walked in the shop. They were insecurities Finn found endearing. He turned, letting Michael's hand skim around his waist to come to rest in the hollow of his back. Time now, nothing but time ahead of him, time enough to slow down and feel the prickles on his skin that radiated out from Michael's touch. Time to appreciate the way his blood yearned towards the other man like a magnet to its pole.

Michael's uncertain gaze grew warmer at Finn's expression. Finn moistened his lips and watched it dip there, as Michael's mouth softened in response. He tilted his head. Michael echoed him unconsciously as he stepped in, the hand on his back pulling him in close.

The kiss began gently enough, almost chaste in its soft drag of hot silk skin across his mouth. The low ache of desire in his belly pumped through his veins and made the air hot around him as he licked along the seam of Michael's lips, pushing with his tongue for entrance. Michael opened to him with a gasp, his whole body yielding under Finn's pressure, giving up control to him, as Michael leaned back on the door to support himself and surrendered.

Finn pushed Michael's coat off his shoulders, rucked his shirt and sweater up under his arms as he filled both hands with Michael's back, running them up his spine, kneading his fingers into the big muscles of the man's shoulders. Michael groaned in that deep voice of his, the one that was like being caressed all over by rough suede, and his hands slid down to cup Finn's arse and pull him tighter.

"Stay," Finn gasped, gloriously crushed, with Michael as hard against him as he was, not quite sure which of them was in charge of this and not giving a fuck either way. "Stay forever."

Michael's hands dipped a little lower, and then he was being picked up—and he was never going to get tired of that, of that casual strength, that promise of the possibility of being overwhelmed. He wound his legs around Michael's waist and kissed him harder, kissed him all the way up the stairs and into the bedroom.

They had the whole afternoon, and Michael took it slow, keeping Finn's wrists pinned in one hand so he couldn't touch himself, working into him gently, slowly, and rocking together until Finn thought he would go mad with need. Michael supported his hips on one arm, picking them up, angling Finn so that he ploughed through stars with every stroke, and when Finn finally got his hands free, he scrabbled against Michael's back and left long red welts that spoke of ownership.

He lost time, fracturing apart under too much sensation. The light dimmed as the sun dipped, and he tightened up under the waves of pleasure until every breath hovered on the edge of pain and he felt scored out, hot, tender, intolerable. It was still too gentle, and he couldn't quite . . .

"Please." Tears leaked from the corners of his eyes, and he loved it but he couldn't, he just couldn't wait any longer. It had to be now or he would die. "Please!"

Michael's hand slid down from where it had been bruising his wrist, closed on Finn's biceps, his thumb digging in. Pain flowered from that spot like the opening of a new universe, gathering the pleasure and amplifying it, pushing it up, harder, until it transformed into something religious, into true ecstasy that washed him out of his body altogether and let him sleep.

Finn woke to find night had fallen and the yellow light of streetlamps was gilding Michael's eyelashes as he lay on his side beside Finn, smiling at him. Michael's hazel eyes looked black as the night sky in that light, warm in the quiet between them.

"Hi."

"Hello." He smiled back, and stretched, his body sore and tired and glowing. "What's the time?"

"It's only about four. Are you okay?"

Four o'clock in the afternoon, and he was waking, his heavy limbs entangled with those of his bedfellow, and absolutely no intention of getting out of bed again until tomorrow. How sybaritic, how delightful.

"I am positively splendid. What was it that you did there, at the end? Because that definitely worked for me."

Michael, bless him, managed to look embarrassed. He shrugged. "You said you liked pain. I didn't want to do anything that would harm you, so I thought I'd try pressure points. Very controllable, not a lot of risk, and you seemed to like it, so . . ."

"It still bothers you, the pain thing?" Finn asked, winding himself a little more closely into Michael's embrace, settling their weight so that they leaned into one another.

Michael kissed the crow's-foot at the side of his eye, and then the corner of his mouth. "I don't get it. But I like to make you happy, and it's hot to me, watching how much it turns you on. I don't think it's going to be a problem for us, do you?"

No, he didn't. But he also didn't want to talk about it anymore. He'd had it with serious for today. The plan for the rest of the evening included food, a shared shower, more naps, more cuddling and, perhaps if he was up to it again by the end of the evening, more sex. This morning had been angst enough for the rest of the year.

A lock of Michael's hair curled over his ear now; it was getting shaggy. Finn tugged on it because he could. "You know what's a problem in this relationship? It's the fact that I'm starving. Get out to that kitchen and make me a sandwich."

Michael burst out laughing, shoved him in the chest, and wriggled away to pull on boxers and slide out into the cold. "As a one-time celebration for the end of your life of crime, okay. But don't think I'm making a habit of it."

He padded away, leaving Finn to wallow in warmth and softness and semisleep. Lights flicked on in the kitchen and the hall. Finn almost called out to him to make food for the ghost too, but remembered in time that he had lost them. He hoped they were well. Maybe the shelters were opening, this close to Christmas, and the ghost too had a warm place to sleep. He hoped so.

"The book club boys think I'm making you up," he said, as Michael brought in hummus and olive sandwiches on ciabatta bread, and two cups of coffee held in one hand. "Every week I tell them you're coming and you never arrive. I'm thinking a Christmas party, and you'd better show up or I'm replacing you with that hot farmer with the shotgun."

Michael sipped at his own coffee, trying unsuccessfully to smother his smile. It was the smile Finn liked best out of all his expressions: sweet and gentle, surprised by joy.

"Well, I can't have that. I'll be there."

CHAPTER
TWENTY-TWO

Two weeks later, and they were into December. The keel of the boat was complete and the skin of her almost finished except for caulking. She was a handsome-looking thing already, slightly wider, slightly more comfortable looking than the average narrowboat. He took a series of photos of her with his phone, intending them for the internet, where he was blogging about the build in an attempt to drum up future custom.

Sarah caught him as he was stashing the tools in their safe, the metal of the locking box burning his fingers with cold, and his breath coming like steam in the blue twilight air. She had wrapped the coverlet from her bed around herself, a padded cone of scarlet quilt topped with the ruffled tight black curls of her hair.

Coat for Christmas, he thought, as her small hand emerged from the wrapping and offered him a fiver.

"Rent for November, Mr. May."

It probably wasn't appropriate to be filled with pride for her. Her renaissance was all her own doing—well, with a little help from Tai—but he accepted the fiver like she was the Queen offering him a knighthood.

"That's fantastic. Thank you." He heaved a deep breath, wasn't sure what she would make of this, or what Jenny and Finn might make of it either, but damn it, she was a child still. She should not spend Christmas on her own in the boat, watching all the families come together without her. "You got plans for Christmas?"

Sarah stepped back towards the open air—the shed was wall-less on one side, to facilitate the movement of boats in and out. She usually talked to him here, where it was impossible for anyone to block the exit. "I . . ." She studied her feet. "No, I won't bother anyone. I'm fine."

"Tai didn't ask you?"

She felt happy enough with him to glance up at him with an expression that told him he was an idiot. "They don't do Christmas, Mr. May. They're Taoists."

He laughed. "I guess I should have thought of that. Then do you want to have Christmas dinner with me?"

Her eyes widened, she took another step back, and he rushed to clarify, "With me and my boyfriend and my friend Jenny from London. We could even . . ." It was not quite the cosy Christmas he'd envisaged, but hopefully there would be other years for that. "We could go to a restaurant, where there would be other people around."

She scuffed the floor with the toe of her new shoe and looked torn. He knew he didn't deserve her trust, shouldn't push for it, but he hoped for it nevertheless.

"I suppose I am your niece, after all," she said at length, making him smile. "It would look a bit odd if I didn't."

"That's wonderful!" He didn't move forwards, didn't try to hug her, just smiled and watched her walk away. Moments later, he heard the distant flurry of yipping that said little Tyson was overjoyed to have his owner home. Then he spent three hours afterwards, worrying what Jenny and Finn would think. Would Jenny think it was illegal? Immoral? Would Finn think it was too much trouble? Would he be jealous? Would he be angry Michael hadn't told him before?

He returned to the house to dress for the book club party. The prospect of Jenny's arrival had driven Michael to finish his slash-and-burn reclamation of the house. The walls were now stripped and repainted, all the furniture thrown out and the skip had been taken away.

Nowhere was taboo to him anymore. He had wiped the memories clean with hard work and several coats of cheap white paint, but the place still had a chilly air, and a stark, unfurnished emptiness he found repellent. He had moved the boxes of his own belongings into his parents' bedroom and done what he could with inflatable mattresses in the spare room and his own, but in comparison with Jenny's cheerful little flat, it was still a mausoleum.

Time to worry about that tomorrow. He shaved and struggled into his best suit, the charcoal-grey one that made him look taller, added a silver-blue tie and silver cufflinks, grabbed a bottle of good wine in a bag with a bow on it, and set off for Finn's.

The bookshop windows glowed and glittered as he walked down the main shopping street. Even in a procession of shop windows full of Christmas kitsch, the bookshop stood out, real oil lamps in the window, swags of real greenery—ivy, fir, and holly—tied with red ribbon, scenting the air like Narnia. A live tree in a large paper-covered planter was bedecked with ceramic pomanders filled with dried fragrant flowers. But Finn had decided against taking the organic thing too far, because everything had been lightly brushed with sparkles, and even the floors were pricked with light.

Finn's eyes widened at the sight of the suit. He ignored the proffered wine to step in and stroke both hands down Michael's lapels, tuck his fingers into Michael's waistcoat pockets, and lean up to kiss him, marking his territory to the sound of wolf whistles from the main room.

"I'm buying you clothes for Christmas. Good clothes. Look at you!"

"Fuck." Michael peeped into the main room and found at least twenty men staring back. "Don't leave me alone."

"I don't intend to." Finn lifted a glass of champagne from a tray by the door and pushed it into Michael's hand, proudly walking beside him into the crowd. "I'd never get you back."

"Well, I must admit, I thought you were fictional." A spiky-haired fellow in tweeds held out a hand to Michael, as if to check he wasn't a particularly sophisticated hologram. Michael shook the offered hand, a firm grip, grazed knuckles, and more unusually a grazed palm.

"Michael, this is James, our archaeologist."

Ah, that explained it.

"I have been living in a parallel dimension." Michael tried not to be too boring in front of Finn's friends, but it was hard, since he was in essence a boring sort of person. "But I'm getting in phase now."

James stuck his hand in the air and beckoned across the room to a round-faced Indian man Michael thought he recognised from somewhere. "Idris, come here. I owe you a tenner."

Idris pushed his way through the interested crowd and shook Michael's hand too before casting an inquisitive look on Finn. "Am I to gather that things have finally become sufficiently uncomplicated that you're officially together now?"

Michael took a breath. Finn grinned and squeezed his arm tight. "That's right. If I had a Facebook, I'd be 'in a relationship' right now."

"Well this calls for a drink!" Idris topped up Michael's glass with something from a hip flask, did the same with everyone else, and called, "Cheers!"

After that, things went swimmingly. Michael was adroitly separated from Finn fairly early on, but only to be quizzed on his family, his business prospects, and his intentions, all of which he found easy to answer honestly.

After the fourth friendly warning of ghastly happenings should he ever hurt Finn, he formulated a backup plan of moving to New Zealand if things went wrong. "But you couldn't do anything worse to me than having it not work out with Finn," he said a couple of times, each more embarrassingly earnest as the evening went on. "He means a lot to me."

By the end of the evening, he had progressed to handing his phone around so that the boaties in the group could admire his handiwork. He had two expressions of interest in possibly buying a boat next year, and Nick Scott, event organiser for the Trowchester Festival, had shaken his hand on a gentleman's agreement to buy a boat as a floating chill-out zone that would be used for promotional purposes for the rest of the year. His head spun on the details, but his pocket was full of business cards, so he figured he would email them all back and weed out the nice things to say at a party from the honest offers later.

By the time the final partygoer had been ushered out of the door, it was 2 a.m. Michael was ready to curl up on the floor and sleep there with the imprint of coconut matting all over his face. The sudden silence was a balm. He breathed out as the door shut, and leaned his forehead against it, closing his eyes.

"Not the world's greatest extrovert, I see." Finn drew Michael's arm over his shoulder and hauled him upstairs. "But how about that, we're official now."

"I like it."

"You did very well not to punch anyone, I thought. I'd warned them all you were desperately scary when roused, but I don't think they believed me, and you didn't do anything to confirm it, handing round pictures of your woodwork skills all night. You realise they're going to start asking you round to put up cabinets? I know Idris has a warehouse full of kitchen units he's been meaning to install for years."

He let Finn's voice wash over him like a warm bath, but it was true, a long evening of raised voices and the crush of bodies, and he had not once felt the need to fight his way out of it. The rage that continually flowed as a base note in his character seemed to have settled back inside its channel now, ready to be called on at need, but not in danger of overwhelming him, of causing him to become someone he would despise.

Hard to pinpoint exactly when that had happened, but Finn . . . it had mostly been Finn's doing, one way or another.

"Oh, they have destroyed you," Finn crooned, pushing him into the bedroom and stripping him efficiently of his clothes. He had the idea that some kind of response would be polite, but couldn't think of one, rather enjoying being fussed over like this. "Well, no more parties then. We'll have Christmas on our own. You'll come to me? We can sleep in late, eat what we like, unwrap each other by the fire. That kind of thing."

Michael smiled up at him from the bed. He was slightly fuzzy round the edges and the world was swaying around him like an underwater weed. "I was making you a boat for a present. But I think I've sold it to someone else."

"Just as well." Finn slid in to his side of the bed, threw an arm across Michael's chest and a leg across both of his knees, grounding him. "What I need is cabinets and bookshelves. Cabinets of delight. Someone said to me recently that I should have a section for modern books. And I should, I'm sure. If I only had the space to put them in."

"Mmm." He closed his eyes, relaxing into happiness. This was his life now, was it? Part boatbuilder, part handyman, with an official boyfriend to curl up next to at night and wake beside in the morning? How had that happened in so short a time? How had he healed so much and come so far?

"So what do you say? Christmas at mine?"

Michael remembered Sarah with a little twist of disquiet. After all Finn had gone through to be on the level with him, what would he think of the niece who wasn't a niece? How pissed off would he be to have his Christmas idyll ruined by unwarned-for fake relatives?

There probably wasn't a better time to find out. "Can I bring someone?"

Finn pushed himself up on one elbow and looked down on him in surprise. "I thought you were one of these lone wolf types. Didn't have people. You've had surprise friends up your sleeve all this time?"

"You know what?" Michael reached up to cup Finn's cheek with his fingers, drew him down like the moon for a kiss. "You're funny. I love that."

"And you're drunk. That's not so wonderful." Finn tucked himself back around Michael, his body pressing heavy and relaxed against Michael's side. "But of course. You just met my people, of course I'll meet yours."

CHAPTER
TWENTY-THREE

Finn watched from the display window for almost half an hour before they came. Dark shapes, swathed against the bitter wind and the flurry of tiny white snowflakes, too small to be picturesque. The largest was Michael in his black duffle coat, with a black beanie on his head and his throat swallowed by a massive knitted woollen scarf in festive shades of red and green. Just the way he walked made Finn feel happy—the figure he cut against the icing sugar dusting of snow on the ground, with his shoulders straight and his head high, as though the weight had been lifted off his back.

His partner from London was only an inch or so shorter, but half the width, even shivering in a mock-greatcoat with swirling skirts. He had an impression of an Earth Mother, the coat being hunter green, embroidered all over with ochre roses. Finn approved of the way she had matched the coat with an ochre and madder scarf and hat set, but he approved more of the bright-blue flowery wellies that gave the whole ensemble that little touch of *I don't give a fuck*.

They had a girl with them, a sticklike creature with a bold, beautiful face tanned by the sun of Africa. Michael's unofficial ward. He'd told the story tentatively as though he feared Finn would disown him over it, but God, the child was thin and young, and what decent person wouldn't have done something for her if they could?

Her eyes met his through the window and widened as he rose from the window seat to let them in. A piercing gust of icy air came with them. They filled the hall as Michael shut the door behind them, and the woman gave Finn such a professional look it was like being patted down for contraband at the airport.

"Jenny, isn't it?" He held out a hand, guessed she wouldn't take kindly to a kiss on the knuckles and shook her hand firmly instead. "Let me take your coat."

The child had pressed herself into the corner of the hall not occupied by a statue, but her eyes were still on him, bright and curious and unafraid.

"Sarah?" he asked. "Do you want to take your coat off too?"

"Do you live here?"

"I do."

"Do you have, like, a back garden?"

Her coat was one of those ghastly skiing things, quilted and stuffed with microfibres for warmth. She looked like a larva in it. But something about the way she stood was ringing bells of recognition in the back of his mind.

"I do."

Something to be said for police officers. Both Michael and Jenny had moved to an unthreatening distance away and were watching quite silently, as though they knew something important was afoot.

Sarah broke into a disbelieving smile. "And it's got a metal table in it, and some of them mobile things?"

"Yes." He suspected it now, but he didn't want to put a name to it in case he was wrong.

"And you used to put dinner out on the table most nights, when you was eating yours." Her smile wavered and crumpled. Her eyes filled with tears all of a sudden. "And I used to eat it and I'd look up, and I'd see you sometimes in the window. And it would be . . . It would be like I wasn't alone."

She raised her hands to her face, made a sound like a laugh until it escalated into racking sobs. Finn's own eyes watered in response.

"You're my ghost?" He didn't stop to think, just stepped forwards and threw his arms around her. She stiffened briefly and then turned into him, burying her head in his shoulder, as she wept. "You're my ghost! I've been so worried. When you stopped coming, I thought something bad had happened to you. I didn't know—" He glanced up over his shoulder at Michael who was stunned and suspiciously glossy-eyed behind him.

"I can't believe it." Finn had a good cry himself, for joy mostly. His eyes were closed when Michael slipped his arms around them both and briefly held them up. Then there was embarrassment and overly bright, overly cheerful voices as he passed Sarah his handkerchief, and

Jenny picked the spilled coats off the floor, and insisted on a hug of her own.

"Well," Jenny said, as they went upstairs and proved how small the kitchen table was by bumping elbows as they tried to sit around it. "I was going to be a responsible adult and argue that unofficially adopting a street child is a course of action fraught with um . . . potential grey areas. But now, well, I'm not going to argue with a Christmas miracle. I'm sure—"

As Finn was putting her plate down before her, she fixed him with a grey glare reminiscent of the point of a fencing foil. "I'm sure I can trust you both."

He had to laugh. He'd watched his own friends do the same thing to Michael over and over at the book club party—the ritual warning that they were watching, that they expected good behaviour. He was glad Michael had this strong-faced woman to defend him, and that someone official, someone in charge of records and investigations was looking out for his ghost. His ghost, who was, it seemed, a ghost no more. Fully relaunched into the land of the living, and sitting close by his chair as though she had adopted him.

"I am the epitome of everything trustworthy," he agreed. "Just ask the local magistrate. I'm a man of honour nowadays, I assure you. Now what will you have? I have turkey or nut roast, and I have white wine or red."

Later, after they had decamped to the living room to open presents and eat unnecessary cake among the glitter of the tinsel and the twinkling of the Christmas tree lights, Jenny's mobile phone went off.

"Damn." She frowned at the lighted screen, unfolding herself from the hearth rug reluctantly. "They want me in tomorrow. Suspected triple homicide with a missing eight-year-old."

He wouldn't have noticed Michael's flinch had he not been leaning back against the man, both of them sharing one sofa cushion so that Sarah could spread out on the other.

"I'll walk you home." Michael untangled himself from Finn at once. No argument, like he knew there was no point in protesting, and with Sarah scrambling up after him, her bright face dimmed, Finn thought he understood finally what kind of a despair Michael had been carrying these last months. How far he'd come.

Finn was not going to be leaving him alone tonight.

Night had fallen outside, and the snow had grown thicker and heavier, spiralling down in silent feathers. He crammed in the last corner of his cake and stood, heading for his coat. "Well, a walk would be good. I'll come with you."

Everyone was indoors on Christmas evening, the streets silent. The river rolled black as the sky between banks where the snow was two inches deep. The towpath crunched beneath their feet as they walked, Jenny and Sarah ahead, Finn holding on to Michael's elbow and leaning into the warmth of him. Their breath clouded the night, and every tree they passed shone with outdoor lights, gold and green and scarlet, blue and silver and amber as distant fire.

Sarah hugged him again as she came to her boat, and he realised that was it. She was going to sit in there alone for the rest of the evening while the world celebrated without her. "Are you all right on your own in there?" he asked, looking at it bobbing forlornly on the death-coloured water.

"I have to go." Jenny gave them both a wave as she hurried to her car, Michael following to grab her bags from inside and say a better good-bye in private.

Sarah waited until they'd gone far enough that their footsteps could no longer be heard. "I got Tyson, haven't I? Little Ty'll be wondering where I am already. Besides, it's all right if Mr. May's in the house. It's like you in the window. I know he's up there, and I'm down here, and it's good. But he goes away a lot to see you, and I don't like it when he's not there. I don't like it when it's empty, and there's just me in the boat."

"Have you told him this?"

"No." She toyed with her keys. "He's done too much already. I don't want to ask for more."

"But you'll ask me?" He found himself incredibly flattered by that.

"You never wanted my name. You never even made me show my face to you. I've always known I was safe with you."

Well. He shook his thoughts together and they fell out in a new arrangement. A child was not something he had ever envisaged in his future, but if he had to be honest, this awkward, distant, independent relationship, with a daughter already grown and mostly no trouble at all, was close to his ideal.

"I'll see what I can do."

He found Michael in the front garden, gazing out after the departing lights of Jenny's car. Snow had turned the uninviting shrubs and overhanging pines into a glittery frosting all around him. He turned at Finn's footfall, his face relaxed, wiped clean of lines of stress and pain, and he looked a good decade younger than he had seemed when he first arrived.

"It's just us, then." He smiled. "You want to go back to your place? Or...?"

"Show me the house again. Let me see what you've been up to these past months."

Inside, it was warm. The kitchen had an old deal table Finn recognised from the charity shop on King's Hedges Street, on which was piled a kettle and the makings of coffee. A half-empty bottle and unwashed saucepan of mulled wine scented the air with nutmeg and brown sugar.

Finn took off his coat and wandered into the sitting room, with Michael following him like a student artist following his examiner through a debut exhibition, waiting for judgement.

This time, he felt nothing in the living room. The white-painted walls were blank. A very temporary-looking futon sofa bed sat on the bare floorboards, and a few books dotted the edges of the room. He opened the curtains, so that the light shone down the back garden, and Sarah in her distant boat could see them both.

He ventured further. Dining room, absolutely blank as though the house was newly built. Upstairs, inflatable mattresses in two bedrooms just as empty. A bathroom clean of any imprint, and another featureless corner room that would make a lovely space for an office.

"You've exorcised it," he said, with a feeling of almost savage satisfaction, as he found Michael again, standing silently in the centre of the potentiality, waiting for his verdict.

"Yes." Michael pulled him close and rested his forehead on Finn's shoulder. "I was thinking I could sell it and move in with you."

"Were you now?" Finn tried for indignant. He should have been able to manage indignant, since Michael's assumption that he could move in whenever it pleased him was so presumptuous. But it was also right. Finn had got used to having Michael around the place. He liked the warmth in his bed and the warmth in his heart, and he didn't want to start another year without having it full-time.

"I don't think I have the space for that," he said, and joy came twisting up out of his contrary heart at the thought that he refused to do the expected even in this. "You see, I was thinking I would move in here. Expand the bookshop into the flat. Start selling a selection of modern works, and maybe a little of that electronic stuff. D'you think you could live with that?"

Michael looked him in the face like he'd never seen him before. Then slowly he turned full circle, Finn still in his arm coming with him.

"It's . . . It's all new." Michael frowned, as though he was trying to place a hard concept, but Finn could feel his body tremble faintly from where it was pressed so closely against him. "I took everything out."

"You see, my flat—" Michael had understood his meaning, that was clear enough. It just needed gently coaxing into words. "My flat is very much *my* flat. But this. We could both bring something to this. This could be *ours*. D'you think you could do that? In this place where I don't think you were very happy for a very long time, d'you think I could make you happy in the future?"

He was pretty damn sure he could, but he wanted Michael to be sure too, wanted him to have faith that the bad times were over, that he would never be so cold, so alone, or so broken ever again.

Michael gathered him close, gentle but inexorably strong, and kissed him, deep and thorough and sweet. "You idiot," he said at last, after the deal had been sealed a thousand times over. "You already do."

Explore more of the *Trowchester Blues* series at:
riptidepublishing.com/titles/universe/trowchester-blues

Dear Reader,

Thank you for reading Alex Beecroft's *Trowchester Blues*!

We know your time is precious and you have many, many entertainment options, so it means a lot that you've chosen to spend your time reading. We really hope you enjoyed it.

We'd be honored if you'd consider posting a review—good or bad—on sites like **Amazon, Barnes & Noble, Kobo, Goodreads, Twitter, Facebook, Tumblr,** and your blog or website. We'd also be honored if you told your friends and family about this book. Word of mouth is a book's lifeblood!

For more information on upcoming releases, author interviews, blog tours, contests, giveaways, and more, please sign up for our weekly, spam-free newsletter and visit us around the web:

Newsletter: tinyurl.com/RiptideSignup
Twitter: twitter.com/RiptideBooks
Facebook: facebook.com/RiptidePublishing
Goodreads: tinyurl.com/RiptideOnGoodreads
Tumblr: riptidepublishing.tumblr.com

Thank you so much for Reading the Rainbow!

RiptidePublishing.com

ALSO BY
ALEX BEECROFT

ABOUT
THE AUTHOR

Alex Beecroft was born in Northern Ireland during the Troubles and grew up in the wild countryside of the English Peak District. She studied English and philosophy before accepting employment with the Crown Court where she worked for a number of years. Now a stay-at-home mum and full-time author, Alex lives with her husband and two children in a little village near Cambridge and tries to avoid being mistaken for a tourist.

Alex is only intermittently present in the real world. She has spent many years as an Anglo-Saxon and eighteenth-century reenactor. She has lead a Saxon shield wall into battle, and toiled as a Georgian kitchen maid. For the past five years she has been taken up with the serious business of morris dancing, which has been going on in the UK for at least 500 years. But she still hasn't learned to operate a mobile phone.

In order of where you're most likely to find her to where she barely hangs out at all, you can get in contact on:

Twitter: @Alex_Beecroft

Her blog: alexbeecroft.com/blog

Her website: alexbeecroft.com

Facebook: facebook.com/alex.beecroft.1

Facebook Page: facebook.com/AlexBeecroftAuthor

Tumblr: tumblr.com/blog/itsthebeecroft

Or to be first with news, exclusives and freebies, subscribe to the newsletter: tinyurl.com/Beecroft-Newsletter

Enjoy this book?
Find more romantic suspense at
RiptidePublishing.com!

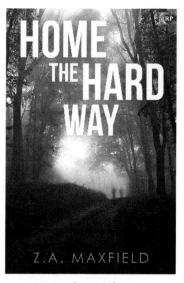

The Two Gentlemen of Altona
ISBN: 978-1-62649-219-6

Home the Hard Way
ISBN: 978-1-62649-146-5

Earn Bonus Bucks!

Earn 1 Bonus Buck for each dollar you spend. Find out how at RiptidePublishing.com/news/bonus-bucks.

Win Free Ebooks for a Year!

Pre-order coming soon titles directly through our site and you'll receive one entry into a drawing to win free books for a year! Get the details at RiptidePublishing.com/contests.

CPSIA information can be obtained at www.ICGtesting.com
Printed in the USA
BVOW07s1701050315

390442BV00002B/2/P